A Killer Story

Tom Vandel

Published by Tom Vandel, 2020.

A KILLER STORY

First edition. July 23, 2020.

ISBN: 978-1393580300

Written by Tom Vandel.

Table of Contents

For Susan and Ruby (and Ben).

A KILLER STORY
By Tom Vandel

"OPTIMISM IS OUR INSTINCT to inhale while suffocating."
- Guillermo del Toro

THURSDAY AFTERNOON

"Okayyy, it's obvious something's bothering you. What is it this time, Kate. Let's get it out."

"I don't know what to say."

"Well figure it out. I'm not gonna guess."

"I don't know who you are, Teddy."

"Here we go. Let me apologize yet again for not being able to read your mind."

"Something has happened. You have something bad you're hiding."

"What? I haven't a clue what you're talking about – as usual! I hate it when you start off a conversation in the middle and expect me to catch up!"

"I'm talking about this."

"What – that envelope? What's in it?"

1

"It was left on our porch – addressed to me."

"What's in it?"

"A picture. An old picture. Of you."

"Show me. Let me see that."

"What did you do before we met? What kind of person were you – are you?"

"I'm the same guy I've always been! I'm your husband, the guy you've been married to for over 30 goddamn years!"

"Stop! Where's this photo from?"

"Give it to me so I can see it!"

"I'll hold it for you. Go ahead, get out your reading glasses. Take a good look, Teddy."

"I don't need my glasses. That was... in Louisiana when I lived down there. It's at a party... on the bayou."

"Who are these men you're with?"

"Just guys I knew in New Orleans. One of them invited me. We were messin' around."

"The guy in the middle looks like he's dead. Is he dead? Look at his face!"

"No, noooo! He was just drunk. Passed out."

"You're lying. Look at his face. He's a corpse. He's dead!"

"He's not dead."

"This is bad. And you don't look too happy either. Who took this photo?"

"Some guy I met at the party – they thought it was funny to hold him up and take a photo of him passed out. Give it to me."

"You're lying. I can see it in your face."

"I'm telling the truth."

"Something bad happened here. And someone wants me to know it. How do they know my name and where we live?"

"I'm not sure."

"You've done a lot of stupid things in your life, Teddy, but this is beyond..."

"Honayyy, come on...sit back down. I'll take care of it."

"Take care of it? What is *it*? I don't trust you, I don't know you."

"Wait, don't go! Honayyy, come onnn. Where are you going?"

"I'm leaving! And I'm taking this photo and envelope. It's addressed to me!"

"Don't go! Come onnn, Kate!!"

Chapter 1 Darkness Falls

Thursday night

I'm in big trouble. The photo left for my wife on our porch today proves it. Bad thoughts bounce off the walls as my fingers drum on the kitchen table. I can't sit here. So I grab my keys and get behind the wheel. Driving relaxes me.

It's a nasty Portland night that gives you the creeps. Greasy fog, lurking shadows, bikers without lights – a good night to be on the road. With surge pricing, I can make decent money.

Uber driving is something I do when bored, which lately has been often. I don't handle boredom well. It makes me restless. Sometimes reckless. My mind starts to wander in search of amusement. It used to be easy to find when I was younger. Not so much anymore.

But I'm not bored now. Not with what happened this afternoon. The delivery of the photo of me in an envelope addressed to my wife, Kate. The argument we'd had sitting at the kitchen table, followed by her storming out. Definitely not boring. I'm about to get caught. I can feel it.

I'd lied straight to her face. The man in the photo she thought was dead had indeed croaked. I remember the night the picture was taken, the night I was introduced to Leroy Dupree and the Agency at a swamp party in a Louisiana bayou.

The other person in the photo standing next to the dead body is Mario. We'd met in New Orleans shortly after I moved there in 1978. He bailed me out when a job he was training me on landed me in jail. Mario introduced me to Leroy and that was the start of my troubles.

That was a long time ago. But try as you might, you can't outrun your past. And if you're not careful it can catch you and take you down. I feel my past breathing down my neck.

My name is Teddy Murphy. Like Eddie Murphy, only I'm a crusty 64-year old white man. In short, I'm a cranky smartass who's getting crankier but not smarter by the minute. You might say I have a bad attitude. I may be showing signs of early dementia, but that's unclear. My mind is slightly disturbed by drugs (mostly minor), booze, and watching the daily news. But whose isn't? If your mind isn't disturbed there's something wrong with you. I'd certainly never vote for you.

My appearance, for those who care, has in recent years taken on the form of a chicken. Poultry in motion. Two scrawny legs, like twigs, hold up a paunch belly that slopes up to a wide head with a few sparse weeds on top and a scruffy tuft of whiskers under the chin.

I've been married to Kate for over 30 years. We're not the spring chickens we once were. Or at least I'm not. I think I'm boring her with my who-gives-a-shit behavior and tired talk, no longer the engaging, ambitious young buck she married. I feel bad for her. And for Jasmine, our only child, a college graduate who lives at home and is hell-bent on getting the hell out of Dodge. I look through pictures of her as a child and I long for that little girl. The one who once said to her aunt who had borrowed a pen, "That's daddy's pen. Don't put it in your mouth." I long for simpler times. But this is my life now. And it's not simple.

Yeah, I'm employed. If you can call it that. I own a one-man global advertising firm called Les Overhead. I am Les, more or less. Professional advertising copywriter – a man of his word. I write ad campaigns, websites, videos, blogs, fridge magnets, everything imaginable. Tagline: Do more with Les. But business has dropped and I blame it, of course, on ageism. Experience isn't worth shit – at least in advertising. And respect for elders? Don't make me laugh.

For a sideline, and kicks, I drive for Uber. It can be amusing. The money's not that good, but I like the customers and action – talking to oddballs, misfits, and everyday Justins and Jennys who just feel chatty. I shoot for more than chat. I want to be entertained.

In a disarming way I strike up a conversation. Then I begin to probe for unlocked doors, windows to the soul left unlatched. Strangers will let you in and unburden themselves if you let them, assuming they'll never see you again.

I drill into veins and mine for gold. Gold in my case being a killer story. A story so good it kills any plans you have until you finish it. A story so compelling that when your pregnant neighbor rushes over in early labor and needs a ride to the hospital you say, "Better call an Uber." A story that grabs you by the throat and takes your breath away. I haven't found it yet, but I'm always looking.

I take along index cards and scribble notes about each fare. I start on the surface, then dig deeper. Here's how the excavation usually goes: "Hi, I'm Teddy. Make yourself comfortable. I'll have you there in no time. What kinda music do you like?"

Then I wait a minute and start the interrogation.

"So, tell me to zip it if you want, but do you have any personal issues or problems I can help you with during our ride? Any secrets or confessions you want to get off your chest? You'll find I'm an excellent listener."

Most folks smile or chuckle. Some cast a wary glance and quickly don headphones. Others will answer any question you throw at them – no holds barred. They'll divulge the craziest shit you can imagine to a total stranger in the front seat who's driving them somewhere. People give up all kinds of dope – personal and literal.

Maybe the rhythm of the road loosens their lips and inhibitions. It's like I'm a robot. An automaton. State your problems, human. Or, I'm a priest. The Uber priest. My Ford Escape a confessional.

To be honest, I could use a priest myself. I have some things I'd like to get off my conscience. For now, I turn on my Uber app and head out.

After two downtown pickups and one in Sellwood, all boring, I get pinged by a fare at one of my favorite haunts – the Goodfoot, a bar on Portland's east side with pool upstairs and live music downstairs.

I'm lucky to find a spot out front. I park and wait. Van the Man, a longtime favorite, comes on the radio – Moondance. I always play the radio. I like listening to stations like XRAY that play local artists, and KISN that plays oldies including actual commercials aired during the 60s. The nostalgia takes me back to times when life was full of passion and promise. Before I took a different path.

As I crank Van up, the door opens and a tall, pale brunette in slim-fit everything unfolds her limbs and climbs in. Gloria (not her real name) says to wait, a friend is coming. I instantly don't like her. She's like white vinegar – sour and dismissive and doesn't look me in the eye. I'm a nobody to her. I'm irked I can't listen to Van with the sound up. But I turn it down.

A full two minutes later a guy runs up, jumps in, and we motor off. In the mirror I see he has tats up and down both arms. Before I can pose a question, she starts hammering and ridiculing him. They're in a fight. He's smaller than her but puts up his dukes. I hear it all. I don't have to turn up my well-honed eavesdropping skills that I employ when people are talking quietly. In this case, I wish I could turn them down.

It helps to be a keen listener. It's a skill I've developed in countless client meetings, tracking two or three conversations at once around a table, usually discussing the pros and cons of the work I've presented for an ad project.

I size up whom to sidle up to, who is on board, and whom I need to win over. In big copywriting projects, like naming a new business or writing a branding campaign or website, getting stakeholder buy-in up front is critical.

In the backseat, Gloria flails away like a boxer, throwing a flurry of insults at the guy, her beau I surmise. She complains he's too rough around the edges.

Roughly: "Portland is more sophisticated than you think. It's not some podunk town. You think you're hot shit, but you're not. This is Portland. It's hip, cool. I don't know if you'll fit in here."

"Bullshit, I'm from LA, I can fit in here!" he bellows, puffing up his scrawny chest.

She busts through his bluster. "You've already been written up once! I don't trust you. You better not be manipulating me!" She glares at him and he looks out the window. I stifle telling her to shut the hell up.

He leans forward, hits me on the shoulder and asks what I think.

"You'll fit in fine," I say. I can't help myself.

In the rearview she stares bullets in my back.

I dump them off at a party in the Pearl. As she gets out, still jabbering nonstop, I flip her off – to her back of course. Don't want her to give me a bad Uber rating.

Two minutes later I get pinged by Cherry, near Burnside. I pull up and see her – something's wrong. She slides in, sobbing.

I'm at a loss for words (it happens). She collects herself as I drive toward her destination. I make a mental note to buy tissues. After a few minutes, I ask how she is.

"Better now," she sniffs. "I just kicked my jerk boyfriend out. He never paid a cent of rent and just sits around getting high. He's such a leech."

"Good for you," I say. "How'd you meet him?"

She starts weeping again. "At a wedddding... Never going to one of those again." I stifle a chuckle in my throat.

I tell her she was smart to boot him. He's an asshole. I've been one so I know. Sometimes I still am. Five minutes later I drop her off at Church (the bar, not the institution) on Sandy. Motto: Eat. Drink. Repent.

Before driving on I check my phone. No messages. I wonder where Kate has gone – my calls and texts unanswered. She hasn't been this mad in a long while. I know I'm in trouble, and not just with her. I can feel my past creeping up on me.

I turn off the Uber app and head home, hoping she'll be there. She's not. I sit on the couch and begin to wonder. What will she do? When we argued she said she didn't know me, but do I really know *her*? Would she do something – like use her court reporting connections to investigate me? I know one thing – she's not afraid to act.

The house is silent. Jasmine, our daughter, is gone – out with friends. Won't be home until after midnight.

Only Ben is there, our half Aussie, half German shepherd rescue who joined the family a few years ago. Extremely bright or extremely dumb (I can't tell), he has a keen nose and a mind of his own and refuses to do as I command unless he agrees with the idea.

He acts like he can see through me and often has a look of reproach that I find disrespectful. He has that look now and I wonder if I forgot to feed him. I can't remember. He eyes me from his perch on a chair by the window, wondering what I'm up to. That makes two of us.

Chapter 2 FOG

If Mario and the Agency were indeed in Portland, I have a serious problem. I don't want to think about it. Looking out the front window I see no one. Just shadows and an empty street. Ben stares at me as I stand to the side peeking through the blinds.

He watches me closely. Looks in my eyes to see if anything is off. I toast some bread and pull some smoked Gouda from the fridge to spread on top. It's gone in two bites.

A drink would be good. But not yet. I need to drive, settle my nerves. So I shove a handful of potato chips in my mouth, walk out the side door, and get in my Escape parked in the driveway.

Leaning over, I plug in my phone and turn on the Uber app. It lights up the car as I look to see how much juice I have on the phone and check for messages. I pull out and head south toward Halsey Street.

Just two blocks away I get pinged. There's no name – just an initial: L. The picture shows a person who appears to be female – pretty face, large dark sunglasses, white scarf. A Jackie O/Audrey Hepburn clone, with skin the color of Morocco.

I hit accept and drive to the location which is across from Normandale Park, down the street from our house. I pull up and see nobody around. I check the app and see L is close by. I sit and wait.

Checking again for messages, I find nothing. Where can Kate be? Staying with her sister? Or our good friends Bill and Steve? I decide not to text them to find out.

In my rearview I see two people walk up and jump in the back – silent. I look at my phone on the dash to see where they want to go. The address doesn't show until you pick up your fare. The moment it pops up I feel an icicle slide down my spine. It's my old address in New Orleans: 1010 Washington.

As my neurons fire, my head is suddenly yanked back by a rope that the rider behind me has looped around my neck and is pulling and twisting hard. His knee is dug into the back of my seat for leverage. I know this move. I've seen it in action. I realize I'm a goner, going out the way I thought might happen. Strangled to death with a rope.

I see a flash and then more flashes and wonder if it's my brain signaling SOS, but then see it's my fare L taking photos, a job I once had.

She (or he) leans in for close-ups. I arch my back and reach wildly behind me with both arms and kick the dashboard like a bronc rider. My boot heel slams down on the radio knob and it goes off, then back on at a higher volume, as I wrench my body and struggle to get free. I can't utter a sound, my breath cut off. My arms both reach toward the rope and I try to wrench free, unable to breathe.

It's amazing what you think of when you're being strangled. In an instant I think of Kate, and Jasmine, and what they would think of me now. I see bad decisions made, wrong forks taken, all in a blur. I think of the brass knuckles in my glove box as I kick on, grasping at the rope wrapped tightly around my neck.

The radio is playing Sonny & Cher – The Beat Goes On. I've always liked it. I'm close to blacking out and I know the game's over after that. In the distance I hear a freight train along I-84, the same lonely sound I've gone to sleep to for years, in our comfortable home and bed just a few blocks away. I feel a deep ache, an acute pain in the center of my chest, at the thought of never seeing Kate or Jasmine again.

I make one last desperate kick with my left leg to hit the car horn – but miss.

Then, just like that, the man releases his grip, lets go with one hand and pulls hard with the other to uncoil the rope wrapped around my neck. It burns. I sputter and cough and try to catch my breath. The person shooting photos jumps out of the car and walks off.

In the rear view I see a man laughing hard in the back seat and I know instantly who it is. The man who led me down this wrong fork over 40 years ago – Mario.

"You shoulda seen ya face," he says, in between guffaws. "You scared shitless, mon! Did ya piss yaself? I bet ya did. Let's see!" He leans up over the seat and I knock him back with my elbow, the only motion I can muster.

He laughs, "T gets a F-O-G! Finallyyy! I knew you would cry, baby cher! You so weak."

I look at him, I want to strangle him – it's Mario but an older, gnarlier, deadlier-looking version than the one I remember. His voice is the same low pitch, with a menacing edge and an oily sheen that flows slow and smooth. You like listening to it, swallowing it, until you realize it's poison.

My chest is heaving and I'm breathing hard, but my mind engages.

"I knew...it was you." I try to keep my voice from shaking.

"No, cher. You had no clue. You thought you were in the grave."

Me, still gasping, "The picture .... tipped me off... idiot." I know from experience you have to face Mario head on. He's sensitive about being considered dumb which is usually what I did – disrespect his intellect. But it's risky. He has a killer mean streak and has never liked me. He's always been jealous of my connection with Leroy, the Agency boss. Dealing with Mario takes bluster and bluff. After all these years, I wonder if I have enough.

He says, "I'll bet you had some 'splainin' to do with that old picture we left fo yo lady."

I can see he loves the spot I'm in. His accent is more pronounced, has more Cajun spice than I remember. He leans forward and I smell brown liquor. Like Courvoisier.

"So, how much ya lady know about ya past, eh T? What's her name? Kate, yes?" With a shiver, I turn around and glare. He wears a black beret from which silver strands of wispy hair curl down his neck.

His face is leathery and lined, like the belly of a gator. He's got a salty goatee and sideburns shaved to a point. I ponder how people change over time and yet stay the same.

"I haven't told her anything," I say. "Not one word. And I'm never going to – to protect her. She knows nothing! So don't you ever contact her or come near her. Or I swear I'll burn the Agency to the ground. And you with it." I try to add swagger to my voice, but I'm no Brando.

"Don't make me laugh, T. It's not ya nature to be violent. You could nevuh do what I do."

"Oh yeah I could, and do it better."

"Shut ya trap 'n drive. Keep yer Uber off. I'll give ya a address."

He reaches in his pocket and pulls out a notebook. I'm impressed. I remember suggesting he carry a notebook back when we worked together on Agency jobs. To keep from forgetting things – like addresses, names, weapons.

He gives me the location. It's on NE 122nd – about ten minutes away. I turn off the Uber app and we head out. As we drive I think back to the last time we met – over 25 years ago – on a cliff in

Montana, the same night I buried a body in a sugar beet field. Mario is thinking the same thing.

"Last time I see ya was in Billin," he says.

"Billings."

"Billins, right. Montana. Been a long time, bro. You tryin to avoid us in Louisienne? Tryin' to disappeah?"

"Naw, just livin'. Livin' legal, unlike you dumb asses down in da swamp." I mock him with a bad version of his accent. I go on, "Who's your run-away cameraman tonight? Not very professional to leave you like that. Just jump outta the car and split."

"Leroy likes photos – you know that. And we got some good ones I bet a you. Oh, yah. But I don need no help with you. We no worry about you."

"Here's why you no worry about me. I don't do Agency work anymore. I retired."

"You can't retire from the Agency, cher, you know that."

"Watch me." I give him a hard look but I know he's right.

I forge on, "So how'd you find me?"

"We no look fo you. But one a Leroy's high school buddies used ta play for Portland State, and he come up for a reunion. You done his Uber ride. He say you ask him buncha stupid questions. He rememba ya from a party at Leroy's back in the day. We track you on Uber and before long find where ya live. Want me tell ya where ya live, T?"

"No thanks."

"You and Kate and ya girl. Jade ain't it?"

"Don't say her name."

"Liah! I know her name not Jade. She's Jasmine. I was testin ya and ya still the dumbass liah ya always were. I ain't stupid – like you."

I keep quiet. Don't want to push it and make him strike. He was coiling like a snake.

"We ain't had no need for ya til now so we let you sit in ya little nest. All snug like a bug, warm and alive. I don't get why Leroy dig ya, mon – he thinks ya smart or something. I'm smarter than you'll ever be. If it were me you'd a been swallowed by a gator long ago." Mario burns me with eyes cold as dry ice.

He goes on, "So, how it feel to get an F-O-G? To be on the receivin' end!"

I'm furious. I want to climb over the seat and throttle him, but I stay where I am, mouth shut tight. I don't want to give him the satisfaction of knowing the F-O-G was as frightening as advertised. It's a good thing I don't believe in god.

F-O-G means Fear of God. It refers to a type of service provided by the Agency. In short, you put the fear of god into someone. Send a message, extract vengeance, deliver justice for an aggrieved party.

Typically, the victim or the victim's family pays for the FOG. It was the cheaper of two Agency services offered – the other being RIP in which the perp's life ends, as you might guess.

The RIP costs more, of course. Leroy laughingly referred to it as "Rest in Piss" because he once emptied his bladder on a man he'd hung. I found Leroy both repulsive and fascinating. He was a cocktail I couldn't put down.

Chapter 3 The Agency

Leroy was head of the Agency, which I was told dated back in his family to post-Civil War Reconstruction. In brief, the Agency is a secret squad of Louisiana vigilante ex-cops and bounty hunter types, mostly from New Orleans and Baton Rouge. They do jobs for people – tracking fugitives, catching criminals, delivering beatings and beyond as needed (and contracted), and scaring the literal piss out of people for payback. Pay up front and you could get almost anything done.

I'd become entangled with Mario, Leroy, and the Agency many years ago and hadn't been able to extricate myself. I'd been trying to get out ever since I left New Orleans in 1979. But as I'd been told many times, there's no quitting the Agency.

But I gotta be honest. I liked the rush of Agency work. Making bad people pay. Not letting assholes get away with shit. With Agency work, adrenaline ran high and the action was always intense. If that kind of thing is addicting, I was hooked. At least I was then. Now, I'm a recovering adrenaholic.

Mario points out the house as we drive by slowly. It's a nondescript home in a neighborhood full of them. People just living, getting by, hiding out.

"That's it," Mario says, "White one with the big bush in front. I been by already and seen it. We go in back. Guy lives alone. Gone in no time." I scan it quick as we drive by without saying anything. My mind turns to Kate and I try to conjure where she might be.

"Turn here." I turn and we continue two blocks to a corner where a convenience store is still open. "Pull in the parking lot." I do it.

"Tonight we meet here, trey o'clock. We hoof over and do our work, scare him to death, split and git. Got it?"

Instead of saying no I don't got it, no I don't got to do it and get outta my car right now, I ask a question.

"What kinda job is it?" As you see, I have a weakness. I'm naturally curious.

"F-O-G, baby. Fear of God. Justice and revenge. Five grand for ya."

I pause and ponder the figure. Five thousand dollars. It'd take a lot of nights and miles driving Uber to make that much. And at least two or three Les Overhead ad jobs to make that much. With Mario, I could make it in an hour – without having to listen to drunks shouting crap in my car or clients spouting bullshit in a conference room.

"The Agency has raised its rates," I say. "Business must be good."

"Ya right, mon. People payin' beaucoup."

I take a good look at Mario. He's thinner and more wiry than I remember. A small dog that likes to attack big dogs. A terrier. I should deliver him straight to the cops but I don't. My name is Teddy and I'm an adrenaline junkie. Don't judge me. Yet.

"So I get five grand for riding shotgun and shooting photos?"

"And ya write the perp's message."

The message was something I'd suggested back in New Orleans on a job where we put a baby alligator in a guy's bed and tied a note to it (the gator not the bed). It was a way to deliver a message, a sentence of justice and retribution for a deed he'd committed. Writing a message for the perp on behalf of the victim's family is one of the value-added services provided by the Agency – along with photos and video.

"We put da fear in him and we gone. Oughta kill him for what he done, but vic's family couldn't agree or cash up. So we foggin him."

"How'd you locate him?" I ask.

"Track him through some state DMV databases. Guy changed names and moved three times. Had fake IDs in names of young kids who died before they got social security numbers. So he got socials in their names. Moved up here a year ago and we find him."

"What'd he do?"

"He's a ped. It's in the note." Mario says. "I'll have a camera for ya. You gotta bring the last rites or whatever you call em."

"Guy lives alone?"

Mario sighs, "Like I say, alone, listen man, pay attention! Jesus H, you still dumb as sheeit. Why the hell I gotta work with you is beyond me. But it be what it be." Mario can get frustrated easily and he was now. He had never liked working with me. He once told me he looked forward to killing me someday.

But Leroy calls the shots and he liked throwing us together – like a cockfight. Leroy likes me. For some reason we click. I've never figured out why.

I think it over. Five grand is huge. My Les Overhead copywriting biz is dropping like a rock and I have mounting debt. Bar bills mostly. And to be honest I'm bored. Life's getting ruttingly dull. A little danger now and then never hurt anyone. This is what I thought.

"You know ya gotta do it, T," Mario says. "It's in ya best interest – and ya family." He raises one pencil-thin eyebrow. I want to stick a fork in his eye but I don't have a utensil. And just like that it happens. My conscience caves.

"Okay, I'm in," I say. "But I'm getting out after this one."

"Yeah, sure thing sugar. We meet here trey o'clock. Don't be late."

"When'd ya learn to tell time?" I can't resist.

"Shup and take me back to the park where ya got me." Done.

Chapter 4 Norman

My heart still beating fast, I drive to Clyde's, a bar not far from our house. As I down a whisky sour and beef tips, memories pour into my mind from dark nights of my past. Seeing Mario is a double shot of déjà vu. I remember scenes from Louisiana I'd blocked out. I'm buzzing when I leave.

At home, Kate and Jasmine are gone. Ben follows me around sniffing my leg, acting as if he knows I'm up to no good.

"Quit following me around, dog. Go lie down." I give him a stern look and he throws it back in my face. I raise my voice, "Get away from me. You don't know what the hell is goin' on."

I sit down and pull out my phone and text Jasmine. Where you? When you comin home?

She gets back to me within a minute. Jasmine always responds fast and expects it of others, which can be a problem. At least for me.

Her text is short: Jack Knife, home 2ish.

It's one of her favorite bars. I respond: Be safe and keep your eyes open.

Yes, dad.

I may be driving Uber late.

You be safe too. You're the one who needs to worry.

I put the phone away and take out the envelope Mario gave me. Inside are notes about the perp's crime and a letter from Leroy. I walk into the living room for my reading glasses and sit on the couch. The letter says:

Dear Teddy,

It's been too long since we've seen each other. Are you avoiding us? Why did you leave? I miss the talks we used to have. Lulu still remembers you – I believe it is one of her earliest memories the day you pushed her in the swing at the fais do-do at our ranch. I wish you had stayed in Louisiana! Now you live far away in Oregon. We have swamps, you have puddles. I prefer swamps. Has the rain washed away your memories of the past? Do you still feel the way you used to? That justice can be decided, and delivered, by anyone? We will find out.

C'est tout, mon ami!

P.S. I love that picture of you we left on your porch. Keep it. I have others.

Leroy didn't sign his letter. He never used his name in writing. Anonymity helps when you are deciding the fate of people.

I remember the day of the fais do-do, which is a Cajun dance party. We ate crawfish and gumbo and drank all day, then went to a bayou dance hall where a Zydeco band played for hours, followed by a "swamp party".

I turn on my laptop and write the message for the perp and print it out.

At 1:00 I get back in the car. Driving Uber might give me an alibi if I need one. First ride is Terrance and a buddy, two drunk Aussies I pick up at White Owl Social Club. They're in the U.S. for the first time. Terrance wants to know if they should hit Vegas.

"Some people say skip Las Vegas," Terrance says. "Why? Should we?"

"Absolutely not," I answer. "Hit Vegas hard. It's the real America – the great down under of the American dream. You'll be right at home."

"What about New Orleans?" I freeze, stiff against the seat. Looking in the rearview I see Terrance with a grin, eyes straight ahead.

"Stay out of New Orleans. You could get in trouble."

I drop them at their hotel and kill time with a few more fares before turning off the Uber app. Don't want to get a fare now. I'd have to decline it, which can hurt your Uber rating. I'm a 4.93. A top-rated driver. Highly respected.

At 2:30, I park at a dark spot near the convenience store where I'm to meet Mario. Nobody around. I reach into my pocket and pull out my little notebook I carry to jot down ideas – ad concepts, taglines, headlines, graphic ideas. Nice thing about being a freelance copywriter is you can do it anywhere. It's all billable time. I could dictate ideas into my phone, but I prefer to write them down and cross them out when they suck. Analog, not digital.

Tonight I work on tagline ideas for a new client, Mongoose Cannabis, a marijuana emporium opening soon on SE Belmont. Searching mongoose traits on my phone I learn that mongooses (not mongeese) live in "mobs" or "packs" with a hierarchy of a dominant male and female who watch out for predators. These ferocious animals are notorious for their ability to hunt and kill some of the deadliest creatures on earth, including the king cobra. With incredible agility and reflexes, a mongoose will attack a cobra by going directly for its head, biting into its skull, killing it fast. And then eat it, venom sacs and all. That's bold – a stone cold killer.

Looking down the dark street, I wonder if I can think like a mongoose. I'm positive I can. The question is, can I act like one? Closing my phone, I jot down a few tagline ideas. I circle one: All creatures welcome, except snakes.

At 2:45 I pocket my notebook and exit the car. From the trunk, I pull out a backpack and put on a black sweatshirt, gloves, and cap. I toss the backpack back in the trunk, lock the car, and take off at a brisk walk toward the convenience store where Mario and I are to meet.

I get there a few minutes early. Right at 3:00 I see a person headed my way. The way he walks I know it's Mario. He steps fluidly with a slight lift of the left hip, a hitch – a black cat with one leg higher than the other, giving him a limp swagger. He could be a zombie. Or freak robot with one bad wheel.

He's wearing a black jacket, dark sweats, wool cap on top, and sharp-toed black leather boots. Both hands are shoved deep in the pockets of his jacket. I'm sure he's packing. Doesn't say a word, just points to follow him. We silently walk to the perp's house and stop across the street.

"Ya ready?" he whispers. "Got the message?"

I nod. From his pocket, he pulls out a phone and hands it to me. I turn it on and check the camera. Then put it in my pocket.

We walk swiftly up to the perp's house and duck around the side in the shadows. We pull our ski caps down over our faces and go through a gate into the backyard. Mario steps up to the backdoor and pulls out a key chain with lock picks. He selects one and in less than 30 seconds he springs the latch and we're inside.

Mario is a viper. He slithers through the kitchen into the hall. We approach a bedroom where we hear soft breathing. I'm one step behind. He pulls a gun from his waistband, steps into the bedroom, flips on the light, and starts yelling.

"Hey Norman, time to wake up! Wake ya ass up, Norm! We found ya!" The pasty blob in bed raises its head. Puffy eyes blink, a fat chin drops. I hear a muffled fart. Instinct kicks in and I clench my nostrils.

"Norman, that day you always fear is here! Is it Norm or Norman? What do we call ya? I know it's not Pete Boggem. That's ya fake name. Ya real name is Norman James Penney. We found ya, Normy!"

"Who...who the hell are-" Mario cuts him off.

"Get ya ass outta bed. Now!"

Norm, eyes blinking like a digital clock after the power's gone out, does as he's told. He stands in the bedroom, hairy chest with pink belly sagging over gray briefs. I pull out the phone Mario gave me and take a few photos. Then I switch to video and start recording.

"What is this, what do you want?" Norm asks, trembling.

"Payback. Do ya believe in karma, Norm? Like they say, karma is a bitch. And she is here for payback. Time you paid for your sins, asshole! Past time."

"For what?" he whines.

"You know for what. For what you did the summer of '77. You remember?" Norman's features tighten and he glances at me. Helpless.

"We here for payback, asshole. For what you did!" Mario looks at me and grins, then motions me forward. I take the note from my pocket that I worked on earlier and begin reading:

"On the night of August 1, 1977 you, Norman James Penney, grabbed an innocent 11-year old girl from a park in Clarksdale, Mississippi and molested her over a period of three days. Her name was Lucy. Somehow, she got away and you took off. You were never caught. But she was. Caught in a web of despair and depression that led to her taking her own life. You, Norman Penney, were the cause. And now, you are the one caught and you are now going straight to hell! Prepare to meet your maker."

The writing could be tighter and uses the word "caught" too much, but it gets the message across.

"Wait, wait, wait, wait - you have the wrong guy," Norm stammers. "I never lived in Mississippi. I swear, it wasn't me!"

"Yeah, was you," Mario says. "We track ya down. Found ya, asshole!"

"No-no-no, please, you got the wrong guy!"

"Any last words, Norm? Anything you wanna say to Lucy's family? Speak now or never." Mario points his gun at the man's forehead. I move in closer with my camera, focusing on Norm's splotchy, pale face. Panic fills it.

"Oh please, no, please, no..."

"I will commence countin' to three. One... two ..." Norm falls to his knees, eyes shut, whimpering, "God no, please, I'm sorry, I'm sorry..." Mario puts the gun barrel to the man's head.

"Three!" He pulls the trigger three times fast. With each click he yells, "Bam!" The gun is unloaded. Norman falls over, shaking, sobbing.

Mario stands over him: "I'd kill ya if I could and I still might! Don't you ever touch a kid again! Cause we'll find ya – and we won't be so friendly next time." He stands back and then takes one big stride forward and swings his right leg like kicking a football, sending his snakeskin boot into Norm's sputtering face, splitting the uprights of his eyes.

I move in closer with the phone, getting good video and audio of them both. Then I pocket the phone and Mario and I split. He stops on a dime in the kitchen, looks at the guy's fridge, and grabs a Barbie magnet stuck to the door. Then we're out the back.

We run to the convenience store and stop. Nobody is around. I hand him the phone I shot photos and video on. In return, he hands me an envelope. I look inside – two rubber-bound stacks of $100 bills. I don't count it.

Instead I say, "What the hell are you doing taking that Barbie off his fridge? You into dolls now?"

"You wish," he grins as he pulls it out shaking it at me. "My little girl digs Barbie – she'll love this." He jams it in his back pocket and then goes on, "We ain't done yet. I'm up here for a two-fer. Got another job tomorrow night."

I'm stunned. No way.

"What are you talking about? I'm not doing another job with you."

"Yeah, ya are. And Leroy wants this one bad, not sure why. I'll find out tomorrow if it's a FOG or RIP." He looks out across the parking lot and avoids my stare.

"Look at me, Mario. I'm not doin' it. Understand? I'm done!"

"Don't be dumb. You got no choice, cher. I don't need to remind ya what the Agency can do."

I know what he means and I think of Kate and Jasmine.

"I text ya tomorrow at three," Mario says. "Be by ya phone." He starts off, then stops and turns, "Forgot to mention, Leroy say hi. Lulu, too – she still remembers ya." I don't respond, just turn and head the opposite direction. A block away I pull out my little notebook and pen. I write: M to text me 3:00 Sat.

Five minutes later I'm back in my Escape. I fire it up and take off – the five grand on the seat next to me. As I drive home, I think about what I've just done, and what I may have to do tomorrow.

.

Chapter 5 Jasmine

Friday morning
The next morning I woke up with a headache. The first thing I did was check my phone. Nothing from Kate. Where the hell was she?

I made coffee, turned on my computer, checked the news. There was no story about last night's job with Mario. I looked out the window and wracked my brain for ways to get out of this. I had to find a way to cut my ties with the Agency. I couldn't do it anymore.

As I pondered, daughter Jasmine emerged from her bedroom, long caramel hair swept down over her shoulder like a waterfall. Her sleepy almond eyes half open, feet shuffling softly across the faux wood floor to the bread drawer. She didn't like to talk in the morning. I took a sip of coffee and let her adjust to the scene.

I was on edge but don't think she could tell. I'd been getting agitated lately and she was used to it. Eventually, I spoke.

"Morning."

As a copywriter, you learn to be concise – to chisel a sentence or thought down to the core. You also learn to shut up and let the client speak, and listen between the lines.

I knew better than to start up with questions for Jasmine. My Uber sawed-off shotgun approach would backfire here. Jasmine had long ago tired of my incessant questioning and probing into her life.

She had clammed up, locked the doors. No getting in. So, I waited her out.

"What time did you get home last night?" she finally said, unable to stand the awkwardness of us sitting silent. She abhors awkwardness. She went on, "I heard you come in really late." Funny how our roles have reversed, I thought.

"Yeah, it was late. I was driving Uber."

"I thought you didn't like driving Uber late."

"Changed my mind. The money's a lot better. The people, too. Turns out I like drunks."

"You're turning into one, as much time as you spend in bars." She didn't laugh. I didn't argue.

Frankly, it would be imprecise to say I'm turning into a drunk – I already am one. In fact, I've been a so-called "regular drinker" for many years. It's a hazard of the job. A lot of good freelance copywriters who have sidelines like mine founder on the rocks. Whiskey for me. And vodka. Gin. Rum. Brandy. Put it this way: I'm an equal opportunity drinker.

Jasmine and I have been drifting apart as we get older. Board games once fun now leave us bored. TV show favorites we once both savored are no longer shared. My card tricks have all been seen, the magic exposed. I struggle to find topics to talk about. And as we spend less and less time together, my heart aches more and more.

It doesn't help that I'm passive aggressive. I take it, take it, take it, then reach my limit and lash out – a mongrel at the end of its chain, snapping out words that hurt and maim. My fuse and chain were getting shorter.

I can tell Jasmine is worried about me. She thinks I'm losing it (her phrase, which is vague and inaccurate I tell her). She claims I sometimes talk to myself out loud and say odd things. Thinks I'm depressed. She's wrong, I'm not depressed. Just utterly bored out of my stark raving mind.

As I've said, I don't handle boredom well. I get antsy. Make bad decisions. My mind gets jacked up and it dares me to do something to shake up the universe. I used to refrain, but lately I've been accepting the dare.

A week ago I was on the Max in the morning coming downtown. I looked at all the blank faces around me, staring zombieish into space. As I got off I yelled, "If you're thinking of quitting your job, do it. You'll be dead before long! Maybe today!" I got a good feeling from it that lasted almost to lunch. I resolved to do it again.

"Dad, I don't know about you driving so late. You're getting old you know." She looked me in the eye for a change. I'm not used to it.

"So. Who isn't?" I said. "I'm fine, dear. But thanks for the concern. I didn't know you had it in ya." This is another thing I've been doing – getting snarky and sarcastic. Anything to amuse myself. I'm losing patience – with everything.

I go on, "Don't worry, I'll be dead before long." Okay, now I'm getting mean.

"Not funny," she said. "What is it with you? You've been acting weird. You're changing. You could have early dementia, you know. Does Uber check for that – dementia, senility?"

I laughed at the idea. She could always make me laugh. Usually when she wasn't trying.

"I am not senile. I do not have dementia. I just forget things once in awhile, like everyone."

"It's more than that. Your personality is changing. You're more negative now, more quiet – not talking as much."

"Who wants to listen," I moped. I hung my head, mostly for a joke, but not entirely.

I went on, "Now that I'm older and know all there is to know, nobody asks me any questions." It's a good line – one I ripped off from someone I can't remember. I have a file full of hundreds of favorite quotes.

Quotes are an excellent copywriting tool – either using them verbatim or as an idea or copy starter. Take a great quote, change a word or two, and you're suddenly a genius. It's that easy.

I think about quotes I like. Here's one: "Sometimes, it's best to shut up." That's from Marcel Marceau, the mime. He knew what he was talking about. But shutting up for me wasn't easy anymore. I was fed up with just about everything. Including myself.

Jasmine broke into my thoughts.

"Know what you should do?" she said.

"No, please tell me," my voice dripping with disdain as I raised my cup and took a sip.

"Write a journal." I about spit out my coffee. Jasmine has never been interested in stories of my past or anything sentimental. It's just the way she is. The idea of her suggesting I write a journal is laughable.

"I'm serious. Write about anything you want. Your life, work, whatever. Talk about your Les Overhead business, give copywriting tips and advice. Or tell your life story, your times in New Orleans and Montana. Maybe it can be a book."

She was pandering, playing to my writer ego. Thinks writing a journal will be good for me – meaning a way to keep my mind occupied and under control.

Little does she know I've been keeping a journal, off and on, for a long time. I've mentioned it to her before but she has obviously forgotten, or wasn't listening. I hate it when people tune me out. It's disrespectful as hell.

Kate, my wife, is an excellent listener – it's her job. She's a professional Court Reporter. She listens to trials, depositions, jail calls, mental hearings, and some of the most depraved testimony that's ever been spoken. She's heard it all and is not unacquainted with the seamy side of the street.

Jasmine spooned up a bite of yogurt and swallowed it. "You know, I'm leaving soon for my Amigos job, right? I'm leaving Monday and I'll be gone for three months."

I racked my brain. Where's she going? Paraguay? Ecuador? Costa Rica? I think she's going back to one of them as a supervisor for the Amigos program she's involved in, but I'm not sure. Could be somewhere new. One thing I do know, I'm not about to ask.

I sat in silence. I thought about Kate and the envelope she'd found on our porch yesterday afternoon. I had a bad feeling, like a boot grinding its heel into my chest. What would she do?

"Where's mom?" Jasmine asked. "I haven't seen her since yesterday."

I don't like to lie, but I can pull it off if need be. "She went to Astoria for a few days. Not sure when she's coming back." The truth is I had no idea where Kate was.

"Why did she just up and leave without letting me know?"

"Her court-reporting work is slow, she needed a break." I knew only the latter half of that was true. She had a lot of transcript work.

"Are you going to Astoria, too?"

"No, too busy." But I was not busy at all – with writing work anyway. My freelance ad business was drying up. As was my memory of the past.

I've told Jasmine that eventually I'll be reduced to four stories, which I'll tell over and over. Then it will drop to two. Then one. We've discussed what that one final story will be.

This depressing topic of my eventual decrepitude used to give us something to talk about, although she's tired of it now. So am I.

I sipped on my coffee. Jasmine was worried about me, but I was worried too – about her. She could be in danger as a result of what I was about to do – or not do – that night.

Jasmine got dressed and left for work at Popina, a Portland swimwear boutique. I had nothing better to do so turned on my

Uber app and climbed into my Ford Escape. Driving helps me think. Almost as much as drinking.

Chapter 6 Mario

Friday afternoon

After a few Uber fares, I pulled over and went to a food cart for some Korean tacos. As I waited, I pulled out my little notebook and read the notation that Mario would be in touch. I kept it out while I ate, to remind myself not to be driving at 3:00 so I could answer Mario's call or text.

At 3:03 I got it. A text that said simply: turn on uber

As a professional copywriter, I hate abbreviated, lower case text-speak. It's sloppy, lazy, unclear. I text him back: No. I'm done. Tell Leroy I'm out.

Mario responds: u will do it turn on uber now

I can't argue this way, so I turn on the app. Within seconds I get pinged by someone a few blocks away. Name is Mo. I accept the fare and drive to the pin – located a block off NE Halsey. From in front of a convenience store a man strides up and gets in – Mario.

Before I can say a word he blurts out, "This Uber thing is slick, man. Let someone else do the drivin'. Nice." I could smell booze and his eyes were glassy. He'd probably found a cannabis store. They're all over Portland and Mario would partake – I knew that.

"We going somewhere?" I asked. I didn't want to sit by this store with Mario in the car. He sat back and sighed.

"We goin' by tonight's venue. I put a address in the app – drive to that. It's near our hit spot – I wanna drive by and scope it." He pulled out his notebook, "The spot we hit is... 6950 Skidmore."

I shifted into gear and we started toward the destination Mario had entered into Uber. I checked the Uber map and saw the route would take us right by the perp's house. Mario got right down to business.

"So, we on tonight. It's a RIP. Good money. Ten K for you." I'm surprised. That's way more than I've ever received on any Agency job.

I told Leroy in the beginning I would never kill anyone or be a part of a murder. Yeah, we'll see he had said. He told me I wouldn't have to hurt anyone – I was only needed for documenting the act. Just take a few pictures. At the time, I didn't see a way out and went along. Besides, once I found out what the vics did I felt they deserved it. Justice administered. And the money was worth any damage to my conscience.

But it's funny about a conscience (or lack of one). It can kick in as you age, and can become a real pain in the ass. It had with me. I realized I was living a life that was essentially worthless. I had never believed in heaven, but wasn't so sure about hell. I didn't like my odds.

"It's over, Mario. Tell Leroy or I will."

"No way, hombre. You are under contract. A verbal contract that is binding in the state a Louisiana."

"Give me Leroy's number. I'll call him. I'm done. I'm dead serious."

"Dead is right, my man! And not just you. How is Jasmine by the way? I see she's taking some college classes." Mario was getting mad and he played his card.

He pulled up a picture on his phone and leaned over to show it to me. It was a screen shot of Jasmine's course schedule at Portland State University. Every class, location, and time. The message was obvious. They could grab her anytime they wanted. Then he showed another photo – Jasmine walking in to work at Popina, the swimwear store. I slammed on the brakes.

"If you ever," I growled, but he cut me off.

"She's safe, as long as daddy does his job. Which he will if he's a decent father. And what about ya wife? She still mad about that photo we left on ya porch?"

I had trouble breathing. I was outraged and under the gun. I didn't utter a word and tried to act calm instead of reaching for his throat.

"All you have to do is get the shots and video, same as always," he went on. "This guy is a bad dude, T. And Leroy is really after this guy – crazy mad. Knows him somehow. He's from Louisiana – he killed his girlfriend. She was pregnant. Cops catch him and he gone to prison. Five years in he somehow got out – as in escaped. Leroy don't tell me how. Dude been loose ever since, til now."

I took it all in and sat silent. How do I get out of this? Escape was heavy on my mind.

Mario went on, "Not only did he kill the chick and her unborn chile, he also kill her poor dog!" I shot a look at him and glared and he laughed hard.

"I'm kiddin' bout the dog. The look on ya face! You hate them dog killers! Remember that guy whose teeth we pulled with needle-nose pliers in the Ninth Ward? You took the guy's dog! That still kills me. Kill a human that's okay to you, but you kill a mangy mutt and you go rabid."

I remembered the incident well. It was vise-grips not needle-nose pliers that were used to yank out the guy's molars. I kept the teeth for some reason and still have them stuffed away somewhere. A memento of the past.

And yeah, I did take his dog. The poor mutt was emaciated – looked like he hadn't eaten in a week. I couldn't leave him. Took him home and fed him. Two weeks later I gave him to the family next door who ended up moving to Lake Charles. I was sorry to see him go. I liked that dog. He was a tough, spry terrier with an attitude and short mutt's complex, always sticking his nose into spots that could get him in trouble. I called him Slim. Still miss him.

"This bastard been footloose for a long while," Mario spat out. "We finally track him down. He got far away but not far enough. Lives alone."

We drove by the perp's house at 6950 Skidmore. It was a pale blue one-story ramshackle with a splotchy yard and bed of wilting flowers. Nothing fancy, but no hovel. We went by slowly and examined the place. It had a driveway. Side door. Fenced backyard with what looked like a garden in back. The scum has a green thumb I thought. Good cover.

"Okay, we go in the back," Mario said. "Meet me two blocks up at 72nd and Skidmore. Let's say 2:00 a.m. Won't take long, then we send Leroy the photos and video and I can get some sleep before heading back south."

From his backpack, Mario pulled out an envelope. Inside was a sheet with background info on the perp. Just a few bullet points to use in writing his last rites.

I dropped Mario off on 82nd Street. No doubt he was staying at a fleabag motel nearby. I didn't want to know where. As he got out of the car he turned with a grin, "I just want ya to know Leroy has given me the green light to do anything I want to you when he's done with you. I can't wait. I'm lickin' my chops." He cackled and pointed a gun finger at me, then slashed the finger across his throat. "Wait'll ya see." He slammed the door and walked away laughing.

I drove off before I could respond. Ten blocks away I pulled over and took out my little notebook. In a scrawl I wrote: Sat 2am RIP 72& Skidmore.

My mind couldn't focus and I needed air, so I went for a walk. Walking is good for contemplation, clearing your mind, plotting an escape, or a murder. My legs carried me, as if they knew the way, to the nearest tavern. I took a stool and started looking at my phone. Texts, emails, photos, the story of my life in digital form. Totally worthless. I felt like pulling the plug. Maybe I'll get reincarnated into a better life, maybe as a dog.

After a shot of Early Times and a couple tall Rainiers, I loosened up and was able to think more clearly. One thing was certain. Mario would kill me, with gusto, once Leroy gave him the okay. And it might come after this last job.

I looked at the bartender who appeared to be over 70. I figured my odds of living that long to be 50-50. I needed to improve those odds.

I came up with a next step. Driving to Fred Meyer on NE Glisan, I bought two prepaid burner phones. Then headed home for a talk with Jasmine.

The house was empty when I arrived. Jasmine was still at work. I sat on our porch swing and watched traffic going by. I went over numerous scenarios, considered various solutions, pondered out-of-the-box options – none of them promising. I went back inside and made a drink.

Jasmine flew through the door around 7:30 and ducked into her room. I gave her a few minutes, then knocked loudly and said I wanted to talk. I heard a heavy sigh, then she slowly opened her door as if it were a block of granite.

"What?"

"Come sit down. I want to talk to you. I bought you something." I knew that would get her. She rolled her eyes and came out. I was so tired of this attitude. I almost went off on her, but I held my tongue.

"What did you buy me?" She might have cared less, but not much.

"I bought you a backup phone. In case you need it."

"What? Why? Why would I need a backup phone?" She was genuinely surprised.

"It's just a good idea to have one. You never know. For safety. In case you lose yours."

"I won't lose mine. I don't want a backup phone."

"Just take it. Hide it somewhere, but where it's easy to get to."

"Hide it? You're paranoid."

"I'm just thinking of your safety."

"I don't need another phone," she said. She looked at me and sighed. "But okay, if it makes you feel good." She was humoring me.

"You know there are hackers out there that can get into your phone, right?"

"Well, sure, but ..."

"It's just good to have a backup. A cheap burner phone. I bought myself one, too. And I've entered the phone number for each of us into both of them."

"Ohhkay...I'm leaving Monday for my job in Ecuador you know. I'm not taking this phone."

"Fine. One more thing. If something bad happens or if your phone falls into the wrong hands, we should have a code so I know it's you. How about Shiny Happy People, that REM song you used to sing as a kid."

"Dad, this is crazy."

"If I ask you or text you what your favorite song is, just say Shiny Happy People...so I know it's you, okay?"

"Are you in some kinda trouble?" She looked me in the eye with legit concern. I was actually touched.

"Please humor me and do this," I beseeched, rubbing my hands together. This is something I learned to do when meeting with clients. Rubbing your hands together shows enthusiasm and interest. It shows you are engaged in the project or campaign.

"If you're ever in trouble, text Shiny Happy People so I know it's you."

Jasmine looked at me, her listless eyes now a little sharper, trying to read my mind. Good luck, I thought. I got up.

"See ya later, I'm driving Uber and will probably be out late again."

"Okay, bye. Be careful, dad." Yeah, right.

Chapter 7 RIP

Friday night
  It's another wicked night. I hit the rainy Uber road, delivering folks to bars, apartments, motels, and illicit affairs all over the city. I crank up the music, not caring if passengers don't like it.

I play a couple sides of Nina Simone, including "I Put A Spell On You." It reminds me of New Orleans in a bad way but I listen to it all. Then I switch to a CD with my favorite Uber-driving song: the 60's hit "Vehicle" by The Ides of March. It's got a sharp, funky edge.

"Well I'm the friendly stranger in the black sedan,
Won't you hop inside my car,
I got pictures, got candy, I'm a lovable man,
I'd like to take you to the nearest star,
I'm your vehicle baby, I'll take you anywhere you wanna go,
I'm your vehicle woman, by now I'm sure you know,
That I love ya, love ya, need ya, need ya,
I want ya, got to have you child,
Great God in heaven you know I looove you."

Around midnight I shut it down and head home. I pull out the perp info Mario has given me and turn on my computer. I do a web search for the guy's name, Nolan Duplantis, but don't find anything.

I open a new file and write out the last rites for Mr. Duplantis – a final death sentence (several sentences to be exact). They state: "You, Nolan Duplantis, are guilty of sticking a butcher knife in the back of your girlfriend, Violet McRae, and leaving her to bleed to death on the kitchen floor on August 24, 1984 in Lafayette, Louisiana. Nice. Did you know she was pregnant? Probably didn't care. You got caught and sent to prison to do your penance, but somehow escaped. Escaped from justice. How'd you do that, Nolan? Who helped ya? Doesn't matter. Tonight, we end your miserable existence, in honor of Violet McRae and her unborn child, and the rest of her family who will dance on your grave. Adios, asshole. Don't hurry back."

At 1:30 I put on my dark sweatshirt, stick the last rites printout in my back pocket, and drive to a street a few blocks from where I'm to meet Mario. I park and walk to our meeting spot. Mario is already there. He's all in black and is wearing a dark backpack. Seems nervous. I figure he's loaded – drunk or high. Most likely both. I know he's armed.

He gives me the phone I used the night before and points the way. We walk silently the few blocks to the perp's address. Stopping in the shadow at the side of his house, we slip on our ski masks and gloves and Mario pulls out his handgun and attaches a silencer. Then, we enter the backyard and step up to the back door. Masterfully, Mario uses his set of lock picks to open it.

Like roaches, we scurry into the hall, outside a bedroom. Mario nods and we quietly enter the room. Pitch black. I sense something wrong, a presence. I pull out the phone. Mario nudges me and flicks on his headlamp.

Light fills the space in front of us and shows something I'm astounded to see: a short, stocky man, totally naked, standing by his bed, holding a kid's aluminum bat.

Mario points his gun at the man and yells "Drop it!" But as he gets the words out the bat crushes his nose. Mario fires, putting a bullet in the man's shoulder but the man doesn't stop and tackles Mario slamming him hard against the wall. They both hit the floor and a framed picture of soldiers in uniform falls and shatters next to them.

Mario and the perp merge into one, each with a bear hug around the other, veins pulsing. In a split second, the man gains leverage and flips Mario over and spread-eagles him. He slams his fist into Mario's face and knocks the gun loose from Mario's hand. The weapon slides toward me and I kick it away, the only instinct I can summon.

The guy pins Mario's arms with his knees and grips him by the throat, digging his thumbs deep into his larynx.

Mario sputters and tries to shake loose, the whites of his wild eyes inflate like balloons. They cast about, then find mine. Staring at me his eyes blink repeatedly, mayday, mayday! Do something!

I grab Mario's pack and pull out a piece of rope. Jumping on the perp, I loop the rope around his neck, twist it hard, and pull it as tight as I can while jamming my knee and full weight into his back. He keeps strangling Mario while I strangle him – an irony I can't help but appreciate. I almost laugh.

The perp tries to buck me off but his shoulder is shot and he can't do it. I lean into his good shoulder and anchor my legs on each side of him.

He lets loose of Mario and reaches around at me, but it's too late. I have him in a hold he can't escape as he tries to dig his fingers under the rope. In a minute he loses muscle response as his brain shuts down from lack of oxygen. I continue to throttle him with all my might as his body goes limp and falls on Mario.

I look at Mario. He's breathing hard, sweat beading his translucent face, fear slowly draining from his body. I'm gasping too and pull my ski mask off to breathe. And then, I come to a decision that shocks me. I still can't explain it.

As if sure of what I'm doing, I retrieve Mario's gun and walk over to him. He reaches up a hand and gasping says, "That...was close."

"Yeah. Like I said, I'm through. So are you. I guess you're not gonna kill me after all, Mario." I point the gun at Mario's heart and fire twice. His jaw slowly falls open, as if trying to ask a question. Did you just shoot me, cher? Then I point the barrel at his forehead, cover my face with my left arm, and pull the trigger again. His skull rocks back and an empty look fills his eyes as his lids drop their final curtain.

For a moment I'm shocked. I've never killed anyone before, and now in less than a minute I've murdered two people – two evil souls dispatched to hell, saving myself and my family. It's astounding. Actually invigorating.

I throw the gun, rope, and mask in Mario's backpack, grab my phone, and shoot a few photos of the dead perp. I get a couple shots of Mario too, just in case I need them.

I then put on the backpack, lift Mario's lifeless body over my shoulder, and start out. In the hallway I see a figure in the dark. It's a kid, a boy about five, sleepy eyes, hair sticking up, wearing a Spiderman t-shirt and pale blue underwear too big for his scrawny butt. He looks at me as if to say: You hurt my daddy.

In seconds I'm out the door. I carry Mario's body a few houses away and lay him down under a rhododendron. Then run to my car, throw Mario's backpack in the passenger seat, and drive back to where I had left Mario. I pop the trunk, gather up his body, and throw him inside.

From his backpack I pull out his phone, a burner like the ones I had bought for Jasmine and me, and call 911. Speaking with an Indian accent I've practiced for years, mostly as a joke to piss off Jasmine who has dated a few Indian men, I report that someone has been shot. I give the address and inform them a child is inside. When asked for my name I hang up.

I drive to the east bank of the Willamette River by Hawthorne Bridge. From the river's edge I gather a large rock and two pieces of broken concrete and return to my vehicle. I dump everything from Mario's backpack into the front seat. Then I strip off my sweatshirt and jeans and stuff them in the empty pack, along with the rock and concrete chunks. From the trunk I grab some duct tape (always have it on hand), and tape the backpack to Mario's body.

Moments later I'm driving across the bridge in my underwear. Halfway across, seeing no vehicles coming, I turn off my lights and stop the car. In seconds, I lift Mario's body out of the trunk and step up to the bridge railing. I fish out the phone and take one more photo of him. Then I toss him over. Silence. Splash. Exit Mario.

Five minutes later I pull over under a streetlight on Stark. I use my phone light to examine the contents of Mario's backpack. There's a five-foot stretch of rope, two hunting knives, a can of mace, a manila envelope with a lot of cash, and the Barbie magnet Mario pocketed the night before. I pick up Mario's phone and suddenly it starts vibrating.

A text. One word: DONE?

I assume it's Leroy. I lay my head down on the steering wheel and think hard. Can I pull this off? No choice, I have to. I wait a minute, thinking what to say. I realize I have to respond.

I text back, mimicking Mario's writing style: done n gone

Seconds later Leroy is back: PHOTOS VIDEO?

Me/Mario: photos comin no video T didn't get it

Leroy: PHOTOS THEN! WHY NO VIDEO?

I grab the phone Mario had given me to use on the job and send the photos I took of the dead perp to Leroy's text number. Within a minute, Leroy is back.

Leroy: DOESN'T LOOK RIGHT. YOU SURE THAT'S OUR GUY – DUPLANTIS?

Me/Mario: yep

Leroy: WHAT ADDRESS YOU HIT

Me/Mario: what you gave us 6950 Skidmore

Leroy: NO! ITS 5950 NOT 6950 WRONG GUY!!!

And with that, my universe explodes. The big bang. My throat constricts and I'm nauseous. It can't be. No! Please god, don't tell me Mario got one digit wrong in the address. No, no, no, no, noooo!

I realize with a kick to the crotch I've murdered an innocent man. I've snuffed out his life, his entire future. And I've forever changed the life of his son, a young boy who knows what I did and will always know, will always remember my face, and who will find me someday and take vengeance. I'm sure of it.

Of course, I've killed Mario too but that was no major loss. He got what he deserved. Justice. At least that's what I'm telling myself. As my mind reels, Mario's phone buzzes again.

Leroy: I WANT OUR GUY DEAD. THE RIGHT GUY! 5950 SKIDMORE!

It seems there's only one thing I can say.

Me/Mario: Okay – but not with T. He wants out and we don't need him.

And that was my mistake – making it grammatically correct. Not Mario's style. Leroy noticed.

Leroy: YOU'RE NOT MARIO. WHO THIS?

Me: no it's me

Leroy: NO. THIS TEDDY?

Me: Mario i swear!

Leroy: WHAT'S YOUR KID'S NAME?

And with that I'm screwed. I rack my brain but Mario had never mentioned his daughter's name that I recall.

Me: it's me man!

Too late. My play is not a winner. Leroy pounces.

Leroy: I KNOW IT'S YOU T. WHERE'S MARIO?

I decide to come clean. With the phone Mario gave me I text Leroy two images of Mario's dead body, in the innocent man's bedroom and on the bridge before I tossed him over.

Me: Mario is dead. The perp was ready for us. Had a gun and shot Mario. I strangled the guy with rope. Had to get rid of Mario's body, dumped in river. Won't be found.

I wait for Leroy to respond. Nothing. I'm sweating. Finally, after two minutes he's back.

Leroy: T YOU GOT FAMILY. DON'T HURT THEM. YOU GOT 48 HOURS. FIGURE IT OUT. THE RIGHT GUY GOES OR YOU GO.

Fear courses through me. What have I done? What am I gonna do? I'm a dead man. After a few minutes I take out my notepad and write: 5950 Skidmore 48 hrs from Fri 3am RIP.

Tired, my mind takes a break. A car passes by and I look up. An old Cadillac. It triggers my memory and I drift back in time, dropping into the depths of my past, like a body slowly sinking into a swamp.

Chapter 8 New Orleans 1978

J **anuary**

At the ripe age of 22, a newly minted know-it-all college graduate, I really only knew two things. One: I was sick and tired of working shifts at the sugar factory in Billings, Montana. Two: I was boring myself to death sitting on barstools drinking Oly with deadbeats.

I had a kick-the-dog mentality that was getting worse. My relationships with the opposite sex had all gone downhill. I'd begun showing up late for dates and not giving a damn.

The cold Montana winter sparked a strong itch to amble south. So on January 21, 1978 (as dated in my journal), a pal named Dick and I put wheels in gear and set out for adventure, glory, and warming. We drove to Texas.

I had a friend, Chuck, who was going to Rice University in Houston. We landed at his place and availed ourselves of the local charms – Lone Star beer, barbecue, and babes. Problem was, the weather didn't cooperate. It was cold and rainy, not the warm sunshine of our quest. So after a few days, Chuck dropped us on a freeway heading west and we extended our thumbs toward Brownsville and the Mexican border.

Over the next two months we made our way down through Mexico to Lake Atitlan in Guatemala, then turned back when we ran short of dinero. We arrived back at the U.S. border in Laredo and hitched back to Houston.

We thought we were hot shit; smart gringos who knew what we were doing. Having less than $100 each left from our foreign sojourn, our plan was to move to Austin to get jobs. My friend Chuck said, "Austin is cool. But I have some friends somewhere else you haven't been." We perked up. "New Orleans," he said with a grin.

The sound of it was alluring, intoxicating, addictive. Dick and I looked at each other and clinked our Lone Stars. Yeah, New Orleans. We were drawn like moths. Or lambs – to a slaughter.

The day Dick and I arrived in New Orleans, March 12, 1978, we hit the ground running. Jobs and cash were needed fast. I parked in the French Quarter and we split up. Dick found a job within an hour, at a sandwich place called Maspero's. I set my sights higher and applied at several top restaurants, but was repeatedly shown the door for failing the "Make a Caesar Salad from scratch" test.

I bought a Times-Picayune and circled two jobs in the want ads. The first was at a new store – Pat's Furniture – opening on Airline Highway in Metairie, a suburb of New Orleans. The second job was bit murkier. In cryptic terms the ad said you could make $150 cash every day. I was curious about the claim, which seemed a lot for a day's work.

Later that afternoon I left Pat's Furniture with a job offer to be an inventory clerk. I told them I'd get back to them in a couple days. What I didn't tell them was I wanted to check out the other job first. I drove from Pat's to a nondescript office in a strip mall on the edge of New Orleans to inquire about the second position.

The job was this: You drive around selling shoddy, overpriced merchandise – all shined up – to unsuspecting people. In small restaurants and bars mostly, when business was slow. I was told I'd get a day of training, and then could go on my own. I would start tomorrow the perm-coiffed boss said. He had proudly mounted his

BA diploma from the University of Miami on the wall of his office. I wasn't impressed. But I showed up the next morning on time.

My so-called trainer did not currently have a vehicle I was told, so we loaded up my Mazda with various watches, knife sets, pots and pans – brand new items that looked nice but were actually shit.

As we drove into New Orleans, my trainer, a decently dressed guy with a roguish manner, rambled on about himself. He had a fluid way of talking – each sentence almost ending, but then flowing on into the next – spoken with an accent that sounded of Brooklyn. He had an oily sheen to him and wore a musky, beach-scented cologne.

He tried to lean his seat back to get comfortable but the merchandise filling the backseat made that impossible. His right foot kept bouncing up and down like he was playing a bass drum. He seemed wired on something.

I asked how he ended up in New Orleans and he told me he was a methadone addict who two months earlier had escaped from New York after trying to rip off his drug dealer.

"Good move on your part," I said. "I mean the escaping part." I hadn't cared what his name was when we first met because I thought I'd never see the dude again. Why pollute my memory. But I couldn't stop myself.

"So what do you call yourself?" I asked. He looked confused and picked at a scab on his hand.

"Huh? Oh, Mario." I told him my name was Ted, but didn't offer anything more. I didn't want him knowing my full name.

The shtick with this job was you would say your company had been involved in a big trade show at the Superdome and had ordered too many products and we were selling them at a loss. For instance, the watches were tastefully displayed in a black velvet case and carried a fancy price tag of $99.

You'd start by asking $75 for one, then drop to 50, then 40, saying it was your wholesale cost, the lowest you could go. Bottom line, anything we made over $11 was ours to keep. It was sleazy as hell and I didn't like it. But I was near broke. Plus, I like talking to people. I figured I might learn something.

We went into a few cafes in mid-morning, after the early rush. Mario would sweet-talk the waitresses. He was smooth. Made it seem like a fantastic deal – a bit of fortune blowing in off the street. People love getting a deal. A silver watch in a black velvet case is very seductive when it's half price. I was seduced myself.

After two hours with about $80 in sales, we were in downtown New Orleans a few blocks from the Quarter, and Mario said to turn left at the next corner. A sign said it was an illegal turn.

I'm a trusting sort, always game to stick it to the man, and decided to do it. A block later I was pulled over by a NOLA cop. When I showed him my Montana driver's license he said that since I was from out of state I had to pay the citation now.

I thought it was a shakedown, but it's standard. Tourists in New Orleans often blow off tickets and leave town. So the NOPD makes you pay fines up front. You could fight it later if desired. At least that's the way it was then.

I didn't have the scratch to pay the ticket. So the cop said to follow him. Ten minutes later I was in the city jail. This was a Friday around noon. I was told I couldn't see a judge until Tuesday. I sat in the detaining cell alone, a long way from Montana. I didn't know a soul in the city and there was no way to reach Dick. My head spun. I felt drunk.

Meanwhile, Mario took my Mazda, full of merchandise, and said he'd call the boss and get money to bail me out. The boss said no way. He told Mario to bring back my car and unload it – he was not bailing anybody out.

Showing honor among thieves, Mario hit some bars and finally sold a knife set. As I was having my fingerprints taken before being transferred to the County lockup across the street, he showed up.

Using the money from the knife sale he bailed me out. We then continued on our sales calls. But I'd already made up my mind about the job.

The jail had a nickel pay phone. I had some change, and called Pat's Furniture to accept their job offer. They asked if I could come out that afternoon to help move furniture onto the showroom floor. I replied I was tied up but would be available to work on Monday.

After that day Mario bailed me out of jail, I forgot about him. Until one night when the cosmos slung us together again.

Chapter 9 Bayou Teche

A pril
       After living on Esplanade for awhile (our landlord Tina we found out later was a he), Dick and I rented a shotgun apartment at 1010 Washington, just off Magazine Street in the Garden District. We'd been joined by another Montana friend, Gary, who had driven down and moved in with us. We caroused hard and drank like the fools we were.

Before long, Dick and Gary got offshore oilrig jobs. It meant going out for three or four weeks at a stretch. When they were gone I spent a lot of time alone, usually going out to hear music at Tipitina's or uptown to the Maple Leaf or Jimmy's. Or just going to bars to play pool.

If I was tired of going out, I stayed home and read. Big, thick books that I thought I should read. I deluded myself and thought I understood them. I felt like I was a man of the world. Of course, I didn't understand shit.

One night I was at our favorite bar in the Quarter, a dark joint a few blocks off Bourbon called The Chart Room. I was there alone when Mario walked in. He was with a loud blonde in a fur coat and tight leopard skin slacks. Both were definitely drunk.

He looked at me from across the bar and I could see his mind cogitating, working out who I was. Halfway through his cocktail he walked over and took a stool next to me. I got a whiff of cologne and bourbon.

"I know you," he said. "Can't remember your name but I bailed you outta jail. You owe me 50 bucks." I was impressed.

"You're good. Hiya, Mario. What's up? Sold any knife sets lately?"

He laughed. "Naw. I'm no longer slingin' that shit. I got a better gig now. What happened to you? I bail you out and you quit on me? You never came back." His eyes were glassy and trying to focus on me, squinting while tilting his head back.

"The boss is an asshole. Tried to screw me." His Brooklyn accent was more pronounced, a sure sign he was blasted. He pointed a finger at me, "Now I remember, you're Teddy."

"That's right. You're not as blotto as you look."

"I got a memory. So what are ya' doin now?"

"This is it, I just drink all day."

"Yeah? Not bad. But I got somethin' better. Maybe a job for ya."

"I don't need a job. I've got one."

"Where's that?"

"A camera store downtown," I lied.

"Really?" He eyed me suspiciously. "You take pictures?"

"Yeah. Sometimes."

"That's good. Got your own camera?"

"I do." This part was true. I had a 35mm Olympus given to me by a friend who had somehow gotten peanut butter on the lens. He didn't want it. I took it and cleaned it up. That got me started taking pictures.

Mario looked me in the eye and stuck his little finger in his glass and swirled it to stir. He took a thoughtful drink then wiped his mouth with the back of his scaly hand. He stiffened up a bit.

"Teddy, this is a better job than before. It's a kick-ass deal and the pay is serious, my man."

"No thanks, Mario. Don't want to end up in jail." He slapped his hand on the bar and guffawed.

"What ya doin' tomorrow?" he asked.

"Why?"

"Meet me here at noon. I'm gonna take you to a swamp party."

"What's a swamp party?"

"It's a bayou partay, my friend, the real thing. Live music, crawfish, crab, beautiful ladies..."

"Thanks, but I don't think so. I was planning to drive over to Biloxi." It was a lie.

He scoffed. "Biloxi! So lame. You're comin' with me, T. You gotta experience the real Louisiana. Bayou Teche. It means snake. Bring ya camera. You'll see some amazing things."

I was intrigued. Sounded interesting and a way out of my bored existence. I decided to go.

The next day I met him in front of the Chart Room and we took off in my vehicle, just like the first time we met. I wanted to drive. I like controlling the wheels. That way I could leave when I want.

Mario told me we were going to a party put on by someone named Leroy at his ranch near Bayou Teche outside New Iberia. It was promised to be an authentic Louisiana country bash with live music, dancing, drinking, cards, and piles of the best crawfish in the Bayou State. I'm a sucker for crawfish. Can't get enough of it. I was all in.

We went through Breaux Bridge south to New Iberia, then drove six miles east toward the bayou. The humidity was debilitating. It felt like you were inside a water balloon. Sweat stung my eyes as I drove us down country roads.

We finally arrived at Leroy's, a spread with a moderate ranch house, two barns (one ramshackle, one big enough for a dozen horses), two corrals, and untold numbers of chickens, goats, dogs (including a 3-legged boxer), parakeets, and other critters.

I was soon introduced to the host. I've never forgotten the moment.

Leroy Dupree was shaped like an icebox – a square block of a man, about five-foot-nine, with well-muscled arms and two thick blocks of wood as legs. The build of a linebacker. He wore a stained white cowboy hat, pressed short-sleeve Panama shirt, faded blue Wranglers, leather belt with silver buckle, and dirt-encrusted cowboy boots. His skin was the color of maple syrup. Ethnicity unknown – part black, part Creole, part Cajun – a mélange of family blood.

He had a thin cigar in his mouth he shifted from side to side as he talked. His voice was a peculiar pitch of both bass and tenor, with tone starting low at the onset of a sentence and rising to high by the end of it.

The sound he made when uttering syllables and sentences threw you off. Your ears had to work hard. It was a gumbo of English, Acadian, country twang, and rebel slang. I could've listened to him read a hymnbook.

In his house, a large table was set up in the living room. Newspapers were taped down completely covering the table. On top were heaping bowls of boiled onions, potatoes, and crawfish. Heads and shells were sucked and thrown on the table, in piles that grew bigger as the day went on. A crowd stood around the table making a mess and talking a mile a minute in sentences I often couldn't understand.

I met Leroy's wife, Evangeline, and their six-year old daughter, Lulu. The little waif was a treat, all big eyes and silly questions. I welcomed her conversation, to be honest. I had been alone for awhile and needed to talk, even if it was with a six-year old.

I won't go into all we did at the party. I drank more than I should, big surprise. I know I lost money playing boo-ray. As the sun went down, I ended up in one of the barns feeding goats and talking to Leroy. We seemed to hit it off. He was a true southern character, with an ingratiating charm and cagy smile. He told me he was a cop for many years in Baton Rouge after graduating from LSU, but left the force and came home to run the family ranch.

We talked about the south, about the civil War of the States (as he called it). We talked about Gettysburg and Robert E. Lee and Huey Long and writers like Walker Percy, Robert Penn Warren, and Tennessee Williams, whom he hated.

We talked about LSU football. And about Professor Longhair, the New Orleans piano legend (whom we'd both seen at the same show at Tipitina's two weeks earlier). We also talked about swamp gators and how to spot them in the reeds at night and how to snap a chicken's neck: "Twist clockwise," Leroy said, and we both laughed hard. We had some shared interests and seemed to click.

He showed me around his ranch and bragged about the two black Cadillacs he owned, each parked behind his big barn. "It's the best vehicle ever made," he said. "You're a fool to drive anything else." He was not impressed with my red, checkered-top, rotary-engine Mazda.

As we drank, he opened up a bit about his operation. It was a cattle ranch that had been in the family for generations. He grew up there, went to the local high school. "We won State in football." he said, flexing his arm.

He explained how his ranch used to be a plantation before the Civil War, back when the long rows of trees that line the front drive were first planted. He loosened his belt and sat back, raised his Dixie and poured the entire beer down his throat. He tossed the empty can on the ground and grinned at me.

"I got another business besides the ranch," he said.

"Really? What's that," I asked, curious.

"I call it the Agency."

"Agency...like advertising agency?"

"Not exactly, but there is creativity involved."

"Sounds interesting. What do ya pay? When do I start?" I laughed, the idea of me coming out to the bayou to work for an agency of some kind, for this character.

"Want to know more about it?" He smiled and took the cigar out of his mouth.

"Yeah, fill me in," I said.

He went on to say the Agency performed services for companies, families, individuals – they solved problems. He didn't explain what these services were, but did say they had a job opening. He wanted to add a new service to his business: Photography. He said Mario had told him I was a cameraman as he called it. Said he needed a camera guy he could trust. And it paid handsomely.

"I think you're the man for it," Leroy said. "I see you got Montana plates. That where you're from?"

"No," I responded quickly. "I bought the car at a used lot when I got to New Orleans. The plates are still good so I kept them on. But I'm from Oklahoma." I said it as if I was proud of it to throw him off. It seemed safer to lie to him. The less he knew about me the better. To be honest, I hate Oklahoma. My grandfather played football for the University of Nebraska from 1924-26 and I'm a big Husker fan. Oklahoma has long been a hated rival.

"Okay, Okie." Leroy took a draw on his cigar and blew smoke toward the rafters. He looked off in the distance. "Tell me, do ya believe in justice? That people should pay for their sins?" I wasn't sure what he was getting at, but I said I most certainly did.

"I do too," he replied. "Now, let me ask you. If you had the opportunity to, how shall I say..." He was about to finish his sentence when the door flew open and Mario burst in.

"Watermelon contest. Let's go!"

Leroy looked at me and jumped up. "C'mon, Okie! You gotta get some pictures of this."

The pictures I took, now lost, show drunken men wrapping a rope around a watermelon and pulling it tight to try and break the melon in half. I tried it. Couldn't do it. Some cracked it and made red pulp seep out, but only one person decapitated the melon: Leroy.

He took great pleasure in it and strutted around like a bantam rooster flexing his biceps like he was some southern Adonis or something. A short man's show of strength and power. Short guys love to show off, and a lot of them have short fuses.

Chapter 10 Swamp Party

When it got dark, the whole party jumped into vehicles to hit a local dancehall. Leroy drove one of his Caddys and one of his gang drove the other. I said I'd drive myself, thinking I could escape later if I wanted and head back to New Orleans. Mario rode with me.

On our way to the roadhouse I told him that Leroy had mentioned the Agency. Mario grinned but I could see a frown in his eyes. He'd seen how much time I'd spent with Leroy and I'm not sure he liked it. He said I could make some serious money – the Agency was busy. I said, "Well, I do have a Marketing degree." He looked at me confused, then slapped his knee and burst out laughing. I didn't think it was that funny.

The roadhouse was hopping. People of every age and color filled the floor, dancing to Zydeco. I danced with Evangeline and a host of her sisters and cousins. It was muggy as hell, swampy. Sweat ran off me in streams. I looked up at one point and saw Leroy on stage playing the washboard. He was stomping around and grinning from gill to gill. It was a blast, and I partook heavily. I was pouring down Dixie beers like a native and dancing drunk like a fiend.

"I love swamp parties!" I yelled to Mario as we stood near the stage.

"This is just the start," he yelled back over the accordion. "You ain't seen nothin'!"

At midnight, the music stopped. The men gathered in the parking lot smoking cigars and a joint that was passed around. I was about to say I needed to get back to New Orleans when Mario piped up, "Leroy, swamp party time? I think Teddy here is interested." Leroy looked at me, spit on his palm, stubbed out his stogie on it and said, "Yeah, let's do it."

"Maybe next time," I said. "I got things to do tomorrow and..." Leroy cut me off. "You can't take off now. You're hammered. You'll drive yourself into the bayou. This won't take long. You can drive, Okie."

I was cornered. So Leroy, Mario and I got in my vehicle and they gave me directions out of town. About ten minutes later we pulled over on a dark road and got out. Leroy told me to bring my camera. I paused, then grabbed it. I had no idea what was up. It was quiet. He was wearing a braided belt made of a lariat. He removed it and wrapped it around his forearm.

We walked a quarter mile to a rusty trailer parked in a grove of cypress trees. Without a word, we walked up to the door. Tried it. It was locked. Leroy stood back ten feet, then charged and busted through the door, falling on the floor.

Mario burst in behind him and flipped on the light. I saw he had a gun in his hand and was headed down the hall. Leroy was right behind him. Seconds later they emerged with a frightened scarecrow of a man. He was rattled. So was I. This was not good. Mario, with gun pointed at the guy's head, told him to get on his knees. The man complied.

"I let you off for poisoning those dogs," Leroy said. "But you had to be an asshole and test me. You had to go out and rob that old black mama on Bayou Teche. That was all the money she had. And then you beat her, break her arm, bust her nose, a 70-year old woman? You're a dog, Tino. Rabid."

"We gotta put you down," Mario snarled. Leroy walked around behind Tino.

"Wait you guys," he squeaked. "She made me mad. Had no respect. I deserve respect don't I? Okay, I'll give the money back. I swear."

"No, you won't," Mario said. "How you gonna do that if you're dead?"

Leroy made a quick motion from behind and yelled something I couldn't understand.

Tino's eyes got big and his arms instantly rose to his throat, gripping at the rope Leroy had looped around his neck and was pulling tight. Leroy pushed him over on his face, put his knee in Tino's back, and pulled hard on the rope, forearms bulging and blood vessels raging in his own neck.

Tino kicked and tried to roll over, his only sound a slight gurgle. But Leroy had leverage. In less than a minute, Tino stopped struggling. His eyeballs slid up under their lids like lemons in a slot machine. Mario stepped up and booted Tino flush in the face, a last boot to his sorry existence.

I was speechless. Finally, trying to control my shaking, I said, "Holy mother of God. You killed him! You can't just kill somebody!"

"Yeah, you can," Leroy said, breathing hard. "If he deserves it. It's justice. You heard what he did. He was beyond redemption. A snake. Trust me." He looked down at Tino, then looked at me. "You said you believe in justice, right? Karma? There you go."

I almost dropped to my knees. It was all I could do to keep steady.

"Get your camera out. You're gonna take some photos," Leroy said calmly.

"No way," I said.

"Do it, Okie, and don't make me ask twice. Mario, go bring Teddy's car up." Leroy was menacing, his voice an octave lower. Mario took my keys and ran out the door.

I took several photos as directed by Leroy. Shots of Tino. Closeups, different angles. A few minutes later, Mario drove up in my Mazda. We carried Tino outside and stood him up against my car, with me on one side and Mario on the other. Leroy took a photo of us with my camera. Then Mario and Leroy threw the body in my trunk.

We drove three miles down a dirt road and pulled over along the bayou, a full moon high above us. A boat was tied to a small dock. Mario jumped in and started the engine.

They placed Tino's body in the boat. Leroy made me take pictures of it. Then he asked for my camera. I handed it to him. He looked through the viewfinder, then raised it and took a quick shot of me. Then he shot one of Mario and me together, handed me back the camera, and told me to take out the film. I wound it up and gave him the roll.

We all got in the boat and took off on the bayou. I was unable to see much except dark forms of moss-draped trees reaching over into the marsh. Like ghouls. Out in the middle, Mario cut the engine and without a word they rolled Tino over the side. In the moonlight, I saw his face drop into the depths, mouth agape as his body slowly sunk and disappeared.

"That big ol' gator will eat well tomorrow," Mario cackled lunatic-like. I gagged and nearly puked into the swamp.

I was shaken, trembling, and in no shape to drive back to New Orleans. Leroy was adamant that I stay at the ranch. I didn't sleep. I kept remembering what Leroy had said on the way back to the ranch, lit up after the swamp party.

He'd said, "The best way to kill a man is to strangle him. You want it quiet. No screaming. No gunshots. And you don't want blood. Blood is bad. Breaking a windpipe and choking the breath out of someone is the best way to do it. I like using a lariat, or garden hose – about five feet is all ya need. Some prefer an extension cord. A rope, or bullwhip, pulled tight is almost impossible to get your fingers around. And when you stick your knee in his back and pull hard enough they don't stand a chance."

I'd never heard anything like it. This guy was talking about murdering someone, as if it was how to rope a goat or kill a chicken. I was repulsed, yet fascinated. I wondered if strangling was indeed the best way to kill someone. But what bothered me even more were Leroy's final words of the night.

"Okay, Okie, you're in. You are now a part of the Agency. And if you ever tell anyone about us, or what you saw tonight, you'll end up gator meat. Just like Tino. Welcome aboard." I was speechless.

The next morning, I drove back to New Orleans with Mario. Along the way he told me more about the Agency. He said he heard the business went back in Leroy's family for generations. To right after the Civil War he thought.

Mario explained that Leroy had connections in the Louisiana Sheriff's Department, the New Orleans Police Department, and other contacts in Baton Rouge. He thought of himself as a sort of Robin Hood of the south. Folks came to him for help in finding missing people, solving crimes, and delivering vengeance. He charged a set fee for each service.

The job we did with Tino was a freebie – a PSA they called it – Public Service Action. Even so, Leroy always paid anyone involved with any job, PSA or whatever.

As we drove, Mario handed me an envelope. Inside was a note. It read: Payment for services rendered to the Agency, made to Teddy the Okie. With the note was $1,000 in cash. "You have to take it," Mario said. Scared not to, I did as told.

In Morgan City, I stopped to get gas. I went in to pay and told Mario I needed to use the can. Mario followed me in to the gas station, but not the restroom, where I removed a shoe and slipped my driver's license inside it.

Back in my Mazda, we drove on to New Orleans.

Sunday was slow in the Quarter. I found a parking place in front of the Chart Room to let Mario out. He pulled out a pen and the envelope that had contained his own Agency payment.

"Give me your driver's license," he said. I shifted in my seat.

"I can't," I said. "I don't have one."

"Bullshit, give it to me asshole."

"I'm serious. I don't have one. I threw it away."

"Give it to me! Now!"

"I threw it away after I got jailed when selling those watches and stuff with you! I got scared. I'm getting a Louisiana license. It's being mailed to me."

"Get out of the car!" We both got out. Pissed, he went through my wallet and all my pockets, then rifled through my pack, glove compartment, and trunk. He got in my face.

"You are one dumbass mother," he said. "You can't hide!"

Then he got the envelope and pen out of my car. "Write down your full name, address, phone and social security number," he said. I took the envelope and wrote out what he asked. I listed my name as Ted Coogan, gave a fake address near Tulane, and made up a bogus phone number and SSN. The only true part was my first name.

He looked it over. "Teddy Coogan? What a hoot. Fits you to a T. Dumbass Okie." He looked me dead in the eye. "Okay, Teddy C, I'll be in touch. Stay safe."

He turned to get out, then stopped and looked back at me. "Listen, you better be careful, man. Leroy may like you, think you're smart or somethin', but he will kill you in a snap if you cross him. You understand what I'm sayin'?"

He leaned in and looked me in the eye. "You're with the Agency now. There's no getting out. You do NOT want to tell anybody or go to the NOPD. He's tight with the force. You could disappear fast, man. Not just you, your entire family. He'll kill them one by one unless you do what he wants. Leroy has tentacles. They reach far and they can hurt."

As he spoke, his hand absently massaged his neck.

I didn't say a word. Mario got out of the car and I sped off, checking my rearview as I headed to our apartment in the Garden District – far from Tulane where I told him I lived. After driving a few blocks I pulled over, took off my right shoe, and removed my Montana driver's license.

My head spun like a disco ball. I thought of gators, watermelons, rope. I turned on the radio and it got worse. The hit of the summer was playing – "Dust in the Wind"... all we are is dust in the wind. I switched it off.

A few blocks from our apartment I parked on Washington, near Commander's Palace. I got out and walked over by the entrance to Lafayette Cemetery and stood behind a tree, checking to see if I was followed. I didn't see a soul. I left my car there and walked home.

That night I lay awake and thought about the shit I'd gotten myself into – and how to extricate myself. I could feel myself starting to rationalize what had occurred. The guy, Tino, had beaten an old woman and ripped her off, and poisoned a dog. Was it that bad that he was dead? I resolved to keep it all to myself, at least for now. But I wanted no contact with Mario or Leroy ever again.

At lunch the next day, I went to a car wash near Pat's Furniture, cleaned my car, and thoroughly vacuumed the trunk. I had a bad feeling the wheels were coming off my life in the Big Easy.

Later after work, I drove to a used car lot on Airline Highway and sold my Mazda. Traded it in on a green '67 Mustang. A new ride would help me avoid Mario and Leroy I thought. At least, that was the plan. But then, I'm not much of a planner.

Chapter 11 Portland

Saturday morning

Waking in mortal dread is worse than waking with a pounding head. A hangover I can deal with. At first, I wondered if what happened last night was a dream. But no such luck. No dream. A living nightmare.

I lay flat on my back in bed and massaged my temples, trying to settle my mind. But the more I woke up the more my brain thrashed about, flopping like a fish in the bottom of a boat.

I sat up on my elbows and caught my reflection in the mirror of our dresser – a lumpy old fart. I instantly looked away. On the dresser were my wallet, a wad of bills, and several cell phones.

Rolling gingerly out of bed, I checked my phone. No new messages. Nothing on my burner phone either. Mario's phone (a burner) had the messages with Leroy from last night. No new ones had come in.

I tried calling Kate, letting it ring until it went to her voicemail. In a raspy voice, I blurted out, "Honayyy, please call me. Where are you? I need to talk to you. I told Jasmine you're in Astoria just so you know. Please call me."

I then texted her: Please call me, let me know where you are and that you're okay!"

Under my wallet was the little notepad I carry around. I opened it and read the last notation I'd made: 5950 Skidmore 48 hrs from Fri 3am to RIP.

I got dressed. In the closet on the floor were the contents of Mario's backpack, including a manila envelope with $18,000 and a Barbie doll. I pulled out four grand, then hid the rest of it beneath a closet shelf. All the while my mind kept turning, like tumblers in a lock, trying to find the right combo to open the escape hatch. I needed a way out of this RIP job.

My memory took over. Reaching into my top dresser drawer I drew out my journal and opened it. I read a couple of the entries from 1978 when I first got roped in with Leroy and Mario.

I thought about writing about the events of last night, but didn't know what to say. I was at a loss for words, afraid to write down in print what I'd done. I couldn't explain my actions. It was like I was a different person. As if a bolt of lightning had struck something primal deep inside – causing an intense reaction. An instinct I didn't know I had.

I made coffee and dropped two frozen waffles into the toaster. A sound made me jump and I turned to see Jasmine's door opening. It was early for her. She came out firing.

"Dad, you did it again!" I looked at my waffles in the toaster. Were those hers? She didn't want me eating her food. But she didn't eat waffles, I thought.

"Did what," I said with a sigh.

"You left the side door open – you not only didn't lock it you left it wide open." She was steaming. I thought back and couldn't recall doing it. It's happened before, but this time I thought I had closed and locked the door.

"I don't recall doing that..."

"Well you did. Who else could've done it? Mom's in Astoria! Who else would just walk into our house?"

"I thought I locked it – I'm sorry. I'm really trying to be better about that."

"Ben will take off you know! Last time he crossed the street and was on Don's lawn, almost on his porch. He could have been hit or killed crossing that street! You can't leave the door open! Any of them! You have to remember to lock the doors when you leave."

"Got it, got it. I know." Jasmine stared at me, then opened the fridge and got out some yogurt. She pulled a spoon from the drawer and leaned up against the kitchen counter. I could tell she had something else on her mind.

"I think I'll stay at Emmy's tonight. We're going out." She seemed nervous, which she never is. I wondered if she was telling me the truth. She was not a good liar, had no facility for it. She always gave the unvarnished truth, painful as it might be to hear.

"Okay, but please stay in touch," I said. "Text me where you are. I'll be gone a lot today."

"Where?"

"Uber driving mostly. And I've got a couple errands. Take that other phone I bought you, okay?"

"Okay." She didn't object a whit. Now, I was nervous. Could something happen to her? I thought not, but looked around for wood to knock on. I tried not to think what I would do if something happened to her. She retreated back in her room.

My waffles sprung out of the toaster like a Jack-in-the-box, jolting me. I stabbed them onto a plate, drowned them in syrup, and wolfed them down. Then, grabbed my computer bag and keys and went out the door, locking it behind me.

I headed west toward the river, unsure where to go, but needing to move forward to keep breathing.

For lack of a better idea I drove to a bar – My Father's Place on MLK. They open at 6:00 a.m. every day of the year. My kind of place. A place I can sit and think and drown my sorrows and liver as needed.

I ordered a tall Tecate with V8 – a red beer. I had learned of the value of drinking red beer from a guy who hustled pool to pay his college expenses. He said drinking red beer when you're in a pool hall all night and playing for money is smart. It gives you just the right buzz to play well, and you seldom lose clarity of mind or vision, or end up hung over.

Along with the beer I ordered the special – meatloaf and eggs. The waffles I'd had at home weren't sitting well. Meatloaf and eggs always sit well.

James Brown was on the jukebox. It was fitting. Music is what feelings sound like, they say. I felt like getting down on my knees. Sitting in the booth, I thought over my life-changing (or ending) dilemma.

I put out of mind the fact that I had, with intent, murdered two men the night before, chopping off their future, leaving two kids without a father. I couldn't deal with it. Besides, I had more urgent problems. The Agency felt like a snake slowly circling me. Or a gator with only its eyes appearing over the surface.

I wrestled with various problem-solving scenarios, conducting a brainstorm with myself – just Les and I. There are NO bad ideas! Think out of the box!

A wide range of actions were considered, none a viable option. A break was taken for a leak and to stretch legs and mind. Then, back in my booth the pondering resumed. I got out my pen and made a T diagram on a napkin. On the top of the T were the words DO IT and DON'T.

Beneath each I jotted down what could happen in each case – whether I go ahead and kill another man (two murders, three - what's the difference), or whether I don't do it and run for my life with family, dog, and conscience. Or, would I take on the Agency. Draw a line, stand my ground, and fight off fate until I feel the rope around my throat.

On the napkin, under DO IT I wrote: Last job, good pay, safe family, bad conscience, could go to prison, or hell.

Under DON'T I wrote: Take money, run for it, probably die, family may die, conscience okay, no prison, no hell.

No choice was made. I didn't like either option. Grabbing at straws, I Googled "ethical decision making" and found an article that didn't help much. In brief, it stated that people often become lazy with their thinking and enter into moral and ethical wrongdoing slowly, step by step. We are so busy with our lives that we don't stop to think about what our moral principles really are.

We just assume we're good folks. Until it becomes obvious we aren't. Like frogs in a slowly boiling pot of water. I needed to turn the heat off.

After another red beer I went back over my ideas and narrowed it down to the best options. A deadline was looming. I had to move forward with production.

Decisiveness can be a problem in the creative industry. A copywriter has to determine which idea is best and be willing to delete all others, kill the babies, including any witty puns and profound thoughts that cry for attention. That was often a problem for me. I usually let the client decide. It was their business. But in this case I was the client. After ruminating over all the options, I put stars by two of the ideas and wrote Plan A by one and Plan B by the other.

Plan A was simple. Beg for my life. And for the life of my wife, child, and future generations of kin. Leroy was big on kin. I would appeal to his sense of family history, honor and service, faith and mercy. I would tap into his literary, poetic side. The side where we had bonded when we first met.

I would bring up his daughter, Lulu, and my own child, Jasmine. I would remind him how Lulu and I got along so well when we first met at his party in 1978. How she sat on my lap and asked me so many questions. How would he feel if Lulu were harmed? How could he take away my loved ones – or take me from them?

Plan B was an entirely different animal. It was to go ahead and do it. Kill the perp, the bastard. His sorry, sleazy life was not worth my own, or that of my daughter. Good riddance I rationalized. But could I really kill someone? I told myself I could and focused on figuring out the best way to do it – to get in, take him out, and escape cleanly.

Getting in was the first step. I'd never learned how to pick a lock – not like Mario anyway. I knew the principles involved, but had never put them to use. I didn't want to resort to a sledgehammer, which I'd been told is highly effective, but of course is loud as hell.

But harder than breaking in would be getting away with it. A second murder in three nights within a ten-block area would draw police and the press like vultures to a carcass. The words "potential serial killer" might appear.

The news would not abate soon – and anyone anywhere, even on a backwoods ranch near a Louisiana bayou, could follow the story as it was investigated. I concentrated on three words: Don't get caught. My new mission statement at Les Overhead.

I chewed over Plan B like a toothpick, rolling it back and forth in my mind. How was I going to kill this guy and minimize the investigation – decapitate it so to speak. The plan needed to account for every eventuality. Unfortunately, account planning is not one of my skills. Creative execution is my area of expertise.

Chapter 12 Ronan

At this point, an astute reader might wonder why I didn't just go to the police and confess the whole sordid story. I thought about that. But what about Jasmine? And Kate? They could disappear. If I took a plea deal their lives would be in danger. I'd still be jailed. I might end up in Louisiana at Angola doing time for the murder Leroy committed the night we met. He could make that happen. Who knows, with Leroy's connections I might be locked up for the remainder of my pitiful life. I couldn't live with that.

Besides, to be honest it was a challenge. I wondered how I could get away with taking this guy out. The adrenaline was kicking in.

In my little notebook, I made a list of tools I'd need. I had them all I was sure, except a sledgehammer. I put a question mark next to it.

Sitting in the booth, I could hear rain pounding the street outside. It was coming down in sheets and the windows streaked tears. It's unsettling what pops into your mind when times get truly dark. I thought of a quote I'd read recently. "When there is no sunshine, be the sunshine." What a crock of shit. If life gives you lemons, I mean real, bad, scary lemons, you don't make any goddamn lemonade. You panic, you freak out, you curl up in a fetal position and die.

"I'm sorry, you need something? I didn't hear what you said." It was the barmaid.

"I said something?"

"Yeah, you said something about lemonade and lemons, I didn't get the rest."

Damn, I thought. Talking to myself? Jasmine was right. Am I losing it?

"No, I was just thinking out loud. I have an alter ego and we talk out loud sometimes. But as long as you're here I'll have another red beer."

"Sure, no lemonade?"

"No lemonade." I wanted to laugh but couldn't. So I went on. "And bring me a double shot of Cuervo with that red beer." I needed to shift into a higher gear.

From my computer bag I pulled out my address book, looked up a number, punched it into my phone. After four rings, an answer. It was Ronan.

"Don't tell me – you've robbed a bank."

"No, a drug store," I said. "I need your help."

"Ha – of course a drug store! Opioids! Good idea. Have you started your heroin habit yet?"

"Not yet, I'm not 70 – don't you remember, I have to be 70 before I take up heroin and golf." It was a running joke between us. I once told him a heroin habit could last for 20 years or more, so why not have a blast your last years on earth. Heroin to relieve the boredom, golf to get a walk.

Ronan Duecker had grown up in Astoria working on fishing boats. He'd moved to Portland and become a Private Investigator and then a cop and detective and then a P.I. again. He was a barrel-chested behemoth, a salty soul and semi-literate fisherman who escaped the graveyard of the Pacific, migrating from catching fish to catching felons. It's safer, he said.

Ronan and I met many moons ago on the edge of Portland. We'd both looked into becoming Private Investigators in the early 90s.

We met at an introductory session for a P.I. training program out in some Clackamas County industrial park. The program taught you how to conduct investigations and surveillance, how to file a report, handle a gun, basic stuff. It was a 12-week course that cost $1500.

At that time in Oregon, you didn't need a license to be an investigator. You could just print up some cards and go to work for lawyers, insurance companies, corporate execs, angry spouses.

Ronan and I both completed the program and kept in touch after that. I picked up some jobs working for lawyers on insurance fraud cases, mostly following people around. Then got into freelance surveillance work for corporate clients who had intellectual property they wanted to protect. Employees often sell trade secrets for money. It was my job to catch them at it. This type of freelance work was interesting and the pay was decent – still is. But I won't go into that now.

Over the years, I've picked up the tools and various accoutrements of P.I. work. I have a few weapons, a police scanner, handcuffs, camera with zoom lens, binoculars and such. I don't do as much freelance P.I. work as I used to, but I keep my hand in it.

Ronan followed a similar path into private investigation. He made some police connections and after working as a P.I. for ten years he became a cop.

He rose to Detective then had a falling out with the Assistant Chief who had a gambling problem he didn't want disclosed. Ronan disclosed it anyway. Shit hit the fan and Ronan took a hike. He still carries a grudge, along with a powerful handgun. That was two years ago. He was now back working private, but still had connections.

"I need your help, big man," I said. "Need you to find a person I'm trying to locate. And his daughter. I need to find them soon, and find out as much as I can about them. Not old stuff, what's current. Cash on the barrelhead."

"T-bone, you dog. What are you into now?"

"It's a long, sad story. I don't want to make you cry."

"You could never make me cry."

"Do you have time to do it? I need all you can get – today."

"As if I had nothing else to do. Let's see, clean out the garage or dig up some trash for you. I'll go with the trash. Might as well make some money."

"Cool. Thanks, RD."

"Okay, gimme the names."

"Leroy Dupree and Lulu Dupree, daughter. Both New Iberia, Louisiana. Name spelled D-u-p-r-e-e. Start with them. One more name if you have time: Nolan Duplantis. D-u-p-l-a-n-t-i-s. Lives in Portland on Skidmore Street. I need info and a photo if you can get one."

"Okay, I'll get to it."

"Get back to me by 4:00 if you can."

"You give me a whoppin' four hours? Why so generous?"

"Sorry, it's all I got."

"Well then shut up and lemme go. I'll see what I can dredge up."

The term dredge was a good choice.

"Don't email it, just call me with the info."

"I'll be in touch. Don't get arrested."

I gathered up my stuff and left the bar. Sleet was slanting outside. I ducked under a storefront overhang and lit up half a Swisher Sweet I had in my coat pocket. I had started smoking again, mainly to give myself something to do.

I blew a cloud of smoke into the rain and tried to read my fortune. Indecipherable.

Chapter 13 Decision Time

S aturday afternoon
     The clouds continued to empty as I drove straight home. I didn't stop at any other bars, which I thought was a positive sign. Maybe I could pull this off.

The house was locked when I got home and it appeared Jasmine was gone. Her bedroom door was closed. I let Ben out and went into the garage.

Standing on a ladder, I reached up to a shelf and took down a large cardboard box that had HALLOWEEN written on the outside. I set it on the ground and looked through the contents. Included were various masks, wigs, hats, gloves, and such. There was also a set of handcuffs with key and a lariat of finely twisted rope.

I took out the handcuffs and lariat and rolled the rope between my fingers. It was sinewy leather, like rawhide. Next I pulled out a skin-tight Mexican wrestling mask I'd bought at the Portland Flea Market about a year ago.

The wrestling mask was called a Blackhawk Lucha Libre. It was striped with black and gold and had red wings that reached up and wrapped around the ears. Two small eye slits were ringed in silver, as was a small opening at the mouth. It was both cool and eerie.

I then tried on a pair of black nylon gloves and flexed my hands. I took them off and gathered up all the items and put them in a backpack that was hanging on the wall.

From a toolbox I pulled out a paint scraper, a few plastic garbage bag ties, and a Bowie hunting knife. It all went in the backpack, which I then put in the trunk of my Escape parked in the driveway. As I shut the tailgate I heard a voice behind me.

"What are you doing?" I about shit myself. Whipping around I saw Jasmine speaking through our kitchen window.

"Oh, I didn't know you were home," I said, trying to be cool. "What's up?"

"I'm going to work. What are you going to do?"

The question threw me. What'd she mean? And yeah, what am I going to do? I wish I knew.

"I'm gonna drive Uber awhile this afternoon, maybe tonight too."

"Be careful. Don't be out too late, dad." We've swapped roles. I could just laugh.

"Same for you, dear. Let me know where you are later. Take that backup phone."

Jasmine shut the window and left shortly after. I went inside, turned on my computer, and began looking for news stories on the incident from last night.

Oregon Live had it. The story read:

Man found dead in NE Portland home

Portland Police report a man was found dead in a home on NE Skidmore Street last night. The deceased was found in his bedroom and the house showed signs of a break in. Early indications are that it was a homicide, police said. Cause of death has not been released.

A Police spokesman said an anonymous caller tipped off Police last night in a 911 call. Neighbors in the area have been asked to report any suspicious activity seen over the last few days. Anyone with information on the crime is asked to contact the Portland Police Department.

There was no photo with the story, no name of whom I'd killed, and no mention of the young waif I'd left fatherless, for life.

I took a photo of the news story with Mario's phone, then texted it to Leroy with a link to the story and a message: News is out.

Two minutes later Leroy got back: HOW'S IT FEEL TO KILL AN INNOCENT MAN?

I didn't respond. Look forward, not back I thought. I searched for information online about the target for tonight: Nolan Duplantis. I didn't find much, but did confirm that he lived at 5950 Skidmore.

It was time for a drive by. I put on a jacket and ball cap and before going out the door grabbed one more thing – my flask, which I filled with R&R.

The rain had let up but steam rose off the road like it was an ash heap. I lit up the cigar in my pocket and chewed over my predicament as I drove toward Skidmore. I tried to focus only on next steps. I was on deadline. My next step was to scope out the perp's address – the correct one.

I parked a block away and took a hit on the flask. From under my seat I pulled out a plastic Ziploc bag containing a curly-haired black wig and sunglasses. I put them both on, checked my reflection in the rearview, then stepped out and walked down the street toward the perp's house.

It was quiet, nobody around. A block away I saw a woman walking her dog, a floppy-eared basset hound. As a kid, our first family dog was a basset – Butch. He was a great pooch, but got flattened by a truck in front of our house and that was that. I cried some serious tears over Butch. One of the few times I've totally lost control of my emotions.

The perp's house was a small Craftsman with bushes in front, a driveway, and fenced backyard. The fence would be easy to scale. I looked closely at the house and yard and closed my eyes and visualized it, so I'd know where to go in the dark. There were trees in the backyard, which would provide some cover. I took out my little notebook and wrote in it: Check on moon for Sunday night.

As I walked by, I thought about knocking on the door and sizing up the man – Mr. Nolan Duplantis. Small? Tall? Weak? Tough? I'd say I was looking to buy a house in the neighborhood and wondered if he was interested in selling. But I decided against it. I didn't want to have any nosy neighbors see me converse with him.

Back in my car, I thought about what to do next. I checked my phone to see if Kate had been in contact. No message. I texted her again: Where are you? I want to talk. Please!

I felt jumpy, so put the car in gear and turned on the Uber app. After a few minutes I got pinged. It was a woman named Nancy who appeared to be about my age. After picking her up, I didn't feel like going into my usual Q&A routine so kept silent as we drove. Halfway downtown she broke the silence.

"Been driving Uber very long?" I wasn't expecting a question and had to think about it.

"Uh, I'd say about two years."

"You like it?"

"For the most part, the money's not great but you meet some interesting people."

"Ever have any problems? I mean like being people being drunk or rude?"

"Yeah, especially at night. But I can deal with it."

She sighed. "Every job has its problems."

"True enough," I said. "What do you do?"

"I'm a behavioral therapist. People tell me their problems." That picked up my ears.

"Really, that's funny," I said. "I often ask people if they have problems they want to divulge. I'm looking for a good story for a book."

"I've got some for you. But if I told you I'd have to kill you. They're confidential."

"Of course. I'd expect nothing less."

"So, do *you* have any personal problems I can help you with?" The question gave me pause.

"Uh, no. I'm a paragon of mental health."

"I doubt it. But good for you."

I drove on and we were quiet. She checked her phone. After a few minutes, I couldn't resist and resumed the conversation.

"Let me pose a philosophical question, a dilemma."

"Okay, what's your dilemma? I'll start the clock." She was quick. I liked her.

"It's not mine. Just a question in general. What if a guy had to do something that is blatantly immoral, but if he doesn't do it someone he loves will be harmed as a result. Should he do it? Is there a time, or circumstance, when morality no longer matters? Where's the dividing line?"

"Hmmm. Well, it depends on how immoral the act is and what the consequences are."

I say, "What if it means killing someone?" I can't help myself.

"Well, morality is a balance. Like the scales of justice. You have to weigh each side, consider the impact and results, and make a decision you can live with – even if it means going to jail."

"I see," I said. "The proverbial gray area."

"I tell patients one way to make a decision is to make a T diagram and write down what will happen in each option. It helps to write things down, pro and con, when making a hard decision. The act of writing seems to focus the mind."

I pondered it. "I believe that's true, at least in my case." She didn't respond. I looked in the rearview and saw her eyeing me, not unlike my dog, Ben.

I pulled to a stop at her downtown destination and she climbed out.

"Thanks for the conversation," she said. "Good luck with your dilemma, or whatever. Don't run off and do something crazy."

I laughed, "Yeah, thanks." I forced a smile, but didn't care for her last piece of advice. As I drove off I thought, she must think I'm an idiot. It put me in a foul mood.

Chapter 14 Plan A

I drove for another couple hours, picking up various fares but not mentioning my dilemma with any of them. I didn't feel like talking about it – I'd flapped my gums enough.

At 4:00 I pulled into a parking lot and texted Ronan to see if he had any news on the three names I'd given him. I said to call me when he had anything. I then called Kate and let it ring until her voicemail came on and I hung up.

I sat wondering what to do when I got a call back from Ronan. I got out my little notebook to take notes.

"What do ya have for me, detective?" I asked.

"Former detective," he responded.

"You're still a detective. You'll always be one. You're an addict, just like me."

"Okay addict, I don't have much dope for ya."

"What do you got?"

"Let's start at the top. Leroy Dupree has a PO box in New Iberia, Louisiana. He has no record, no past complaints or actions filed, a few speeding tickets... Most recent, two years ago someone accused him of stealing their watermelons and that was settled. He's collecting a pension from Louisiana for a law enforcement career that was mostly in Baton Rouge and New Orleans... left the NOPD in the mid-70s for some reason. I didn't find his name much after that. Pays his property taxes. Sponsors local sports teams. Donates to charity."

"Kills people," I barely heard myself say.

"Kills people? That what you said? That little detail escaped me. Of course, wouldn't surprise me knowing you. Nice friends, Teddy." He laughed and went on, "What in God's name are you doing, man? What the hell shit are you into? Who's this Leroy Dupree in Louisiana?"

I didn't say a thing.

"You're gonna get yourself killed someday if you're not careful."

"Don't worry. Just a little project that came across the transom." I laughed.

"Transom? What the hell's a transom?"

"Look it up. It's a good word."

"I will not look it up. Because nobody would ever use that word in their life."

"I just did."

"Who's your client on this little project?"

"Nobody you know."

"What's his name? Or her name?"

"Dashiell Hammett."

"Hey dumbass, I know who Dashiell Hammett is. He's that detective writer. You think I'm an idiot? C'mon, spill it. Who's the client?"

"Okay, he doesn't want his name known. It's Les Overhead."

He laughed. "You are crazy you know."

I wanted to bark back at that, but kept quiet. My thoughts were approaching the levels of alarming and unhinged. Steam was about to blast out my ears and a whistle in my mind was near to blow. I pulled out my flask, took a deep swallow, and wiped what spilled down my chin with my coat sleeve. I almost forgot what we were talking about. Then remembered.

"What about his daughter, Lulu?" I asked. "What'd ya find on her?"

"Lulu Dupree has a PO Box, not the same as her pa – it's in Lafayette. No record or incidents for her either, just like her pop." He went on and I could tell he was reading from a report. "She went to LSU, then transferred to Tulane. Graduated 1992 in English, got a teaching certificate in 1997 – taught school in New Orleans for 10 years, then moved back to Lafayette and is a history teacher at her old high school. Divorced. Was married to a shrimp rancher whatever that is. Two months ago she was elected Chair of the County Humane Society. Plays in a band on weekends – the Bon Temps Outlaws. She's lead singer. Nice looking, at least from her driver's license. Couldn't find anything on her mother whoever that was, and she has no siblings, an only child."

"Really," I responded, thinking of our own only child, Jasmine.

"You know these people?" Ronan asked.

"From a long time ago. I remember Lulu when she was a kid. She was cute then. Haven't seen any of them since."

"Well, they look like a nice group of folks," he said, the sarcasm dripping. "Please don't introduce us."

"Okay, what about this guy Nolan Duplantis?"

"Not much there either. Convicted of murder in '79 and locked up in the state pen. After that there's no record of him. Kinda weird. I'll keep digging on that. I do know he just got his Oregon's driver's license a month ago. Now lives at 5950 Skidmore. And that is it."

"Thanks for not much," I said after a pregnant pause. "Why don't you text me an image of his driver's license."

"Can do."

"Pretty good for an afternoon's work. I owe ya."

"Yes you do owe me," he said. "And I will catch you and you will pay."

"You know I'm good. Let me know what else ya dig up on Duplantis – soon as you can." I was getting antsy and hung up.

Arriving back home, I let Ben out and then checked every room of the house. No signs of forced entry or broken windows. Nothing amiss. Jasmine was at work. I needed to hear some music but it took a full minute to decide what. Finally, stuck in a CD of Buckwheat Zydeco to get me in the right frame of mind for what I had to do.

Checking phones (personal cell, burner, Mario's cell) there were no new messages. I found the text from Ronan of the Duplantis driver's license and emailed it to my Les Overhead address.

Two minutes later I was looking at the man's face on my laptop. I screen-grabbed his photo and printed out a color copy. He had the look of a loser, no doubt. I could pick him out in a lineup. That's him your honor, the killer who took a young woman's life (and the future life of her baby). Lock him away and bury the key.

I opened a new Word file and began writing what I would say to Leroy – Plan A. It had to be compelling and concise. Expressing yourself in short, written fashion is damn hard. That's why taglines (i.e. slogans) cost more than headlines, and company names cost the most of all. The shorter it is, the harder to write and more important your word choice.

I started by invoking our history together and how we had so much in common, so many shared interests, then appealed to his deep-rooted sense of old-world honor and service in the line of whatever Leroy wanted.

I brought up the end of the Civil War, and the honor and compassion demonstrated by General Grant when he let General Lee and his entire army keep their horses and return to their homes. It was time to reciprocate. Let us part ways as friends, I said. Let us bury the sword. I thought he would like that line.

For a rousing finish, I brought up Jasmine and how she is so much like his own daughter, Lulu, who peppered me with questions when we first met at his ranch in Louisiana. Lulu is older than Jasmine but they both have that in-your-face spirit, I wrote.

I wrote he must be proud of her being a local high school teacher, history no less. I said it's great that she plays in a band on weekends – the Bon Temps Outlaws. I love her voice. She's a beautiful girl. And now she's the Chair of the County Humane Department, that's cool. She obviously loves dogs. Just like you and I, and my daughter, Jasmine. I wanted him to know I knew a lot about his daughter. My thinking was that if Leroy thought I could harm Lulu, he just might let me off the hook.

With my notes on screen in front of me, I called Leroy from Mario's phone. I let it ring six times, then hung up. There was no voicemail. Within a minute he texted back: DO NOT CALL. TEXT OR PHOTOS ONLY.

They say technology smells fear. It's certainly true in Leroy's case. He's always been fearful of technology. Reticent to use the latest new thing. Didn't like computers or digital products of any kind – communicated only with burner phones and the U.S. Postal Service which he felt he could trust. He'd only use a computer in rare instances, like checking on a murder. Otherwise he let his minions handle the digital dirty work.

He was like Crazy Horse – never wanted his image to be taken, printed in the paper, produced in a mug shot, captured for eternity. Never wanted his voice to be heard, his slightly lispy speech pattern recorded, presented as evidence in his undoing.

You can read people by their writing. Leroy's writing was often in all caps. When you use all caps you're yelling your message I tell clients. So make sure that's what you intend to do. I'm sure Crazy Horse Leroy intended to yell at me, but I noted he didn't use an exclamation point, which meant he wasn't as mad as he could be. I struggled to think positive.

I texted him back: Will take photo of what I have to say and send it.

With Mario's camera I zoomed in on the computer screen showing the copy I'd written – Plan A. I took a couple shots in case one was blurry. I then texted the photos to Leroy and waited.

I realized they might be the most important lines of copy I'd ever written. Promoting and preserving the brand known as me. Was the content spot on? The tone correct? The call to action, or in my case inaction, strong enough?

It didn't take long to find out.

Leroy texted back: NICE TRY. YOUR WRITING HAS IMPROVED. BUT NO, IT MUST BE DONE AND BY YOU – BY TOMORROW NIGHT. AFTER THAT I'LL LET YOU GO. I SWEAR ON THE GRAVE OF ROBERT E. LEE.

I think he loved General Lee more than his own mother. I texted back: WHY ME?!

Leroy: YOU'RE THE ONLY ONE I CAN TRUST.

Me: I'll turn myself in.

Leroy: NO YOU WON'T. TO MUCH TO LOSE.

I took notice of his spelling error – writing "to" instead of "too" much to lose. He was slipping I thought. I'm always proofing, looking for typos and grammar errors – on billboards, ads, menus, beer labels, anything with words.

Leroy was a literate type who read a lot and knew good writing. In this case, his grammar was off but the content was spot on. He was right, I had too much to lose. I brought out the hammer - Lulu.

Me: Aren't you worried about Lulu? I have connections, too!

Leroy: I WILL GOUGE YOUR EYES OUT.

Me: Funny. That's what I told Mario when he threatened Jasmine.

Leroy: YOU GOT NO EYES ON LULU. I DO ON JASMINE. DO IT!

He was right. I threw the phone on the ground and put my hands over my eyes. Plan A was down in flames. I'm screwed. I rocked forward and began hitting my head on the desk. It didn't knock any sense into me so I stopped.

With one finger, I hit delete and made my letter to Leroy disappear, then turned off the computer. How could I kill this guy Duplantis? He'd already been convicted. It would be like killing another innocent man – two in three nights. Mario I didn't consider innocent so he doesn't count.

I bent over and picked up the phone and put it back in my pocket. My mind shifted course and gears began turning. It was on to Plan B.

Chapter 16 Ben

Ben. Where is he? I looked all around the house calling his name. No sound, not a whimper. Did he get out? Did I leave the door open? Or was he taken? I opened the back door and there he was, sitting on his haunches, waiting. The dog who will not bark.

Ben is a rescue from Texas who was shipped by truck to Seattle. Kate found him online and we drove up and stayed at my cousin's house while we checked him out.

He's about two-foot tall, black and butterscotch in color, with big paws and a wide face with brown marble eyes that seldom blink and make him look like a wolf.

To kill time, I took Ben for a car ride. When I say the words "car ride" (or as Kate would quip, "bar ride"), Ben's tail wags like windshield wipers on high. I leashed him into the seatbelt in the backseat and took off. Car rides are a love we both share.

I lowered the windows and the fresh air did us both good. Ben stared out the window, his nose a couple inches out, trying to sniff out the world we were passing through. I did the same.

To scope out the scene again, I drove by the perp's house. Nothing had changed. There was no vehicle in the driveway and Duplantis was gone. Ben looked at the man's house and studied it as I drove by. It almost seemed his brow furrowed, as if he sensed something odd there.

From driving Uber, I knew a park was close by with an off-leash area. Frazer Park. It's a hidden gem of a spot with a grassy hillside and a ring of tall trees, with a grade school on one side and houses behind a high fence on the other. There's seldom anyone there.

Ben knew where we were as we pulled up. He shook his head briskly and stood on all fours. I felt a chill, not from the air so much as from dread. I could feel myself shutting down, sinking under the surface, unable to do anything to save myself, or my daughter.

Sitting on a swing at Frazer Park I felt as low as I've ever felt. It was more than depression, it was a nervous breakdown that I felt was bearing down on me, flowing like wet concrete into my mind, about to set up. It was getting hard to think, hard to make a decision.

I walked over to where Ben was poking around a few bushes, then saw a little farther out on the hill an enormous tree. It twisted out of the ground and spread into branches that resembled the bony, knuckled fingers of a gnarled hand reaching up from the underground.

The sight of it rocked me. It was both beautiful and violent, an expression of the natural world that was frightening to behold, even in daylight. I imagined it at night – imposing, monstrous, a devilish silhouette swaying in front of a full moon.

The tree had a thick branch that stuck out horizontally about twelve feet off the ground. It had lime green moss growing on the top side, which reminded me of the trees that formed a gauntlet down the dirt road to Leroy's ranch, and of a tall rope swing that Leroy's daughter Lulu would sit on while I pushed her.

I remembered learning how to tie a hangman's noose – and eventually being able to do it blindfolded. I used to practice it at night in our apartment when Dick and Gary were out on oilrigs and I was tired of going to bars alone.

Leroy used to have contests to see who could tie a noose the fastest. I won once. It was a proud moment for me. But I've never had the opportunity to put the skill to use.

And in a snap, I saw it. An escape. A release. An end to the madness. I laughed hard, so hard that if I'd had booze in my mouth it mighta blown out my nose. I laughed until I was literally shaking.

Ben stared at me and tilted his head. His ears came forward and I could tell he was reading my mind. He knew my plan. He was thinking, "Are you bat-shit crazy?"

I stared right back at him and heard myself say, "I'm not sure. Maybe."

So, it was on to Plan S: Starts with s, ends in cide.

I'm convinced that hanging is the best way to do yourself in. It's bloodless. No brain spatter. No ruined carpet. Easier on the poor soul who finds you. Simple and clean (other than what might run down your leg out of your bowels).

All you need is something to tie around your neck and a place where you can let gravity do its thing. Cops like it, too. Makes the investigation easy as pie. You can put the incident to bed, bury it, and move on to something serious. That was something I learned in Louisiana from Leroy, during my formative years.

Chapter 17 New Orleans 1978

June

My swamp party experience with Leroy and Mario had shaken me to the bone. They'd murdered a man right in front of me and implicated me in the process, with my own camera and my own car. Their contacts in the NOPD and State Police made me leery of turning myself in. They could get off and I could end up in a Louisiana jail, and prison, for years to come. And would they do something to my family?

When I last saw Mario, I'd told him I worked at a camera shop on Canal Street and that I was from Oklahoma. I'd given him a fake address and fake name – Ted Coogan. I'd sold my Mazda and bought a Mustang trying to cover my tracks.

One might wonder why I didn't just leave town? All I can say is, I got cocky. I thought I knew what I was doing. I thought I could dodge these guys. And to be honest, I didn't want to get scared out of the experience of living in New Orleans.

By the time June rolled around I figured I might be in the clear. I was enjoying the Big Easy immensely. I'd been to the Jazz & Heritage Fest where I wandered around wide-eyed tossing down Dixies and assorted cocktails like a man dying of thirst.

Dick and Gary still worked on oilrigs for weeks at a time. I enjoyed going out alone, trying new places, sniffing around for good times and adventure.

I'd risen from inventory clerk to credit manager at Pat's Furniture. I took credit applications from customers and called them in to finance companies. You didn't need to be a genius to do it. I liked talking to the customers – people of all stripes.

One day, Stan Best, one of Pat's better salesmen, came to my desk with a customer seeking credit. He was a tall, thin man around the age of 70 with the blackest skin I'd ever seen. He had a scowl on his stony, intimidating face and his creamy, red-veined eyes stared directly into mine.

I looked at the sales invoice to see what he was buying and how much he needed in loan. I started off like I always do. "Okay, sir, please have a seat. I'll ask you a few questions and see if we can get you a loan for those bunk beds and dressers you want."

He leaned over and sat down, silent, never taking his eyes off me. It was unsettling.

I said, "Can I get your full name please?"

With a deep growl he said, "Coogan, Theodore." He stared hard and I felt a chill. His long, bony nose looked like it might stab me. The catfish po'boy I'd had for lunch flopped over in my gut.

"Your name is... Theodore Coogan?"

"That is correct, young man," he snapped, the words sounding like bones breaking. I knew then I was nailed. It couldn't be possible that this "customer" had the same exact name as the fake name I'd given Mario when we last met. He didn't look like a Theodore. I didn't know what to say, so went on with the credit app.

"Um, what is your address?" My voice tremored.

"2919 38th Street, New Orleans, Louisiana." The instant he uttered the number my heart stopped. It was our family address in Billings, Montana – where my parents now lived. My mouth went dry.

"Okay, what's this all about?" I said quietly. "Mario send you? I assume you're not here to buy bunk beds."

"Hell no, I ain't buying no cracker bunk beds!" he said. I thought he was gonna hit me. "I got a message for you." He reached into his shirt pocket and took out a piece of paper and slid it across the desk. I read it.

It said: Mario will pick you up at your place at 7:00 tonight. Be there. We know where you live – 1010 Washington. And we know where your family lives in Billings, Montana. Be ready at 7 sharp."

The man snatched the note back, stood up, and walked like a shadow out the door.

I was struck dumb. My heart pounded and it was an effort to get up and go in the can and splash water on my face. How did they find out where I worked? Where I lived? Where my family in Montana lived? Mario was right. Leroy had a long reach and I'd just seen his tentacles.

IT WAS A FRIDAY NIGHT, sultry as hell. Even though we had AC in our apartment I sat outside on the front porch. Sweating. A few minutes after 7:00 a black Cadillac pulled up across the street, out of which emerged Mario from the passenger's side. He scanned the area, then walked up to our porch with a lopsided grin.

"I told ya, didn't I? You can't run and hide. The Agency will find you, Teddy Coogan, aka Teddy Murphy." He burst out laughing and stood on the steps in front of me.

"Did ya like meeting Theodore Coogan today? That was a kick. I was there – pretending to buy a sofa set. The look on your face, man, I wish I had a picture of it. You musta shit your cheap-ass seersucker pants."

"Yeah, that was a nice trick. Who was he, your granddad?" I tried to sound unafraid.

"Shut up! He's a former Baton Rouge police captain who is now 85 years old! Still sharp and knows how to put the fear of god in folks. Like you!" He bent over double laughing and I could see his bumpy, serpent-like spine showing through his tight silk shirt.

"Your man didn't scare me," I lied, trying to spit but failing. "So how'd you find me?"

"You're an idiot, that's how! Leroy knew you'd probably run off and sell your car after the swamp party and so we began checking the DMV and sure enough the very next day after our par-tay you went and traded your Mazda in on a Mustang. We got your address off the bill of sale and ran a background check on your true name – Ted Murphy."

I cursed myself for doing exactly what they thought I'd do. Selling my car. Bad decision. Mario went on, "We know everything about you now. Even where you went to high school – Billings East or something." It was actually Billings West but I didn't correct him.

"I followed ya to work one morning – Pat's Furniture. Ain't exactly no camera shop on Canal like ya said. You got a problem with lyin'." His grammar seemed to have gotten worse.

"Listen and listen close," I said, trying to conjure Bogart, "I don't want anything to do with you guys. I haven't told a soul what I saw that night in the bayou and I don't intend to. You don't have to worry."

"That's right, we don't have to worry," he shot back, emphasis on we. "You're the one who has to worry. You have a lot to worry about, fool! Starting now if you don't get in that Cad and go with us. Get your camera and film and let's go." He looked like a viper, ready to strike.

"Where would we go?" I asked, trying to buy time.

"You'll find out. You're gettin' off easy tonight. We're just puttin' the fear of god into someone. The Agency calls it an F-O-G. All you have to do is take pictures. And you get a grand for a couple hours work."

"A thousand bucks? And all we're doing is scaring somebody?" I was now feeling more curiosity than fear. That was as much money as I'd make in a month at the furniture store. Maybe this wouldn't be so bad I thought. And this is how it happens.

"We'll be done and back in about two hours no sweat," Mario said.

"What's this F-O-G thing, fear of...god? What does that mean?"

"We put the fear of god in 'em, make them see Jesus. Let's go."

I looked down at the beads of perspiration on my arms. It was a muggy night. I knew that Caddy would have AC.

He went on, "Of course, if you don't wanna do it, just stay home. In a few days you'll end up in the hospital or somewhere else less hospitable. Got insurance?" He threw his head back and cackled. "Do the smart thing, man. Get your goddamn camera and get in the Caddy. Now. I'll wait here."

I didn't know what to do, but found my legs carrying me up the musty stairs to our apartment. Our bathroom had a shower with a window that looked out over neighborhood roofs. It was the only way out other than down the front stairs where Mario waited.

I considered climbing out the shower window and making a run for it. But run where? With what? I had about 30 dollars on me. I had to play the cards I was dealt, without knowing the game. Sucker bet.

Chapter 18 Leroy

In a minute I was in the backseat of the Caddy and we were heading down St. Charles toward downtown. Leroy was in the backseat with me; one of his Agency staffers at the wheel. They called him Domza. I don't know if that was a first name or last. He appeared to have some Indian blood in him and had one of the ugliest mugs I'd ever come across – with acne scars pockmarking his neck and face like red ants at a flesh picnic. It pained me to look at him.

Leroy eyed me and said, "So, you're not some dumb Okie from Oklahoma? You're really from Montana?"

I looked at him and smiled, "Howdy Leroy, nice to see ya again. No, I'm not from Oklahoma. I misspoke."

He grinned, "You're one funny character, mon cher. You're lucky I like you." Mario turned and leered at me. Leroy went on, "I don't blame you for trying to hide your identity. I'd a done the same thing. But I wouldn't a picked Oklahoma. Only idiots are from Oklahoma. Or is that Iowa? Idiots out walking around – isn't that what they say? I know you're no idiot. You've proven that by gettin' in this vehicle."

"We'll see," I said. "The jury's still out." Leroy laughed and I said, "So what are we doing? Where we going?"

"We're paying a visit to a man who needs to be taught a lesson. Simple as that."

"Why? What'd he do?" I tried to act nonchalant and looked out the window at the stately old homes flanking St. Charles. The area reeked of history and mold.

"The monkey got himself elected to office and then turned his back on his friends who helped him get there. And he's an embezzler and is having an affair with a married babe who I happen to know. And he beats his wife and kids. And doesn't pay his taxes. And kicks dogs. What more do ya need?"

Mario and Domza cracked up at that and I was left wondering what was true and what wasn't. My world was spinning out of control, again. I was nauseous.

We got on the freeway and went over the Crescent City Bridge to Algiers, across the Mississippi from New Orleans. I'd never been to Algiers. After a few turns we pulled into a parking lot at a Holiday Inn. The tone inside the vehicle turned cooler as Domza shut down the engine.

"You sure they're in there?" Leroy asked Mario.

"Yeah, we've had a tail on him all day and he's here for his little rendezvous." He pronounced it "ren-dez-voo" and I wasn't sure he was joking.

"Okay, we all go in. Teddy, you too. Take all the pictures you can. I want shots of the dude and the dame. Comprende? Let's get ready."

Mario reached into a backpack and pulled out two guns and four ski masks. He gave one of the guns to Domza and handed each of us a mask.

"Put this on – unless you want your face to be seen," Mario said. I thought about arguing, but held myself in check and put the mask on, adjusting the eyeholes so I could see. We went inside the hotel and up to the third floor, to room 322 – I still remember the number. With no pause Mario knocked on the door and said in his most charming voice, "Room service – complimentary champagne for our guests."

There was a rustling and footsteps, then a soft woman's voice said, "Champagne? Just a minute." I stood holding my camera, wearing a black mask that covered my face, wondering what the hell I was doing. How did I get here?

I didn't have long to ponder it as the door opened slightly and Domza threw his body into it and busted through, breaking the shiny brass chain that held it closed. We all rushed into the room and Mario knocked the woman back against the wall and she dropped to the floor.

He pointed his gun at a fat, pale speckled man in bed who pulled the bedspread up to cover himself. His creased pants and shirt were folded over a chair.

"What the...!" the man shouted. He didn't finish his question, obviously knowing the answer.

"Shut up!" Mario said. "Get up, now! Or you'll be dead in that bed in a few seconds." Domza reached over and pulled the bedspread from the guy, exposing him.

His rolls shook like jello as he jumped up, naked as a jaybird. I was frozen, not wanting to take a photo. Leroy gestured to me to start shooting. I snapped a few pics of the walrus and one of the woman cowering on the floor. The room reeked of perfume.

"Let's go," Mario said. "You're coming with us." Domza grabbed the guy by the arm and started pulling him towards the door. The perp picked up the bedspread off the floor and wrapped it around him as we all headed for the exit. It all happened fast. Last I saw the woman she was sobbing, crouched in a fetal position on the floor.

Once in the Caddy, with the perp wrapped in the quilt and sitting in the backseat between Leroy and me, we headed back to New Orleans. We all kept our masks on and Leroy did most of the talking. In essence, he explained to the perp that if he didn't play by the rules he would end up in the river. It was more colorful than that, but still kind of cliché. It felt like a movie. Or a preview of a coming attraction.

The perp didn't say a word. I could feel him trembling next to me, the pastel blue and pink bedspread pulled up to his thick neck. While crossing the Mississippi back into New Orleans Leroy said, "It would be so easy to tie your hands and toss you into that river. I'd love to do it. Seriously. It would give me great joy. But not tonight, jerkwad. Next time, for sure. Count on it."

The perp sputtered, "I hear ya, I'll do whatever ya want. I swear." He was scared shitless. I thought I detected a scent of urine.

We drove on into downtown New Orleans and turned down an alley close to a diner where Dick, Gary, and I often ate late at night – the Hummingbird Grill. They serve a turkey dinner on Sundays with all the trimmings for $2.99. It was a dive diner with soul where street people gathered.

"This is your last warning," Leroy said, still in his mask. Gesturing to me he said, "Get out and let this creep outta the car."

I opened the door and let the creep out, still wrapped in the fluffy hotel bedspread. Mario jumped out too and ripped the bedspread from the guy, tossing it back in the Caddy. I noticed he had something shiny in his hand. It became clear what it was when he swung his fist at the perp's face, splitting the forehead open in a deep gash. Brass knuckles. I'd never seen them used before and I admit I was impressed. It was as violent a blow as you can deliver with a fist. I could see how handy they might be and I resolved then and there to get some knucks of my own.

The perp staggered back from Mario's blow and fell on his ass. Mario stepped forward and put a gun between the perp's eyes.

"Watch this," he said in an evil-sounding voice. The perp's eyes closed tight. Mario pulled the trigger three times. I instinctively blocked my face, expecting blood to fly my way. But nothing happened. Click, click, click.

"Next time I'll take the safety off," Mario said with menace.

From the car I heard Leroy yell, "Pictures!"

I snapped several quick pics of the naked man, trying to keep my hands steady as I focused. Suddenly, Leroy emerged from behind me and said, "Gimme the camera! Give it to me!" I handed it to him and he pushed me forward. "Stand next to him, now!"

I shook my head and stood still. Mario grabbed me and shoved me near the naked perp and Leroy took a picture. Then Leroy motioned to Mario and in an instant Mario had ripped the mask off my head. I heard the camera click just as I was starting to duck my head. I heard several other clicks as I bent down and turned my back to Leroy.

"Let's fly!" Mario said, darting back into the front seat. I was frozen for a moment, then stumbled forward and got in and we took off, leaving the perp in the alley, one hand on his forehead, the other covering his crotch.

We sped uptown, removing our masks and trying to catch our breath. Leroy tossed the camera to me. "Take out the film," he said.

I shouted, "You bastard Leroy, why did you have to take my photo? I did what you wanted!"

"Just precaution, my friend. Relax. You're new to the Agency. We don't trust you yet. These pictures will be kept on file and nobody will ever see them – if you do as you are asked."

"And what if I don't! I'm not just gonna do whatever you tell me to do! No way, no way. This is one thing, but..."

He cut in, "You'll never be asked to do anything crazy – like kill someone, trust me." He snickered, "I don't think you could do it." I glared at him, furious.

He went on, "I thought Montanans were cowboys – tough dudes! You're weak. You could never kill anybody. Mama's boy." He dragged out the last two words, mocking me. As if it was a joke – the very idea of me killing someone. I hate being mocked.

Ten minutes later I was back at our apartment. Before getting out of the Caddy, I gave Leroy the film and he handed me an envelope with ten 100-dollar bills. It had all taken less than two hours, just as Mario predicted.

As they were about to drive off, Mario opened his door and threw the bedspread out on the sidewalk. "Get rid of this," he said. "Or keep it for yourself, but I'd wash it first." I heard them all laugh as he shut the door and they roared off.

I picked up the bedspread and ran upstairs to our apartment. Later, in the middle of the night I took the quilt out to my car and drove five blocks to the Mississippi River and tossed it in. I then went home and took a shower to get the scent off me.

The excitement of the night – my first official Agency job – took awhile to wear off. Lying open-eyed in bed, I tried to rationalize what had occurred earlier. I wasn't sure what the perp had done but I was certain he deserved retribution of some sort. And we provided it – and taught him a lesson in the process. I had to admit it was funny, leaving the naked man on the street in downtown New Orleans.

I eventually got to a point where I was comfortable with myself and fell asleep. The next day I woke up a different man – richer in money, poorer in morals. Morals are overrated I joked to myself, without laughing.

I did laugh two days later though when I saw a news item on page four of the Times-Picayune. The headline read: *Parish Councilman Mugged in Bizarre Incident*

The story went on to say:

Local Parish Councilman, Healow Hoggins, may have been mugged in downtown New Orleans Friday night but his staff says he has no memory of what happened. What's certain is several witnesses saw him walking down Royal Street with no clothing and bleeding from a head wound. He could not recall what happened or how he lost his clothes. Police are investigating but have no suspects as of now. Hoggins has not returned calls from reporters and members of his staff have offered no comment.

The following few days were uneventful, though I did take some of the money Leroy had given me and sauntered down the street to Commander's Palace for one of the best dinners I've ever eaten – Boudin Stuffed Quail. I still remember it like last night. I can taste it.

Chapter 19 Marley

New Orleans in July was stifling. We would go out at night just to cool down in bars. One night we met a character from Alabama named Burt Juliano. He had flaming red hair, a red beard, and a voice like a grandfather with phlegm. It would have been hard to listen to if what he said wasn't so damn funny. He was a pharmacist at a drug store who felt it was his duty to sample every product he sold. He was about halfway through their stock.

My work at Pat's Furniture continued but I didn't get any more visits from Theodore Coogan or any Agency staffers. I wondered if the Agency had cut me loose. Did the photos from the last job not turn out? They may have been blurry. I kept looking for signs of Mario or Leroy but saw none. Until one hot, sultry night in late July.

That night, Dick, Gary, Burt and I went to a concert at a place called The Warehouse on the Mississippi River. It was the reggae king, Bob Marley.

The Warehouse had a concrete floor and people brought big sections of carpet to sit on. Nobody told us. We had no carpet – shag or otherwise. We stood the whole night.

Bob Marley started slow, swaying his body side-to-side and getting into the swampy feel of the evening. As he went on, song after epic song, he became more animated and eventually was swinging his dreadlocks back and forth in the air like whips. You could see the sweat flying off his braids in little arcs, like a sprinkler. It fell in drops down my own face as well.

There was a bar at one end of the Warehouse and we all ventured up for a drink. Standing in line, I saw two men talking animatedly at the end of the bar, near the can. One of the men was Leroy. He was pointing his finger in the other man's chest and talking fast.

The man talked back and it was obvious they were arguing. Then Leroy's arm shot out and slapped the man across his face. The dude was stunned and Leroy did it again, harder the second time. Leroy then erupted in a fusillade of words as the man kept his mouth shut, eyes down.

Nobody around saw it, or they didn't want to interrupt. I kept quiet. We finished our drinks and returned to our spot on the concrete floor where we watched the end of the concert.

The next day, returning home from work, I found an envelope with my name on it attached to our front door. Inside was a note: Wasn't Marley great? Saw you there with your crew. Good news, you've been promoted. More jobs, more money. Stand by.

It was unsigned but I knew it was from Mario or Leroy. I'd be lying if I said I was distressed to get it. I wasn't. I was definitely curious. Stand by for what I wondered.

I was keen to find out and it wasn't long before I did. Three days later I had another note waiting for me when I got home from work. It said: Agency job tomorrow night. Be ready with camera at 9.

The next day I bought three rolls of film at a drugstore and was sitting on our front porch at 9:00. Punctual as before, a Caddy pulled up. Mario stuck his arm out the window and motioned for me to get in. I did. Domza was again at the wheel and Mario was in front. Leroy wasn't in the vehicle – it was just the three of us.

Acting tough I said, "I'm not sure I'm going through with this, but what are we doing?" I didn't disguise my interest very well and Mario noticed.

"So, you a little more willing to go with us tonight?" he asked. "You startin' to wise up. A grand in ya pocket will make any fool wise up – even a loser like you."

"Yeah, well, I'm not doin' it if I don't like it. What's the job?"

Mario looked back at me in his side view mirror, "It's another F-O-G. Fear of God. Make that fear of Gar." He looked at Domza and they both cracked up. I didn't get the joke and lowered my window to let the marijuana scent out.

I won't go into all the details here but in short what happened is this. We drove to a house near Lake Ponchartrain, not far from the UNO campus, and picked up a dog – a feisty mongrel with a mean disposition and teeth it liked to show off. It was thin as a greyhound and its ribs made ripples in its splotchy skin.

The dog was frightening to behold. Truly a beast. His name was Gargoyle, due to how he resembled the mythic creature. He sat on his haunches, his jaw open in a wide grin baring his fangs. His dull eyes were set deep under a furry, bony brow that reached across his forehead. A caveman dog.

We leashed Gargoyle and got him in the car. Domza then drove us to a different house – somewhere in Metairie. Gar sat next to me in the backseat and stared at me for an unnerving amount of time. He could've torn off my nose and swallowed it in seconds if he cared to. I didn't make a move.

We finally pulled up in front of a ranch style home with manicured grass and a lawn jockey out front. Mario walked to the door, knocked on it and waited. The door opened slightly and Mario went in. Domza quickly got out and took hold of Gargoyle's chain leash and said, "Let's go." Camera in hand, I followed them inside.

In the living room, Mario was yelling at a middle-aged black man in gray boxer shorts and faded blue terrycloth bathrobe. I started shooting photos from different angles and tried to hear what Mario was babbling about. It was something about one way or another.

Mario didn't have a gun, or at least he didn't show one, which surprised me. But the perp was nervous as hell. He kept looking at the dog. Gar was growling, pulling hard on the chain. He only knew one thing. He was hungry. He wanted to eat. And it appeared this meaty stranger was at least worth a bite.

From his jacket, Mario pulled out an envelope and unfolded a piece of paper. It was a document of some sort. He had a pen on him.

He handed the pen and document to the guy and grinned. The perp eyed the demon dog drooling ten feet in front of him and made a swift decision. He signed the document.

We were out the door seconds later, Gar barking like a car alarm. I knew what his barks meant. He was yelling, "Bite, bite, bite, eat, eat, eat!" He was hungry and mad. I could see why. He had the meaty guy right in front of him and then he got dragged outta the house once the perp signed.

We talked about it and decided to swing by a fast-food joint for a few burgers to feed the dog. He wolfed it all down in less than five seconds, then we headed back to drop him off where he lived. He'd stopped barking and we all sat quiet on our haunches – I remember it well because a song came on the radio I'd never heard. "Lou-Easy-Ann" by J.J. Cale.

"Lou-easy-ann, I hear you calling back to me,
Lou-easy-ann, I hear you calling back to me,
Lord, I'm going back to New Orleans,
Lou-easy-ann has set me free."

In a way, I related to the song. I felt Louisiana had set me free from my past. Made me strong. I felt confident, as if I could do anything.

After that night, I started getting more jobs (I called them gigs to make them more legitimate) from Leroy and the Agency. It was a thrill to be honest. I'd never felt more alive – which I admit sounds like new age bullshit and I'll deny I ever said it but it's true. Plus, I was making killer money – long before killer became an adjective.

The gigs varied but typically included one of three subject areas: money, justice, and vengeance. With a dash of mayhem mixed in.

Sometimes it meant making somebody fork over what he or she was obligated to pay. Leroy and the Agency made sure folks lived up to the agreement they'd struck, whatever it was.

All I did was snap pics. I did not plan or condone the violent aspects of these Agency matters. I did not abet the crimes in any legal sense.

I do, however, admit I was there. I was there when they cuffed the owner of the Toulouse Street movie theater and wrapped him with 35 mm film and almost set him on fire in the projection booth.

And I was there when they dragged a scofflaw behind a skiff in some sewage canal near Houma. Man, did he ever stink. I've no idea what happened to the photos from that one but I'd love to see them because they were some of the best pics I ever shot. It was a beautiful night on the bayou. I remember the sky was violet – purple like a bruise.

I learned a lot on these night (and day) ventures. In essence, if you show up with a weapon or a mean-ass dog and a take-no-prisoners attitude, you can scare the holy bejesus outta anyone. You can make them do anything. It's a power that can go to your head if you're not careful. And I was feeling pretty heady those days.

Chapter 20 Ali

In early September 1978, my father and brothers came to New Orleans to see me and have some fun for a week. They slept on bunkies (mattresses) from Pat's Furniture, lined up in our apartment hallway.

Arriving two weeks before them was Muhammad Ali who was in town to fight Leon Spinks for the heavyweight championship.

In the week leading up to the fight, which local wags had dubbed "The Battle of New Orleans", Ali had workouts in a gym near downtown. The workouts were open to the public.

My dad and brothers and I went to a workout and watched Ali spar a couple rounds. After the workout, he began regaling the crowd. He spoke for 20 minutes straight, covering all sorts of topics, including apartheid in South Africa. It was impressive. He also jawed about how he was going to demolish the jack-o-lantern, gap-toothed Spinks.

At the training session, I happened to spot Leroy off to one side. He saw me the moment I saw him. I went up to him immediately, to keep him away from my dad and brothers.

Leroy said, "Isn't Ali something? The guy's brilliant. An assassin. He's gonna destroy Spinks."

"Yeah, I know," I said. "Spinks is a dead man. So Leroy, you come to town to see his workout?"

"Of course. I've got a little business to do, too."

"I'll bet you do. Hope it doesn't include me." I stole a glance to my brothers who were watching Ali as he commanded everyone's attention. They didn't see me talking to Leroy.

"So, you have some buddies with you I see," Leroy said. "Wanna introduce me?"

"No, you don't want to meet them." I looked him in the eye to show I meant it.

"Who are they?"

"Just some friends." Ali threw some shadow punches and said something funny I couldn't hear that cracked people up. I scrambled for a different topic of conversation but before I found it Leroy spoke again.

"It's funny, your friends look kinda like you." He stuck his elbow in my ribs and grinned wide, gator-like. It was muggy and I felt a drip down the back of my neck.

"You think so?"

"Who's the older guy?" Leroy motioned to my dad, who was focused on Ali.

"My boss, from work. He's the manager. He likes boxing." I didn't need to add the boxing detail but I did, which is a telling sign for someone lying. I was lying for all I was worth, as if the lives of my loved ones depended on it.

"Looks to me like the old man is your pop, and the guys are your brothers – you all look alike." I froze, didn't say a word.

"So they came down to Nawlins to see ya? That's good. Family is important."

I didn't respond, just stood watching Ali fling his wit. I said we had to go and went back to my dad and brothers. We left to beat the crowd.

Ali beat Spinks in 15 rounds, reclaiming the heavyweight crown for the third and final time. I paid 50 bucks and watched it in the

Superdome with 70,000 other rabid folks, including my friends, Dick, Gary, and Burt.

Leroy and Mario were at the fight as well – in row five. Leroy had on a yellow, open-necked Panama shirt with dark slacks. Mario wore his ever-present black leather jacket, with a white shirt, bolo tie, and beret. I'd brought binocs and I remember zooming in on Mario.

At the end of the bout, after the ref raised Ali's arm in victory, Mario jumped on his chair and started flailing his hands in the air, his fingers spaced like claws as if he were a gator or a mongoose.

In my journal, my scratchy handwriting describes the night of the fight in brief. I wrote how Joe Frazier sang the Star Spangled Banner and didn't mangle it, which surprised me. I wrote how I saw Sylvester Stallone and Lorne Greene and other celebs sitting near ringside.

After Ali and my father and brothers left town, life got back to normal. Normal being I'd go on a job with Mario a couple times a month. Nobody was killed in these little forays, but messages and pain were delivered. I found it fascinating.

The funniest was when we left a baby alligator in some big shot's bed. He was royalty with one of the top Mardi Gras parade krewes and had been caught in an affair by his wife. She knew of an apartment in the Quarter he used for his hookups and we were able to break in and leave him a gift.

We blindfolded a 2-foot baby alligator and tied its legs to a bedpost and left it under the sheets of the guy's bed. Gators stop thrashing when they can't see anything.

I wish I coulda seen the adulterer's face and snapped his shot later that afternoon when he pulled those sheets back for his little tryst.

After tying the gator down, I mentioned that maybe we should leave a note. Leroy liked the idea and I had my pen with me, so we grabbed a piece of paper and I wrote: *Congrats on your new baby! Cheat again and his mama eats you.*

Leroy howled and slapped me on the back. He thought it was hilarious. He carefully placed the note inside the sheets and we turned out the lights and left.

It was strange. Doing these jobs was like an out-of-body experience. It felt like being in a homemade movie. I was a supporting actor, playing a role. It wasn't the real me.

As official photographer, I caught every episode and escapade on film (including the baby gator). I gave every roll to Mario or Leroy so they could provide proof that the Agency had completed its assigned task and collect the fee.

I got the hang of the work and did my job well. I even got some brass knuckles out of it. Mario got them for me from a bartender at Pancho Villas in New Iberia. They were used, one of several extras kept behind the bar.

When Mario gave them to me he said, "Here's your knucks, ya owe me thirty bucks." I remember being struck by the rhyme. Mario could wax poetically without knowing he was doing it.

Brass knuckles take some getting used to. These were made of iron, not brass. Solid brass would be too heavy I was told. Leroy said you could break your fingers if you didn't use them right. You have to use a rolling punch with a glancing blow – not straight on. The technique protects your fingers and delivers more damage to the recipient.

Truth be told, I've never been on the receiving end of a brass knuckle punch. But I've heard it's extremely painful. Staggering. Debilitating. A well-delivered blow to the head, sternum, or spine can take you down hard. And you may not get up.

Those who know history, particularly World War I, may recall that brass knuckles were used in hand-to-hand combat in trench warfare. That's slugging it out. Those with the toughest mettle win.

Knucks, without a doubt, have a violent history. And I do love history.

On the advice of Leroy, I bought a watermelon. I propped it in the corner on our kitchen counter and started slugging it night after night, getting used to the knucks. Dick and Gary were offshore on rigs so they never witnessed the nightly melon bashing. The cockroaches were out in numbers though, crawling out of their foxholes to watch (everybody loves a fight). I gave it to them. I'd try to stomp on the roaches with my boot heels when they scurried for a better viewing spot.

I remember once squashing one flat and seeing his guts ooze out. I raised my knuckled fist and sneered, "Got you sucka!" I leaned down over the flattened cockroach corpse, "My species rules!"

Smugly, I walked over to get a paper towel to dispose of the carcass and when I came back the roach was gone. I stared in disbelief. That roach was dead! But he had somehow sprung back to life and escaped – his life redeemed. Either that or his buddies came out and dragged him off, an act of roach heroism I've never heard of, but I believe is possible. Can roaches not be heroic?

Slugging the watermelon was like hitting the bag for a boxer. It was a workout. I'd put on a Professor Longhair record and mix up a batch of julep punch, then start punching. It was a release. A way to blow off steam without causing a ruckus in some bar.

From then on, I started carrying the knucks in my pocket when I went out at night. Feeling a bit tougher, a bit angrier. Looking for a fight. Almost.

Chapter 21 Last Call

As the end of 1978 approached, the allure of New Orleans started to fade. I got tired of partying, tired of the people.

When I told locals I was from Montana they looked at me like I was a Martian. They'd heard of Montana (like they'd heard of Mars) but had no idea where in the universe it was. And when I suggested they visit this amazing U.S. state they acted as if it was the most ridiculous thing they'd ever heard.

Why would I go all the way to wherever the hell Montana is when I live in New Orleans, the epicenter of life, was the prevailing opinion. I was tired of the uppity attitude. Dick and Gary had also had enough.

So we all decided to quit our jobs at the end of December for a little escape. Our plan was to take a trip to Mexico and Belize for a month. Kick back on one of the islands. Then return to New Orleans for Mardi Gras. After that, my schedule was open.

On December 15, 1978 I gave two-weeks notice at Pat's Furniture. I didn't give notice to the Agency because I hadn't officially decided to quit. I was just taking some time off and didn't feel the need to tell them. I wasn't sure what they'd do.

The Agency was silent in December. Apparently the vengeance and retribution business is seasonal like other industries. People are less prone to harm someone during the holidays. But once the New Year kicks in, watch out for blood spatter.

At least that's what Domza used to say in his baritone brogue. He didn't talk much but when he did you had to listen. Just for the sound of it. He would have made a great Sioux chief.

On New Years Eve we were all in the Quarter – Dick, Gary, and I – hitting our favorite spots and sidestepping all the falling-down-drunk Penn State and Alabama fans in town for the Sugar Bowl. Penn State was ranked number one that year. Alabama number two. I didn't give a shit about either team.

That night we were trying to meet up with our pharmacist friend, Burt. He said he'd be on Bourbon Street. Shortly before midnight I spied him on a corner intersection buying a Lucky Dog. I still remember he had an orange plastic cone on his head. With his red hair and red beard he looked like a gnome – a conehead Yosemite Sam. I wish I'd had a camera.

As I reached for his shoulder I suddenly felt a sharp pain and I spun down on the street. A car crossing Bourbon had hit me, rolling over my ankle. It wasn't much but the collision fractured a bone.

I saw the vehicle was black and instantly thought it might be Domza and Mario, but it wasn't. Somebody stopped the driver – it was a young drunk from Tennessee in a black Trans-Am – Tennessee license 1L 8599, which I memorized in case I might have to seek compensation.

I couldn't walk. So, Dick, Gary, and Burt fireman-carried me around. We ended up at our favorite haunt, the Chart Room. None of us felt any pain.

My firemen cohorts decided to go across the street to have a drink at another bar. I stayed where I was, on my barstool talking to Margaret, the Chart Room's exemplary bartender. I don't recall what we discussed but I'm sure it was important. Subjects like justice, vengeance, gin, vodka.

Then of course, right on cue, in walks Mario. On his arm was a blond woman in a blue chiffon dress that hugged her tight. She was leaning toward Marilyn Monroe and almost getting there. They didn't appear happy – as if they'd just finished a fight. He lit up a smoke and ordered drinks and they sat silent. Then he saw me and came over.

"Happy new year, Mario," I said. "Glad to see you're still standing."

He was blasted, weaving in a tight circle. I was blasted as well, but seated.

"You don't get around much do ya?" he said. "This the only bar you drink in?"

"I like the atmosphere," I said. "The drinks are cheap. So is the talk. Speaking of which, I wanna talk to you."

"You should go to better places, cher – the money you're makin'."

"Yeah, about that money. I'm laid up for awhile. I got hit by a car tonight."

"Sure ya did." He looked back at his date, not happy. He licked his lips and said, "Listen, the Agency is slow now but come Mardi Gras it could get crazy. So don't go far."

"Viva Mejico! Viva Zapata!" I slurred and laughed hard. He looked at me clueless, then returned his focus to his date.

"I'm heading south, amigo," I garbled. "Comprende?" Mario appeared to not hear me. Or didn't care. As if I wasn't worthy of being given his attention.

Taking a drag he blew smoke in the air and said, "I gotta go. We'll be in touch before Mardi Gras." He looked up at Margaret behind the bar and smiled. She smiled back in a way I sensed she had a familiarity with him. As he turned to go he said, "Find yourself another bar."

"Wait, I wanna tell you something!" I blurted. I leaned forward to grab his sleeve and missed, almost spilling from my seat.

I yelled, "Mario! I knew you when you were a drug addict from New York – remember? When you were hocking junk and got me thrown in jail! Don't act like you're better than me!" And then I lost purchase on my barstool and crashed to the floor with a bang.

Mario looked back with a sneer and shook his head. Then returned to his seat, tossed back his drink, and grabbed his date by the arm and pushed her out the door. I didn't see it but I heard the sharp sound of a slap, hand on skin with force – followed by a short, piercing female wail.

"You asshole, Mario!" I yelled.

Chapter 22 Mardi Gras

In early January 1979 we made our trip to the Yucatan and south to Belize and out to a little island called Caye Caulker where we flopped on the beach and drank cheap rum.

We eventually reversed course and landed back in New Orleans a week before the kickoff of Mardi Gras. I had my cast taken off and a new walking cast put on. No more crutches.

We gave notice on our apartment. Dick and Gary planned to drive straight back to Montana. I wasn't sure where I'd go but it was far from Louisiana. We planned to leave shortly after Fat Tuesday and go out with a bang.

As the parades ratcheted up during the early days of the festival, we hit different neighborhoods, standing along the street, drinking champagne, catching beads and tokens tossed from the floats of various krewes. But as the major parades approached, the weekend before Fat Tuesday, a fat problem arose. A police strike.

The police shutdown made Mardi Gras in 1979 different from any other. Tensions were high and both sides, city and police, were not about to give in. Right up until the end, neither side caved.

With no deal in the works, all the NOLA krewe captains met at the Howard Johnson's Hotel downtown and voted to cancel the last few days of Mardi Gras parades in Orleans Parish. They released a statement saying they refused to be held hostage by the Teamsters. The Teamsters union was led by Vincent Bruno who was related to

New Orleans mob boss, Carlos Marcello, who I was told was a nasty piece of work.

The cancellation didn't mean the end of the party. New Orleans favorite pastime is to party – no matter what, police strike or not. Someone die? Let's party. Saints win a big game? Lose a big game? Let's party. Ali beat Spinks? Let's party. Hurricane coming? Hunker down and open the bottles, y'all.

Some of the krewes relocated their parade to Gretna or other suburbs. Others just pulled the plug. Local residents were not happy. It was the first peacetime cancellation of Mardi Gras since Reconstruction following the Civil War.

The city had to scramble. They called in the National Guard to deploy troops to the French Quarter for Fat Tuesday, which even with normal police presence is off-the-charts wild. In 1979, with no police anywhere, Fat Tuesday in the Quarter was out of control.

It started early. I'd received a message from Mario to meet him in the Quarter at the corner of Dumaine and Burgundy at 8:00 a.m. I was sure this would be my last job, but wasn't sure if I'd tell Mario and Leroy.

We'd been out late for several nights prior so it wasn't easy getting up. My roommates slept in. I told them I was going out and would meet them at the Chart Room around 2:00.

I connected with Mario and Domza at the appointed spot in the Quarter. Their black Caddy was parked at the curb. Mario walked over to a pay phone on a brick wall outside a bistro and made a call – I assume to Leroy. He came back and said, "We're on. A spotter has the target – he's not far. We're gonna snatch him at the Drag Queen contest. Let's go."

"What are we doing? An F-O-G?" I asked.

"I don't know yet, Leroy will know. We're gonna meet him."

I had a bad feeling. This was my last Agency job and I knew the money would be good, but I was nervous, more than usual. I tried to remain cool.

We walked over to Bourbon Street and a few blocks down to where a crowd was gathering. People were lining the street four deep to see the Drag Queen Beauty Contest, one of the more colorful parts of Mardi Gras.

A flatbed truck was parked in the middle of Bourbon. It had a long ramp leading up to it. Contestants would sashay up the ramp onto the flatbed, do some twirls like a model on a runway, then stroll back down the ramp.

The costumes were like nothing I've ever seen. Glittery gowns with 10-foot feather headdresses and crowns, long gold silk dresses, purple capes, with wands and scepters that were used to point to the gods above and friends in the crowd. An oompah band played and people applauded every entrant.

We worked our way through the crowd to where the spotter was standing against a wall. Mario walked up and the spotter (I assume NOPD or ex) pointed out the perp. The target wore a cream-colored jacket, purple satin shirt, and off-white seersucker slacks. He had on a cheap, gold glitter hat that a tourist might buy.

As the drag contest went on, we stood about ten feet back of the perp. He was with some friends it appeared, and I wondered how Mario planned to snatch him. As nervous as I was, I was also curious. What was going to happen here?

There were no National Guardsmen in sight. Someone said the closest one was perched on a ladder about three blocks away, trying to keep an eye on everyone. Fat chance.

Once the contest was over and a winner announced, the throng began to disperse. Mario walked up to the perp and whispered something in his ear. The guy rolled his eyes and grimaced. He didn't like what Mario had to say, whatever it was. Then Domza went up and grabbed the guy's arm, twisted it behind his back, and pushed him over to a brick wall.

"Spread your legs," Domza said. "Seriously?" the guy responded, then did as he was told. Domza frisked him, then handcuffed him. He made it look like an arrest. People watched but didn't seem concerned. They'd seen it before. The perp's peeps stood around us, unsure what to do.

"I thought you guys were on strike," one of the man's friends said.

"Gotta keep the city safe," Mario said. "He's wanted for questioning. Step back and let us through."

Nobody stopped us and we walked away in the direction of the Caddy, near Dumaine and Burgundy. We had to wait at one point while a mock Mardi Gras jazz funeral marched down the street. It felt like we were heading to a funeral as well.

Chapter 23 Ball and Chain

When we got to the Caddy, Leroy was there. We all got in and drove off, the perp in the backseat between Leroy and me. Mario rode shotgun and Domza drove as usual.

We headed out of town west toward the bayous. The perp knew he was in trouble and started trying to talk his way out of it – whatever "it" was. I was still trying to figure it out myself. Leroy let him present his case, then finally had enough.

"Stop your pathetic whining, you know what this is about. You know you-"

The perp interrupted, "I told the police everything I know about that, and I was cleared. No charges filed. I've no idea what happened to those girls. You know that."

"You did it," Leroy said, voice rising. "You know you did it, I know you did it, the police know you did it, the girls' families know you did it. And if you don't admit it and tell us where the bodies are you won't live past noon. I shit you not."

"I swear I did not take 'em! I don't know what happened to them. I'll go to the cops."

"Yeah, good luck with that." Mario said.

I wanted to know what this was about so spoke up. "So what'd he do?" I asked Leroy.

"Nothing!" the perp said.

"Here's what he did," Leroy said. "He kidnapped two eight-year old girls about 20 years ago, molested them most likely, and killed them both. They were riding bikes and vanished without a trace, just like that." Leroy snapped his fingers. "This guy here did it – everyone knows. But he was just lucky enough to get away with it – so far. No charges were ever filed. But it's 99% sure he did it."

The perp responded, "Like I told the investigators, I knew those girls but didn't see them that day. Never laid eyes on them. Somebody else did it. Not me!"

"Shut the hell up," Leroy said. "You may not have heard but a few days ago one of the girls was found." I looked at the perp and saw his eyes widen a bit. "That's right," Leroy said. "Her skeleton was discovered tied to a tree in the woods. Some guy found her remains while out hunting, actually his dog found her. But nobody knows where the other girl is. She wasn't there. So the question is, what'd you do with the other girl?"

The perp was shaken. He didn't say anything for a second, then "I want my lawyer."

Leroy laughed and said, "We're way beyond that asshole. You have only one option – tell us where the other girl's body is! Or you'll vanish just like they did."

Leroy went into detective mode and started hammering the perp with questions and threats. We continued on driving and turned onto a gravel road that led towards a swampy area. The perp wouldn't say a word at this point.

So Leroy changed topics. He talked about how a few weeks ago he'd gone to a prison auction and swap meet held at Angola – the Louisiana state penitentiary.

"They were getting rid of a bunch of vehicles, furniture, sinks and shit," he said. "I saw some old balls and chains that prisoners wore back in the day. They were just rusting in some shed, so the prison sold 'em. I bought a dozen."

According to Leroy, the balls were made of iron and weighed about 18 pounds each. They came with a four-foot stretch of heavy chain attached.

I was the only one who seemed interested and I questioned Leroy about it.

He explained how balls and chains were used in the U.S. prison system for many years. Inmates at Angola (called "The Farm") worked 60 to 90 hours per week planting and harvesting cotton, corn, and sugarcane. Prisoners wore a ball and chain all day, causing gangrene and shackle sores, until finally the practice was ended.

The balls and chains were stored away and forgotten. Leroy, a fan of history and violence, decided he wanted to preserve the past and picked them up for a song. He didn't say what he planned to do with them.

When we came to a fork in the road, Domza turned right and said, "It's just a mile or two from here." A few minutes later we pulled up to a bridge crossing a bayou lagoon. We came to a stop in the middle of the bridge. The water had an oily sheen and I saw a rusted car door half-submerged on the other side. It was a nasty looking swamp.

Domza, Mario, and Leroy jumped out. Leroy pulled the perp out of the car and said, "Put your hands against the vehicle and spread your legs," as if we were going to frisk him again.

I got out and stood to the side, camera at the ready. Domza opened the trunk and reached in to heft something out. It was a ball and chain, one of those bought by Leroy at the prison auction. I snapped a few shots of the ball and chain and the perp.

Domza dropped the ball on the ground and leaned down to bolt it to the perp's ankle. The perp said, "What're ya doin'? You're gonna leave me out here? No way! I can't walk back with this!"

"You ain't walkin' anywhere," Leroy said. "Question is, can you swim with it?" The perp didn't say a word. He was way more nervous than I was. I focused on my job and took more photos.

"How deep is it here?" Leroy asked Domza.

"About 15 feet. Over his head at least."

"Okay, this is it. You either tell us where that other girl's body is or in about one minute YOUR body will be at the bottom of this piss pond, with this ball and chain attached. Nobody will ever find ya. But I bet a gator will – and you'll eventually get chewed down to a skeleton, your bones settled for eternity right down there." He pointed to the dark, still water beneath us.

"Talk or die, now."

"Believe me I would but I don't know what happened to that girl, either one of them!"

Leroy nodded at Mario. Mario stepped forward and he and Domza picked up the perp and dangled him over the bridge, head down pointing toward the murky swamp. Leroy picked up the iron ball and stood next to Mario.

"Where is she?" Leroy yelled. "I'm not asking again."

"Wait, wait, wait!" The perp shouted.

"I'm about to drop this ball," Leroy said. "And when I do your life is following it."

"Okay, okay! Lemme up, I'll tell ya!" I looked up and saw egrets circling overhead, curious about the drama being staged below.

"You better not be lying. We got shovels in the trunk and we're gonna dig her up. You're going with us. So you better be right."

"Okay, okay! I'll tell ya! Pull me up!" I leaned over the railing and saw the perp struggling. I thought about taking a picture but was afraid I might drop my camera in the drink. Leroy yelled, "Get him up! See what he has to say." Mario and Domza pulled the guy back up on the bridge and Leroy dropped the iron ball.

"Your next words better be true," Leroy said. "Last call!"

The perp was breathing hard, gasping to get it out. "I'm...not saying... I did it, but...I think I know... where her body is."

"You think?" Mario said. "You better know and not be lying! Or I swear I'll..." Mario's lizard tongue flicked out as he spoke.

"You know the tire factory... near the old Plaquemines Parish ferry landing?"

"Yeah, off the Frontage Road." said Leroy.

"There's a tool shed in the back... by the chain link fence. She's buried inside the shed – under some tires and junk."

"If we go there right now are we gonna find her?" Leroy asked.

"Yeah, she's there. At least she was 22 years ago."

"I swear, if we don't find her there I guarantee you'll be the one buried there."

"She's there, you'll find her," the perp said. I believed him. You could tell he'd given in. "It was an accident. I never meant to kill them."

"Yeah, sure it was," Leroy said, and he bent over to pick up the iron ball. He nodded at Mario and Domza and they grabbed the perp and lifted him up. The perp (now admitted murderer) tried to kick out with his unshackled leg.

Mario and Domza wrestled him over the bridge railing and Leroy looked at him, smiled, and said, "Hold your breath, asshole!"

And then Leroy heaved the 18-pound ball into the air and Mario and Domza let go of the perp. He screamed as he dropped like a stone into the dark void below. A cannonball splash plumed up from the watery black hole as the murderer disappeared into oblivion. The egrets above were shrieking. I was shocked. It was an R-I-P right in front of me.

Leroy then turned to me and pulled out a gun. "Mario get that other one," he said. Mario walked over to the trunk and leaned in to pick something up. I heard it before I saw it – the sound of a chain, like a rattler hissing and shaking its tail.

I froze as I saw Mario lift another ball and chain from the trunk. It hit me, I'm a dead man. That ball and chain is meant for me. I was headed down to the bottom of the bayou with the murderer they'd just sunk there. My heart beat furiously and I dropped my camera.

Mario sneered at me. Domza looked at Leroy, then at me with surprise. He didn't seem to know about it.

"Nice knowin' ya, but you talk too much," Leroy said with a fierce look. And as I blinked what I thought was my last blink, Leroy raised his gun and pointed it at my head. Then suddenly he spun around and shot Domza straight through the Adam's apple. I couldn't believe my eyes. A small hole appeared in his throat and blood spurted out like water from a squirt gun.

Domza reached both hands up to his neck and stuck a finger in the hole, trying to stop the crimson flow.

Leroy stepped toward him and said, "You talked. I told ya not to. Didn't I? You told her some things you shouldn't have, chief. You shoulda stayed away from her, like I told ya. Let this be a lesson to ya – in your next life." Leroy laughed maniacally, then raised his gun and fired two rounds through Domza's forehead. Dead man number two.

My knees buckled and I retched. I leaned up against the Caddy so I wouldn't fall over. The world spun around me like I was on a fair ride.

"Get that chain on and let's go," Leroy said. Mario bolted the chain to Domza's leg and they lifted him up. I picked up my camera and stepped forward. Leroy hissed back, "No pictures!" I lowered the camera and stood back as they upchucked Domza over the bridge railing. His body fell, pulling the chain in a sickening rattle over the rail followed by the iron ball, which Leroy lifted up and dropped over into the bayou. Adios, Domza.

We jumped in the car and went back the way we came. I was speechless. Unable to think clearly. Mario was now driving and he turned to me, "Scared the holy shit outta ya didn't he? Your face was white! A marshmallow!" His face broke into a wide grin. His two gold-capped teeth seemed to glisten.

"Why'd you do that, Leroy?" I was finally able to mutter. "Why, man?"

"Sorry, I was just messing with ya – and I needed to get the drop on Domza. You did good, T!"

We drove about five miles to a bait shop where Leroy made a call from a pay phone outside. After a few minutes, Leroy came back and said he'd called a detective and told him where to find the girl's body. They would confirm recovery of her remains and get back to him. He said someone was coming to pick him up and told Mario to take me back to New Orleans.

Leroy leaned down to the open window and said, "Your money's in the glove box." Mario opened the glove compartment and handed me an envelope full of cash.

"Gimme the film," Leroy said. I removed the roll from the camera and handed it to him.

"Why no pictures of that last ball and chain?" I asked, regaining a smidgen of nerve.

Leroy peered back with an edge in his eyes. "The client didn't request 'em."

"The client being you?" I said.

Leroy didn't answer, just smiled. "Be good, Montana. Don't get in trouble in the Quarter. Cops aren't workin' ya know." I looked closely into his face. Is this what the devil looks like? I wanted to remember it. It'd be the last time I'd ever lay eyes on him.

Mario and I took off with me now sitting up front. As we headed back to the city, I asked him what had just happened. Mario said Leroy liked a certain babe and Domza didn't know it and he jumped her too. She ended up liking Domza more and Leroy does not like to lose. He told him to lay off and I guess he didn't.

Mario didn't know if Domza had told her anything verboten, but he doubted it. Domza was solid he said. He wouldn't spill anything, even if he was drunk. But Leroy was not someone you provoked. And if you and he liked the same woman, you better step aside.

Mario pulled to the curb a few blocks from the Quarter to avoid the crowds. As I got out he turned to me, "You saw what happened out there. That bayou could swallow you up too. Too bad it was Domza, not you. Maybe next time. See ya soon, cher."

Mario pointed his hand like a gun at me, then sped off. I said to myself, "No you won't, cher."

When he was gone, I sat down against a building. I was exhausted, physically spent, emotionally dead. I wondered how I came to this spot in the road. How did I let this happen to myself. It didn't seem real.

I tried to tell myself that the perp, the murderer of two young girls, got what he deserved. I could rationalize that. But what happened to Domza wasn't right. It certainly wasn't just. And it meant I was in more danger than I had naively thought.

I turned the whole situation over in my mind numerous times and concluded there was only one sane option. Run for my life. After Fat Tuesday was over.

I met Dick, Gary, and Burt at the Chart Room at 2:00 as planned and we commenced celebrating Fat Tuesday for all it was worth. There wasn't a cop in sight, nor a National Guardsman. They were mostly deployed up and down Bourbon Street, two blocks over.

My memories of that afternoon and night in the Quarter are minimal. I remember throngs of people, in costumes and without, dancing in the street. Music came from balconies and bars. It was all a blur.

Years later I talked with Gary who shared his own memories of the day. He said that when we connected in the Quarter I was white as a sheet, like I was about to lose it. He thought I was more hung over than he was. I didn't tell him the real reason.

People that year said the lack of law enforcement made it the best Fat Tuesday ever. Anarchy reigned. But anarchy gets old. So does drinking yourself under a table. We took the St. Charles streetcar home that night, then I went into my room, packed all my stuff, and collapsed on my bed.

The next morning I rose early, took three aspirin, loaded my car, and said adios to Dick and Gary and the cockroaches. They were severely hung over – Dick and Gary, that is – maybe the roaches, too. I wasn't hanging around. I wanted out of my southern gothic adventure, away from my reckless youth.

I got behind the wheel and headed toward the freeway. It was quiet as I drove out of town. I wasn't sure where I was going but I knew one thing: I'd had my fill of the legendary New Orleans. I belonged in the Northwest. Montana. Oregon. Somewhere far from crazy people. As I drove I kept checking my rearview, a habit I continue to this day.

The route home was not straight. I meandered through Texas, New Mexico, Arizona, and California stopping to see friends along the way. Landing in Missoula, I took refuge at the home of a longtime buddy.

My plan was to lay low. Get myself together. And move on with my life – less recklessly. I made a valid effort. For awhile.

Chapter 24 Portland

Saturday afternoon

When I got home from taking Ben to Frazer Park, I took out the rope I'd put in my trunk and brought it and Ben inside. I sat at the kitchen table and tied a hangman's noose at the end of the rope. Then I grabbed a kitchen chair and took the chair and rope outside and put them in the trunk of the Escape.

Next, I punched some numbers into my phone. After a few rings, a woman's voice answered. It belonged to Rose, a freelance graphic designer I often worked with on ads, websites, and other creative projects.

She'd recently left design behind and become an artist and was making a good go of it under the name Mary Pason – a play on Perry Mason, her favorite TV lawyer. She was still one of the best designers in Portland. Seriously knew her shit and could Photoshop your face off. Plus, she was always up for something a little out on the edge.

"Rose Marie, Les Overhead here," I said.

"Hey, hi! What's up, Les? How's it going wherever you are these days?" she laughed. She was always quick to laugh. I liked that about her.

"Going well, going well, hope with you, too. Sorry to call on a Saturday, but I have a weird, warp speed job and need your help if ya got time. It's fast turnaround, but the money is good and it's a fun one."

"Did you say weird? I love weird," she said. "What is it?"

"It's a morbid birthday tribute for a friend. Similar to what we've done before. But we would need to meet today. One layout is all we have time for – I have the image to use. And you won't believe this..."

"Yessss...?"

"I need final art by 5:00 pm tomorrow."

"Sweet, no time for revisions!"

"Exactly." We both laughed, then agreed to meet at 7:00 at the Thirst, where I knew a good band would be playing. I would give her the copy and size specs there.

Next, I called another number, sat back, and waited until a man finally picked up. I knew my name probably wouldn't come up on his phone, but he would eventually answer. He's relentlessly curious. Like me.

"Yeahhh?"

"Lex – this is your buddy T-bone, in the flesh."

"Whatttt, are you serious my friend? You are still living? I think you would be dead by now. I guess old copywriters never die. Like cockroaches – you used to say." His memory was spot on and his English had improved. His Slavic accent, however, was still thick as beet soup.

"I've got a job you may like, Lexor. It's a tough one. And it needs to be quick – coded and ready by tomorrow night. A hush-hush job. I'll make it worth your while. End of story. Your turn to talk." A full five seconds went by before he responded. His breathing indicated he was still there.

"Theodore, you amuse me. My friend, it would appear you are in some trouble, yes? And you know me, I do like trouble. This intrigues me. You say it is a tough one? I am curious to know what you mean by this adjectiva tough. It is an adjectiva, am I right?"

"Yeah, adjective. First, I need you to see if it's possible to hack into something – a website. I need to add a new page to it, so it is seamless with all other pages. I need to know by midnight if you can get in or not. If we can, I'll get you the page to upload. It stays up for about three hours, then you delete it. No footprints, no trace. That's it."

"You want me to hack into a site," Lex went. "And then insert a secret new page for some unknown reason?"

"Yeah, so to speak."

"Do I get to know this reason?"

"It's a birthday joke on a friend."

"That is quite a joke. And illegal. Yes?"

"I'm willing to take the risk. And I'll pay you well for it."

"How can I resist such a mysterious offer. Okay, let's go down this path. See if we can find an open gate for this so-called birthday tribute. If anyone can find a way in you know it is I ... or is it me?"

"I," I said. I then gave him the name and url for the website to hack into. He wrote it down and said he knew of it, and yes it would not be easy. I gave one last instruction before hanging up.

"Don't email me. Call or text only – by midnight tonight. Do your magic."

"Over and out, boss man." He hung up.

I poured myself a glass of R&R and made one last phone call – to an individual who shall remain nameless at this point. I told him of a delivery I might be sending his direction Monday – what it was and where to pick it up. I didn't say what to do with it.

Going to my computer, I brought up the image of the driver's license for Nolan Duplantis Ronan had sent me. I opened a new Word document, then added a screen-grab of the driver's license photo at the top and began typing.

Twenty minutes later I finished. I proofed the copy, printed the document, and pulled a Flash drive from my drawer. I loaded the document on it, then ejected the drive and stuck it in my front pocket.

Before shutting down the computer I checked the weather forecast. Tonight would be clear, with a full moon. That's good, I thought.

Turning to my phones, I checked for messages. None. Then tried calling Kate but got no answer. I texted Jasmine and asked her what time she got off work.

Jasmine: 7:00.

Me: I want you to come home after work. Don't go out.

Jasmine: Why?

I knew why, but I didn't want to alarm her.

Me: Because I'll be out and Ben will be here alone. He misses you.

I don't know if Ben missed her or not. What I was worried about was someone grabbing her.

Jasmine: Okay.

Me: Talk later. See you at home tonight.

I set down the phone and rubbed my eyes. I needed a cocktail and some tunes, so I poured another glass of R&R and put on Leonard Cohen. It was starting to get dark.

Chapter 25 Escape Bag

Saturday evening

I must have fallen asleep because I woke with a start an hour later. The clock said 6:00 but I couldn't remember if it was morning or night. Assuming it was night I got up, unplugged the phones I'd been charging, and made myself a turkey sandwich. I wolfed it down in minutes and thought of what I had to do that night.

Going to my desk bottom drawer I pulled out an envelope. On the front were the words LOCATION – $AVE. Inside was a piece of paper with a set of directions: *Lone Fir Cemetery Go past entrance 300 ft to MARTIN, 100 ft south to YATES, 3 feet west of YATES, dig.*

I folded the paper neatly and stuck it in my pocket, then went out to the garage and grabbed a flashlight from the toolbox and took down a shovel from the wall. I put them all in the Escape, jumped in and took off.

Ten minutes later I was at the Thirst. Rose hadn't arrived yet. The band was one I liked and had seen many times. The Deadstring Family Band. A loose ensemble of 70s country rock that made me wonder what happened to that old jean jacket I had.

I bought a Pacifico and stood near the bar. Before long, I felt a tap on my shoulder and I heard a cat-like voice say, "Hey Les." It was Rose. We hugged and I got her a drink. It's a crowded, narrow space in the Thirst, so we moved to the back out of the way.

When the band took a break, I suggested we go outside. We walked out around the corner and I pulled down my hat as I started talking.

"So, about this rush job."

"Yeah, I'm curious. Sounds cool." She rubbed her hands together and grinned.

"I have a friend whose birthday is in a few days," I said. "He used to be a reporter at the Oregonian but got laid off and has always been pissed about it. So, for his birthday we're gonna make something with a fake Oregonian news story. I have his photo and the copy to go with it. We need to make it look as much like a real Oregonian story as possible – identical. Same font, same spacing, sizing, margins – everything. So go online and see how they format news stories. Then make a page with the photo and copy I give you. What do ya think?"

"That is hilarious! I love it! What are you gonna make?" I'd expected this question and prepared for it.

"A blanket. We're gonna screen print it on a blanket." It made her laugh. I hated lying to her.

"Well, this one'll be fun. Ya need it when?"

"Let's say by 5:00 tomorrow? That enough time?"

"Should be. I'll let you know if not."

"Okay, and can you give it to me on this Flash drive - instead of email it to me? I can come get it if you want or we can meet. It would be better not to email me. I'm having computer problems."

"Sure, let's talk tomorrow."

"Okay, here you go." I surreptitiously handed her an envelope that contained the Flash drive with the photo and copy, the pixel dimensions for the art, and ten 100-dollar bills. She took off shortly after and I went back in the Thirst. I sat on a barstool, letting the music and booze ease my mind a bit.

After the music ended, I got in my car and checked for messages. None. Tried calling Kate again. No answer. Where the hell is she? I was getting pissed.

I texted Jasmine: Where are you? Let me know. Now.

She should be home soon I hoped. I turned on the engine and checked for some music on the radio while I waited for Jasmine to respond. XRAY was playing classic country – guys like Ferlin Husky, Conway Twitty, and George Jones. I tried to focus on the lyrics to take my mind off my situation.

After ten minutes with no response from Jasmine I began to worry.

I texted her again: Answer please – where you?

Five more minutes and nothing. Now I'm nervous. I try calling and she does not pick up and with each ring the thought that she's been taken ratchets up. It will force my hand. I'll have to do what I don't want to do. And just how would I do that?

Getting into his house was the first problem. As an ex-con, he'd no doubt sleep with one ear open. It would be hard to get in without making a sound. Of course, on the other end of the spectrum, a sledgehammer would do it. It would make a big bang, but if I could bust in and waste the guy before he knows what's up, I could be gone in a flash. He can't have a gun, legally at least, being an ex-con.

As I'm doing my due diligence, my phone buzzed.

It was a text from Jasmine: Sorry, battery died. Just charged it. I'm home now.

I bent my head over in relief and the weight on my shoulders lifted a tiny bit. She's safe. So now what? What do I do with this Nolan Duplantis? I didn't know.

Jasmine texted again: Where's mom?

Me: Still in Astoria. Her phone had problems, she's fine.

Jasmine: Are you guys in a fight or something?

Me: Kinda, but no big deal. She'll be back soon. We'll figure it out, like we always do.

Jasmine: When are you coming home?

Me: Soon. I think we should switch to the burner phones.

Jasmine: Noooo, why? That's a hassle.

Me: Just to be safe. I want to try them out.

Jasmine: No, you're getting paranoid. We can talk about it later.

We would definitely do that, I thought. But I had one more thing to do. I drove to Lone Fir Cemetery.

Lone Fir is Portland's oldest graveyard, established in 1855. Many pioneers and early-day luminaries are interred there, buried beneath grass and pine needles, amid beautiful old firs that stand guard.

I parked near the front gate and when I was sure nobody was around I took out the chair and shovel I had loaded in my trunk earlier. I placed the chair next to the iron fence. The cemetery closed at sunset, but you could easily climb up and jump over the six-foot fence and get in. Once I was up and over, I reached through the fence and pulled the chair up and over to my side, where I could use it to get out.

It wasn't hard to find my way under the full moon. I unfolded the paper in my pocket with the directions I'd written down many moons before. I walked down the main road 300 feet and spotted the tombstone for MARTIN.

I turned left, and walked about 100 feet south through gravesites to a stone marker set in the ground with the name YATES. Three feet behind the tombstone, in front of a large pine tree, I began digging.

I was looking for a portal. An escape hatch I'd hidden in that precise location many years earlier. The hatch was actually a black rubber bag, wrapped in duct tape, buried two feet down under a bed of pine needles. It's often called a Go Bag, or Escape Bag. At the time I buried it, over 20 years ago, I thought I might need it.

It's always a good idea to have a Go Bag ready. You never know when your life will go off the rails.

The moon was bright enough that I didn't need my phone light. I worked fast under the sheltering tree branches. In five minutes I had the bag in hand. I filled in the hole and smoothed it over with dirt and pine needles, then took the bag and shovel and walked back to the fence where the chair sat. I stood on it and jumped over. Reaching through the railed fence I pulled it up and over and placed it and the shovel and Go Bag in the back of my vehicle.

About ten blocks away I pulled over. From the glove box I got out a knife and cut open the bag. Inside was a Canadian driver's license that had my photo with a different name: Addison Thompson. It listed a street address in Edmonton, Alberta.

There were also two stacks of bills bound by rubber bands. I counted it - $22,220. I thought I had buried more, but couldn't remember for sure. Also in the bag was a Canadian Social Insurance card. Their version of a U.S. Social Security card.

A law enforcement contact I made in Portland in the early 90s (still employed so will remain nameless) connected me with a guy in Moose Jaw who produced fake Canadian IDs and forged documents. It was his hobby or something. He excelled at it. Once I had the identity of Addison Thompson I had the forger update it every five years, renewing the license and changing the picture. I always wore a hat and glasses in the photo and grew a beard to make my face more unrecognizable. I added more money as the years went by, for inflation.

Canada, and particularly Edmonton, was a good spot to escape to because of its size and location – big enough to hide in and cold enough that nobody would follow you.

Chapter 26 Ronan

J ust then, my phone rang. It was Ronan.

"Make my day," I said.

"Found out some more about your Nolan Duplantis. I was able to get behind Louisiana's Angola wall. They don't make it easy."

"I've heard. Whaddaya got?"

"Nolan Duplantis was convicted of murdering Violet McRae and her unborn child in Lafayette, Louisiana in year 1-9-7-9. He was incarcerated in Angola prison and..."

"I know, and then he escaped."

Ronan paused. "Escaped? Naw, he never got loose. Served 37 years and got out in March of 2017. Moved here two months ago looks like."

"Wait, he didn't escape?" I asked. "You sure it's the same guy? I heard he flew the coop."

"Nobody escapes from Angola, man. This is our guy. It's all on his sheet. Convicted of murder in 1979. Victim was pregnant, so he got the double whammy. Evidence and testimony looked solid. His blood was on the scene. Slam dunk. No write-ups while in the pen. Model prisoner I guess – for a murderer. Served his sentence and got kicked earlier this year. Moved to Portland shortly after."

I was dumbfounded. Leroy was wrong. The perp had served his full sentence and had never escaped from prison. Why did Leroy lie and why did Duplantis still need to die?

"I guess I have wrong intel," I said. "Thanks, that's all I need for now."

"Okay, Bone. Sometime you'll have to tell me what this is all about."

"Yeah, maybe sometime."

"If you need anything else, send up a flare."

"I'll do that. See ya."

After hanging up, I sat in my car and wondered. Why does Leroy want this guy dead so bad? I decided to text him: You lied. Duplantis did his full sentence. He did NOT escape! Why kill him now? Who wants him dead, why?

I waited but received no answer. A few minutes later I texted again: Justice was served. He did his time. I'm not doing it.

Leroy then got back to me: THIS GUY IS A SERIAL KILLER. HE NEEDS TO BE DEAD!

I didn't respond. It was clear he wouldn't tell me much. I had to make a decision and soon. I decided to check with Lex, to see if he had any luck getting inside the website I gave him.

He picked up on the second ring. "Hey, you said I had until midnight."

"Yeah, I know," I said, "But time is short and I need to make some decisions. Any chance of getting in there?"

"Not yet, but I ran your problem by some friends I have in faraway places and they are at this very moment looking into it. I expect to be enlightened soon."

"Can we trust these friends of yours?"

"I always do and have not been disappointed yet," he laughed. "I didn't tell them anything about you, Theodore."

"Okay, get back soon." I hung up and turned on my vehicle to head home. That was the destination, but I didn't quite make it. I stopped at Tony's, a neighborhood tav just three blocks from our house – for one last pop for the night. They serve a concoction called a Chicken that I'm partial to – vodka, seltzer, and a squirt of grenadine in a tall glass.

I watched Sportscenter on ESPN and sipped my drink. The Blazers had blown a late lead and lost to the Jazz. I grumbled under my breath, why can't people do what they're paid to do – like make a goddamn free throw. How hard is that?

By this time, I wasn't in a stupor but was heading there. When I felt my pocket move, I knocked over my drink trying to get out my phone.

It was a text from Jasmine: Someone on porch! What do I do!

With fumbling fingers, I typed back as fast as I could: go basement hide furnace room im coming

I then bolted out the door of the bar and began sprinting the three blocks to home. I thought I could run there faster than get in my car and drive. As I ran, bending my head under branches over the sidewalk, I cursed myself for stopping at Tony's. Why? Why? I should have been home with Jasmine.

When I got to our house I ducked down and went to the garage and grabbed a bat. I crept up to the side door. It was locked. I took out my keys and opened it slowly, listening. Not a sound.

I yelled out "Jasmine! Jas! Where are you?" I walked through the kitchen, bat held high, into the dining room. And then I dropped the bat and fell to my knees. The front door was wide open. Jasmine was gone.

I couldn't breathe. What had I done? Where's my daughter?

Sitting on his haunches in the living room was Ben. He sat motionless, eyes staring right through me wondering, "Where were you?" and "What are you going to do now?"

I passed out.

Chapter 27 Kidnapped

Sunday Morning

The first sound I heard was a lawnmower. It hurt to hear. Reminded me of everyday life. The kind of life I once had, when Jasmine was a tyke and I would walk her over to Normandale Park and push her on a swing, jumping in front of her as she swung down toward me, stepping aside at the last second, the mad dad matador.

Those times seemed to be from a distant era. From a time and universe where my heart and bones didn't ache like holy hell. I slowly sat up from the floor and wondered how I got there. Ben was sleeping on the couch.

I got up and splashed water on my face. Did not look in the mirror. I found my phones and sat down at the kitchen table and checked for messages. Several had arrived while I was passed out on the floor. One from Leroy to Mario's phone. One from Jasmine's burner phone to my burner. One from Lex, my coder/hacker, to my personal cell.

I opened the one from Jasmine first. All it said was: SHP

My mind skipped. Wait, what? SHP? I tried to figure out what SHP meant. I couldn't. But it couldn't be good if it was sent from her burner phone to mine. I pulled my little notebook out of my pocket and looked through every page. Finally, in scrawled lettering I saw SHP – Shiny Happy People = Jasmine SOS

I knew what SOS meant. Like a fire hose to the face it hit me. Jasmine had disappeared last night. Had she been kidnapped? Taken by Leroy's vipers who'd slithered into our house and carried her off while I was sitting at a bar three minutes away?

I texted back: Shiny Happy People?? Where you?

In seconds, I got a response back on my burner phone.

Message: I'm okay. Don't know where I am. But don't try to rescue me, daddy.

The word daddy made me freeze. She never in her life has called me daddy and she'd never do it now. Was it a signal? Or did someone have Jasmine's burner phone?

I texted back: What band do I like best?

Jasmine has always known Van Morrison is my favorite.

Burner: Professor Longhair.

Jasmine didn't know anything about Professor Longhair. This was not Jasmine. I called the number. It rang five times and I hung up and texted back.

Me: Please don't hurt my daughter. Let me talk to her.

Burner: Don't worry, daddy. Just do what they say. Bye.

Me: I know this IS NOT HER! I wanna know she's okay! Call me!

Burner: She's okay. FYI, I like her hair. Don't text back.

I set the burner down and picked up Mario's phone and checked the text message from Leroy.

Leroy: YOU FORCED ME TO TAKE HER. SHE'S OKAY FOR NOW, IF YOU DO WHAT I SAY.

Me: Okay!! Don't hurt her!! Leroy, please! I'll do it tonight. I swear! But I wanna know she's okay. Where is she?

Leroy: I WANT EVIDENCE. WHEN I SEE IT MY GUYS WILL LET HER GO.

Me: Who has her? Tell me where she is!

Leroy: DON'T INSULT ME! DO THE JOB. TURNING OFF PHONE.

A dark fog descended over me. What a pathetic excuse for a father, husband, human, I am. I walked into the bathroom and took a long leak while sitting on the john, too tired and distraught to stand up. I reread the messages from Leroy. His grammar was spot on, no typos or errors. The content was clear, concise, and to the point. He was sharp this morning.

As I sat on the throne, I had trouble focusing. My brain was a whirlpool of thoughts, memories, lies, and murder – a gumbo of madness. I needed help. A plunger. I thought about calling Ronan and bringing in a few select cops but decided I can't get others involved in this – yet. I had to figure this out on my own.

I tried to imagine where Jasmine was – some little hotel room under the guard of who knows who, not far away I bet.

Grabbing my personal cell I opened the message from Lex. Just four words: We are in business.

Yes! I immediately called him.

He answered, "It is I, your Slavic genie." His accent was more robust than usual.

"So, you got in?" I said, my voice rough as sandpaper.

"Ya's, boss, we are good to go. These colleagues of mine found a crack in the wall. They can insert whatever you want into this crack, Jack!" He laughed at his use of American slang. Then he got serious. "This is one time only you understand. In and out."

"That's all I need. Just this one time. What about covering their tracks?"

"It will be bounced from a server they have accessed to other servers in various parts of Asia and Africa and I think Iceland and Wyoming or someplace and it will be scrubbed of any trace of the source. Once we pull it off the site, those who try to follow will find the footprints lead nowhere. How killer is that?" I about dropped my phone at hearing killer.

"You guys are good," I said. "Your hackers cost us a presidential election and ruined the country but I'll let that go. Let's do it. I'm still getting the art ready. I'll have it later this afternoon. Let's meet at seven tonight unless I get back to you."

"And where shall we have this conference?"

"Remember that place we used to go and play pool on that warped table, with the great jukebox?"

"Yeah, sure. Roadside Attraction. It's named after that hippie book."

"Right, let's meet there – seven o'clock."

"See you there, Theodore. I will have details on where to send the fee."

While I charged the phones I jumped in the shower. Showers are good for thinking and I had a lot to ponder. I wondered if I should kill the perp tonight and not take chances with this crazy Plan S. Jasmine's life was hanging in the balance. And if anything happened to her, Kate would kill me – literally. That is, unless Leroy beat her to it.

I let the hot water run off my shoulders as I tried to talk myself into what I had to do. It was true Duplantis had done his time and justice had been served. But he was still a murderer. We can't escape the fact that he killed a woman and her unborn kid, with malice. No big loss for the world. Nobody would miss him.

If I did everything right I could get away with it. One more murder to add to the two others I'd committed two nights earlier, what's the difference? If I'm going to hell anyway I might as well go all the way.

I tried to summon the primal surge I'd experienced when I strangled the man and shot Mario. I needed total buy-in. But I couldn't muster it. All I felt was sadness and disgust.

In a change of clothes with a cup of coffee down, I felt better. I took Ben for a walk. He sniffed around the porch and front yard as we left, as if trying to get a scent of Jasmine, or of those who'd taken her. I walked him around the neighborhood keeping an eye out for black Caddys.

Back home, I put Ben in the backyard, then went inside and made a list of items I needed at the store. I tried to stay calm, even though my daughter had been kidnapped from our home less than 12 hours before. I wrote down peanut butter, mayo, tortillas, juice, and yogurt. Then added one more item: facial cream.

I grabbed the phones, put them in the pocket of my jacket. As I was about to go out the door, one of my phones began vibrating. I fumbled it out of my pocket, almost dropping it on the floor. It was a text on my personal cell. From Kate. Finally.

She said: Let's talk. Noon at Grant Park playground. Come with answers and the truth.

I waited a minute, then texted her back: Good! See you there.

It escaped me what I would tell Kate – about Jasmine, about us, about all the rest of it. In a light, misty rain I drove to Fred Meyer to buy the items on my list, as if I was a normal, decent human shopping on a Sunday. I didn't fool myself.

Avoiding bars on the way home, I put the items purchased in the fridge, except the facial cream which I put in the trunk, in the backpack with other tools I had placed there the day before.

I had an hour before meeting Kate so spent it driving past various motels near the edge of Portland. No Cadillacs with Louisiana plates. No vehicles at all from the Bayou State. It deepened my state of despair.

Chapter 28 Kate

Sunday Afternoon

At noon as planned I was at Grant Park, standing under a tree by the playground. I watched mothers and fathers with their kids, pushing them on swings, just as I once did with Jasmine. Remembering the past can be painful.

Five minutes later, I saw Kate walk up. I went out to meet her. With pursed lips, she said let's walk around the track. We headed that way, not speaking. I knew to wait for her opening salvo before uttering a word. I was walking in a minefield.

Once we were by ourselves on the track she started talking. There was a low razor edge to her voice that she only used when seriously mad. It sliced me open.

"I want to know what you've done. Now. The truth. Before you say a word, I want you to know this could be it. I may be gone. What you tell me is going to decide. But first, where is Jasmine? Do you even know that? I tried to reach her this morning. She hasn't responded."

I paused, still unsure how much I would tell her. I couldn't tell her about Jasmine – not yet.

"Jasmine is at work. She called me on Popina's phone. Her own phone's battery died and she doesn't have a charger." The content was plausible, but my lower lip would not let me lie and gave me away. It started trembling. I couldn't stop it. Kate knew instantly something was wrong.

"What, you're lying aren't you. Tell me the truth!" Her eyes bored into mine and I was overcome. I broke down, unable to speak a word. Kate had no pity for me and waited until I was able to collect myself.

"Be very careful what you say next," she said.

"Okay, this is the god's honest truth, and I am so, so sorry. I thought I could control this shit but I'm not sure I can."

"Oh no. Oh no..." She shook her head, knowing what was about to come was not good.

"Jasmine was taken by some guys I knew in Louisiana, vigilante ex-cops working for a man named Leroy Dupree who has a business called the Agency that I used to do some work for when I lived there and unless I kill someone they want dead...tonight..." I didn't go any further.

"Oh my God, what have you done?" Tears poured down her pained face. Words stumbled out of my mouth in a bum rush as I tried to explain why I hadn't called the cops, how Jasmine could be killed if I did.

"I'm calling police! We need an Amber alert!" She frantically reached for her phone in her back pocket. I grabbed her wrist and squeezed hard.

"Don't! We can't! Once those thugs hear it they will be gone and we'll never see Jasmine again. Believe me! But I know how to get her back!"

"Are you crazy?" She looked at me wide-eyed as if I was indeed insane.

"I know how to deal with these guys."

"No, no, they left that photo of you on our porch?"

"Yeah." I went on to explain how I got connected with Mario and Leroy, and how I became leveraged by the Agency.

I told her I was through with the Agency and this was to be my final job. I told her I would not kill the man – and I didn't think I had to. She looked at me stupefied, like I was an alien in a museum display case. Do not touch.

"I don't believe this. You can't be serious!"

"It's true – all of it. I'm sorry. I had no idea it would come to this." I was suddenly worn out.

"Who is this person you're supposed to ...." She couldn't finish the sentence.

"His name is Nolan Duplantis. A bad dude who murdered his girlfriend and daughter. Leroy wants him dead and says I have to do it, nobody else. I told him no and then they took Jasmine last night. If I don't do it, tonight, I die – or Jasmine disappears. Or both."

She quietly sobbed. I could tell she didn't know what to do. Then in a low voice she said, "How would you know how to do something like this?"

"I know how to do it if I have to. I know where he lives. But I have a better idea that will get us Jasmine back, and I won't have to kill him."

She didn't respond. Weeping was taking it out of her. Kate finally collected herself and turned toward me.

"What is this stupid idea of yours?" Her eyes hardened. "How do you propose to get her back, genius?" she said, spitting out the last word. "If I don't like it I'm calling the police and you're going to jail."

"No, no. You go to the cops and you could lose a daughter, and a husband," I said.

"I don't care about the husband," she responded. I deserved it.

"Okay, it will take a bit to explain so let me talk. I got it all figured out."

I proceeded carefully, unreeling my plan like a movie, scene by scene, building to a climax and resolution where we all live happily ever after. I left out the part about me killing two people two nights before. That was old news. I was focused on the present and I was as logical and practical as possible as I laid out Plan S.

She responded as I expected. "Are you out of your mind? What is wrong with you? You can't possibly be serious!"

"It will work! I know it will! And I won't have to kill anybody. Leroy just needs to see the photos and one local news story and that's it. He's afraid of the Internet. He'll take one look at the photos and news story and that will convince him. Jasmine comes back safe, we're free, and Leroy is out of our life. Nobody will ever know!" I should have stopped right there, but like a hack writer who needs editing, I added one more line – a weak one.

"It's the best idea we've got," I said.

"Who's we? Don't include me!"

"Okay, okay." I stared straight at her, unflinching.

"This idea is crazy! This is the best you've got?" And then she uttered the words that set me off.

"You can do better." Rage seized me upon hearing it. She knows those words drive me mad, and have for many years. As a freelance copywriter, she has always been my editor and idea judge. Time after time, when I present her with ad concepts or headline ideas she just says, "You can do better."

It frustrates the hell outta me. I yell back, "What's wrong with them? C'mon - give me better feedback! Be more specific! C'monnnn!"

She'll just repeat, "You can do better." And I'll stomp off and curse her and sulk, and then go hammer out more ideas which are almost always stronger and prove her right. It's exhausting.

But this time, a deadline was hanging over our head. I didn't have time to draft up a second round of ideas. The deadline was near. We had to act soon.

I stopped on the track, started speaking semi-loud and turned the volume up as I spoke. Nobody was around.

"You can do better? That's what you say? Now? Jesus Christ, you know I hate it when you say that! Let's see YOU do better! What is wrong with the plan – what can be improved? This is the best idea we've got! At some point, you have to pick an idea and put it in motion. How many times do I have to tell you that! What do you think I've been doing!"

I was rolling now. "I've been racking my brain for two days! Do you think I'd just roll over and not do anything! You think I'd just let my daughter be kidnapped and not do everything I can to get her back safely! Are you really that dense? Seriously? You have no idea what I'm capable of – you're right, you don't know me at all! Take a good long look – this is me. And this is us!"

Her eyes seemed covered with a gauze curtain. "Our daughter," she said.

"What? What do you mean?" I said trying to catch my breath.

"You said my daughter, she's our daughter."

My chest heaved, I wasn't in shape for sustained yelling. My shoulders slumped and I mustered, "Go ahead, do whatever you want. But what happens is on you. Not me. You're the one deciding this. Can you live with that?" She looked me in the eye and didn't respond.

I went on without emotion and divulged more details of the plan. I could tell she was listening intently. Then I hit on an improvement to the plan, an addendum: Kate. I could use her help in pulling this off, if she was up to it. As I spoke her features seemed to turn to stone, her face ashen.

We talked and walked one more lap around the track. Then she said, "I'm leaving."

"Where? Where are you staying?"

"I'm not telling you. Don't follow me."

"I'm not gonna follow you. But don't go home."

"You think I'd go home?" she snarled.

"No. I don't."

"Okay, what do you want me to do?" she sighed.

"Meet me at 8:00 tonight at that church parking lot where I showed you how to drive a stick."

She walked off zombie-like and got in her car. As I drove off, I felt it went well, all things considered. She wasn't freaking out and I wasn't headed behind bars. Speaking of bars I thought, why not. But I decided to avoid my usual routes and haunts and headed elsewhere.

Chapter 29 Rose

I got on the freeway and drove downtown and made my way through the homeless denizens of Old Town to the train station. I parked a block away, then reached under my seat and pulled out the curly black wig and sunglasses I kept stashed there. I put them on and went inside the station and bought a one-way ticket to Whitefish, Montana – on the Amtrak Empire Builder leaving the next morning at 6:30 am. I wasn't sure who would be getting on.

Before getting back in my car I called Rose, my designer. She told me she had the art ready and could meet anytime.

"It looks cool," she said. "Just like a regular news story. So funny."

"You're good," I said. "Can't wait to see it. Let's meet at six tonight. Do you know the Jupiter art gallery, by the Doug Fir?"

"Yeah, I've been there."

"They have a show opening this afternoon. We could meet then."

"I've shown a few pieces there. I wonder who's showing."

"I'm not sure."

"Six is good for me. Don't let me buy any art!" She laughed and we hung up. I scribbled the time and place in my notebook.

I got back in the car and tried to think what to do next. Still needed to figure out how I was going to break in to the perp's place tonight. I didn't trust my ability to get in the back door, in the dark. "So go in the front," I heard myself say.

And then in a snap, I knew what to do, and how to do it.

After getting home from the train station, I discovered I'd left Ben outside in the rain. He came in and shook water all over the kitchen, obviously pissed. He sniffed all around the house and checked rooms for humans then returned and looked me in the eye and I read his mind. Where's Jasmine? I didn't respond. Then he walked over to his bowl and looked up. Feed me, now.

I poured him a bowl of dry food and added warm water for gravy – the way he likes it. For myself, I heated up a can of chili and threw a tortilla in the oven.

I checked the phones for messages and finding none I plugged them in to be charged and ready for the night. I needed recharging, too. So after eating, I sprawled out on the couch and took a nap.

It was an hour later when I heard one of the phones vibrating on the kitchen counter. With aching bones, I stood and walked into the kitchen and picked up the phone. It was a text from Leroy: BOBBY WITH YOU?

What? Who the hell is Bobby? What's he talking about? I sifted back through memories and could not recall Leroy ever mentioning someone named Bobby. Then the phone vibrated again.

Leroy: IS BOBBY LEE WITH YOU? GET BACK TO ME!

I decided to text back: No. Is that a problem?

Leroy: WHO THIS?

Me: Who do you think? Are you losing it?

Leroy: WRONG PERSON. DELETE THESE TEXTS!

Interesting I thought, Leroy mistakenly sent me a message meant for someone else. Perhaps someone in Portland, who may be holding something dear to me. The message also meant that Leroy was slipping.

"Bobby Lee," I said out loud. I went on speaking to no one, "Bobby Lee Dupree could it be? Leroy's progeny? But Ronan said Lulu's an only child. That's wild." I looked at Ben who had raised his head upon hearing me babble.

"I'm a poet and don't know it," I said to no response from Ben. He just stared back. I could tell he wanted a car ride, not poetry.

"Alright," I said. "But before we go, I gotta get a few things."

He followed me as I grabbed all the phones and put them in my jacket pockets, then went to my office desk bottom drawer and pulled out a manila envelope. It contained two items: a single key and a Portland Police Detective's shield with my photo, slightly outdated. On the badge in bold print next to the photo was the Detective's name: Les Overhead.

The badge was actually real, an old one Ronan no longer used – from his early days on the Portland force. I told Ronan I wanted to borrow the badge for a Halloween party. Sorry to say I haven't returned it.

It was easy enough to find a local artisan (Portland is crawling with them) who could replace Ronan's name with Les Overhead – my alter-ego business partner. I put the badge in my jacket inside pocket, then took the key and went downstairs to a bedroom closet where I have a gun cabinet. I unlocked it and took out two guns. One, a powerful and intimidating 9mm Beretta semiautomatic handgun I'd bought at a pawn shop in Butte, and the other a .40 caliber Glock, a subcompact pistol that's light and easy to conceal.

I also grabbed my silencer to use with the Beretta if needed. It wouldn't totally mute a gunshot but would hush the volume enough for my needs. Last, I took out two boxes of ammo and was about to lock the cabinet when I remembered one more item – brass knuckles. They might come in handy so I added them to my collection of arms.

Ben had been waiting patiently as I gathered the guns and he now wanted to go. I put the weapons in my backpack in the trunk with the other gear, then got Ben and put him in the backseat.

We headed north towards Skidmore. I wanted to drive by the Duplantis place one more time to survey the scene. Again, Ben had a wary eye as I drove by the domicile.

A car was in the driveway – a white Honda Civic. Looked like high mileage and the tires appeared low. I scanned the front of the house and side and then saw a figure in the picture window.

It was hard to gauge the body size but he seemed slight, or at least that's what I told myself. About my height. Bony-looking. Could I take him down? Who knows. But I saw he wasn't wearing a cowboy hat. That made me feel better. Cowboys are tough bastards and they like to fight.

Driving on for my meeting with Rose to get the flash drive, I cranked up XRAY-FM. I knew Radio Bandolero would be on – vintage rarities. Obscure ear worms they call them – from psychedelic to psycho.

Ben didn't mind the volume, just curled up and went to sleep. I wondered if he would dream as he often does, whimpering softly, his top leg hitching, as if trying to run but being unable to. Chasing a small critter, or being chased by a big one.

"See anything you like?" I said to Rose when I found her at the gallery just after 6:00. "I think you should buy this."

"No, you're supposed to stop me from buying something," she said. "You're a bad influence." She laughed. Little did she know how bad I truly was.

"Didn't I just give you $1,000 yesterday? I think you should blow it."

"God, I wish. I have to buy paint. And heat. And food."

"And guns," I said, a thought that I accidentally verbalized.

"Ha, yeah, guns. I forgot. Everyone should have one!"

We looked at some art then walked outside. On the sidewalk in front Rose handed me the flash drive with the news story on it. She had a printout and unfolded it. It was perfect. The design, formatting, type font, colors, and photo of Duplantis from his driver's license were all spot on.

In a caption under the photo was the name Nolan Duplantis. It looked totally legit. I folded up the printout and put it and the flash drive in my pocket.

"So, how you gonna use it?" Rose asked. "You said a blanket?"

"Yeah, we're screen-printing it on a blanket," I lied. "To keep him warm and comfy in bed, and in his coffin."

Rose cackled, "That is so sick!"

"Yeah, I know." I felt bad about lying to her but that didn't stop me. "It'll make a great gift. He'll love it. He's got a sick sense of humor."

"This should make him laugh for sure."

We talked some more then took our leave. The rain started pouring and I ran to my Escape. I was planning to go home to check Rose's news story on my computer but her printout showed me it was good.

All I needed to do was give Lex the flash drive and have it ready to load. I'd hold onto the printout, in case I needed it. It was time to head for Roadside Attraction and my meeting with Lex.

Chapter 30 Lex

Arriving just before 7:00, I found a booth in the back. Roadside Attraction is a ramshackle bar just a dozen blocks from the river, central east side, with a fire pit and porch swing in front and a dark, low-ceiling lounge in back. It has a jukebox to kill for. Nina Simone. Muddy Waters. Badfinger.

Precisely on time, Lex strolled in scanning the small crowd gathered at the bar. I stood up and he saw me and nodded. After getting a drink – vodka straight it appeared – we sat in the booth and clinked glasses. I had soda water in mine.

"I know why you like this place," he said.

"Why's that?"

"Lots of weird people and nobody notices you. You are invisible here, Teddy. Too old to matter to anyone. Beneath attention."

"Very astute. But it's mainly the decent drinks and tunes I'm here for. And meeting my weird friends."

"Yes, cheers to that. And cheers to our good fortune in this little illegal escapade we are engaged in. I hope you don't get caught."

"You mean we don't get caught."

"No, I mean YOU don't get caught."

"I don't intend to."

I looked around for some wood to knock on and seeing none I tapped my fist to my forehead. Lex took a swallow of his drink. He examined me for cracks. I tried to show no weakness. He reached over and gave me a small piece of folded paper. It had the coordinates for a money transfer I was to send to a certain offshore account. I put it in my pocket and withdrew the flash drive Rose had given me with the news story art loaded on it. I slipped it across the table to Lex.

"This is the news story," I said. "The only version. Do not lose it. I will call or text you when I want it inserted on the site. It'll be around eight tomorrow morning. Make sure you're up and ready and your phone is charged. I'll give you the word when to remove the news story – it could be a few hours after it goes up. Then, destroy the drive."

"I am not an amateur. You don't have to tell me all this, Theodore. I will be ready. Now, let me do something more important."

"What's that?"

"Destroy you at pool."

"That I can't let you do." We then proceeded to play a best of three. He won two. Then we bumped fists and we left.

It was close to 8:00 by now. I needed to go meet Kate. The adrenaline was starting to kick in. The closer the deadline, the tighter the noose.

I drove to the church where we were to meet and arrived at 8:00. She was already there, sitting in her Subaru. I parked next to her.

"We'll go over behind those bushes and trees," I said, "but first come over here." I opened my tailgate. I dumped the contents of my backpack out in the trunk. There were black gloves, a Mexican wrestling mask, handcuffs, brass knuckles, duct tape, a jar of white facial cream, and two guns (fully loaded, one with silencer attached).

Also in my rig was the rope I'd tied in a noose and the kitchen chair I'd brought from our house. My black rubber Go Bag was there as well, with money and fake ID inside.

"Where did you get all this?" Kate asked, taken aback.

"Fred Meyer and Target mostly," I said. "Got the mask at a flea market. The chair is from our house."

"These guns and handcuffs and, what are these – brass knuckles?"

"Just things I've picked up over the years. Accoutrements in case I need them. I never really use them."

"I do not know who you are. I am... dumbfounded." A feather could've knocked her flat.

"I seldom use any of this stuff," I said as natural as can be.

"I wish I could believe you. Nothing you do surprises me anymore."

I looked at her and tried to smile but wasn't successful. I then put all the tools needed for tonight, including the weapons, in the backpack and carried the pack to the secluded area behind the church.

When we were behind the bushes out of sight I took the Mexican mask, gloves, guns, and handcuffs out of the pack.

"Wear these," I said giving her the gloves. "And I want you to try this on." I handed her the mask. "It'll cover your face and make it look like you're a man, my backup. He'll never know who you are, and if you act tough and serious, that's all we need."

"I'm supposed to wear this?"

"Yeah, to protect your identity and throw him off. You just need to point the gun at the guy while I get him handcuffed. The rest of it I'll handle. Simple and easy. You may want to bring a book to read." It was a joke to lighten the mood, but it didn't lighten shit.

"Don't try to be funny," she said.

"Sorry. Try the mask on."

She put it on and I had to admit it looked great. The black mask, emblazoned with a hawk's red wings on each side and sharp gold claws around her eyes, provided a surreal effect. It gave her a whole new persona and attitude.

"Can you breathe okay?"

"Yeah, I guess," she muffled.

"You may be wearing it awhile. You might be able to take it off at times, when not around the perp, but keep it on otherwise."

"Perp? Did you really just say perp?"

"I say perp instead of his name. You should not say anything, no names. I'll say his name at the start to show him we have the right guy, but you don't say anything. If you need to talk to me, whisper so he can't hear you."

She took off the mask. I then gave her the handcuffs. "You won't need to do this tonight, but here's how to put on a set of handcuffs."

"I'm not putting handcuffs on anybody. I'm not touching anyone!"

"You won't have to – I'll do it. But just in case, it's a good skill to know." I was all business now.

"Get those out of my face," she said. "I won't be handcuffing anyone, ever. And that's no lie." Emphasis on lie. She didn't laugh but her attempt at sarcasm was noted. A positive sign. A sign that maybe we could pull this off together. Kate has always been sharp and brassy and I was counting on her being that tonight. In spades.

I gave her a gun and showed her how to hold it, standing straight with legs wide, arms extended out, aiming at a target, in this case a pine tree.

"It's fully loaded. The safety is on – see? You turn off the safety like this. And when you aim and shoot..." She cut me off.

"I'm not shooting anyone! I'm not hurting anyone! Except maybe you."

We practiced for a little while longer as I explained the sequence of events I had planned for the night. I detailed how we'd get in, what would happen afterwards, and how the night would play out, ending tomorrow morning with us getting Jasmine back. She didn't interrupt, which could be good or bad.

"Am I in a dream?" she asked after I was done. "Is this really happening?"

"This is real as hell, and we gotta be on our game." On our game, I thought? Did I just say that? I was turning into a caricature, a cliché. I needed a drink.

I returned everything to the backpack except the Glock and handcuffs, which I put in my coat pocket.

We walked to Kate's car and I tossed the backpack in her backseat. She would carry it into the perp's house after I'd taken control of him.

"Okay, you know what to do," I said. "This will work. Everything's in place. We can do this!" I laughed at myself with my pre-game speech. Kate saw how pathetic it was, but she stayed silent to her credit.

I went on, "Follow me and park where I do. It's on Skidmore, not far. When I go up to the door, have the backpack on and be ready. Put on your gloves and mask before you go in. Give me about 30 seconds, then come in. Don't panic. It'll be quiet and safe. Don't worry."

I don't know if I've ever tried to sound more confident. As much for Kate as for me.

"I can't believe I'm doing this," she said. I can't either I thought.

"We're doing this, and it's going to work. Trust me." She stayed quiet and I forged ahead.

"Let's do it." I gave her a hug. She didn't hug me back.

As I drove off, I looked in the rear view and saw Kate get into her Subaru and start to follow me. Then I saw Ben, still asleep in the backseat. Oh shit. I forgot he was there. Now what? It was too late to take him home so he would be going along for the ride.

In the mirror I saw him sit up and look outside. Then he turned to me. "What are you doing and where are we going?" he asked. I said, "We're going to visit someone. Stop talking."

He shut up.

Chapter 31 Duplantis

Sunday Evening

The rain stops for the moment, as if the clouds have parted so the gods can watch this Sunday night show. It's dusk. I turn down Skidmore and park a block from the home of Nolan Duplantis, murderer. Kate parks about 50 feet behind me and waits in her car.

I take out my burner phone and text a message to the kidnappers: It's on tonight. Do not harm Jasmine. Let me talk to her.

Within a minute I get a response: Good, do it! Your girl fine. We're watching TV.

Then they text a photo. It's Jasmine sitting on a decent motel room bed watching TV. She's not tied up or blindfolded. Nothing to keep her from screaming. Strange.

I then text Leroy on Mario's phone: It's on tonight. I'll send photos – be ready around midnight. Charge your phone.

I stick the phones back in my pocket and with nobody in sight I get out of the Escape and give Kate a thumbs up. I then take the detective badge from my inside pocket and walk down the street to the Duplantis house.

With a deep breath, I give three firm knocks to the front door. I hear the TV and it's soon muted. I try to look bored, tired, non-threatening.

"Yeah, who is it?" I hear. I know he's eyeing me through the peephole but I don't look there. He'll see an old fart who does not look threatening in the least.

"Les Overhead, Portland Police. I'm a detective looking for a Nolan Duplantis. Nothing serious. Just want to ask some questions related to a recent incident in Louisiana. Here's my badge." I hold up the detective shield to the peephole. I'm not wearing gloves which should make him less nervous. There's a pause. Almost there I think.

"It won't take long," I say. "I know you're on parole from Angola but I'm not here investigating you. We're investigating someone else you may know."

I figure he has to be curious who it is and I'm right. The door slowly opens and he asks, "Who?"

"I'll tell you – can we talk inside?" I ask. "Just a few questions."

Slowly the door opens and he lets me in, his eyes on my badge. He's my size, with a better head of hair and a slight potbelly not fully covered by a purple LSU Tigers t-shirt. His skin is pale, almost translucent. His eyes are a watery gray and his eyebrows have wild hairs sticking out like weeds in all directions. I smell stale breath or it could be his clothes. Like old carpet.

"Thank you, sir." I say, looking him in the eye. "I appreciate it. Sorry for the inconvenience." I step forward into his home. I now have about 30 seconds before Kate arrives.

"Do you know a man by the name of ..." I pause as if to remember, then reach into my pocket as if looking up the name. In an instant, my gun is pointed between his eyes.

"Easy now. Put both hands straight up and step back to the wall. If you do one thing wrong your life is over. But you can live through this if you do as I say. I don't wanna kill you. But believe me I will if need be. Turn around and put your hands on the wall."

He does as I instruct, not saying anything.

"Do you have anything in your pockets?"

"Just my wallet and phone."

"With one hand, take them both out and toss 'em on the floor. Keep your other hand on the wall." He does it and I say, "Sit down and cross your legs. Put your hands behind you." While I have the gun at his head, I wonder where Kate is. It's been more than 30 seconds since I came in. Did she run? Freak out? Is she paying me back by leaving me to do this alone? I pull gloves out of my back pocket and put them on, then go on speaking.

"You're about 95% dead, but you do have a chance. There's one way out of this. Remember, I do NOT wanna kill you. But I will in a heartbeat. Trust me."

I glance at the front door. Where is she? This is not going to be easy to do alone. Then I see the door timidly open and she leans in – a figure in a wild-colored wrestling mask covering her entire head, wearing a dark blue jacket, black gloves, and a backpack. It spooks me to see her.

I glare at her for being late. She removes the backpack and takes out the Beretta with silencer attached. She slowly raises her arms and trains the gun on the forehead of Duplantis. She stands in a wide stance with arms extended as we practiced earlier. I have to admit she looks tough.

I close the drapes and take out the handcuffs.

"I'm just putting cuffs on for precaution, okay? My buddy here is one mean mother and he'll put a bullet in your brain if you make one move. Once we have the cuffs on, I'll tell you why I'm here, and with luck we'll all get outta here alive. Got it?" He nods, silent. I can tell he's thinking fast.

"Keep your hands behind you and don't move." I kneel over him and snap on the cuffs.

"Okay, now I'm going to put duct tape over your mouth, another precaution. You'll be able to breathe okay. We just want to keep you silent while I tell you what's happening. Then I'll take the tape off. Understood?"

"What the hell is this? I know who sent you." Duplantis says. His voice is deceivingly deep for a scrawny guy. He could have been a DJ.

"You're no detective obviously," he says. "What's this about? What do y'all want?"

"You're about to find out if you shut the hell up. Let me put the duct tape on."

"You don't need it. I won't yell."

"Yeah, maybe so. But the sooner you shut up, the sooner we'll get through this."

He sighs heavily, nods slightly. Kate keeps her gun on him as I take the duct tape out of the backpack, tear off a piece, and stick it across his mouth. He's silent and secure.

There's a rocker and a couch in the living room.

"Take a seat," I say to Kate, pointing at the rocker. She looks at me and points at herself. "Yeah, we're gonna be here awhile. Might as well relax." Her eyes are wide and I can tell she's frightened, but she takes a seat.

"Are you okay?" I ask Duplantis. "You can breathe alright?" I want him to be calm. He nods.

"Okay, I'm going to talk for awhile. Listen closely." I kneel down and look Duplantis in the eye.

"You're supposed to be dead now, as of about one minute ago. I've been hired to kill you – you don't know the person who hired me but they want you gone. Tonight." He looks at me and nods his head.

"You may have an idea why these people want you dead. It's retribution for the young woman you killed in Louisiana – Violet McRae. Did ya know she was pregnant? That was a pretty vicious murder you committed. Two murders counting the unborn child. Looking at you I wouldn't think you have it in ya. I guess I'm not a very good judge of character. Well, justice has come knocking, my friend. Be thankful you're not still in Louisiana or you'd be in a gator's gut. But you hit the jackpot this time. You got me as your executioner. But here's the thing, I honestly and sincerely do not want to end your pathetic life. I kid you not, Nolan, I don't want to kill you, but I will do what I need to do."

I don't say anything about Jasmine being kidnapped. He doesn't need to know. But looking at him, his eyes seem to signal he knows more than I think.

And then there's Kate. She'll be hearing most of this for the first time. I wonder what she'll make of it. Will she get up and walk out the door?

Duplantis stares at me as I kneel in front of him. His unblinking eyes show hatred now. Fear becomes confusion becomes hatred. A natural progression of emotions. I expect it.

"I know you served your full term at Angola – what was it, 30 some years? That couldn't have been easy. I feel bad for you, really. You get far away to Portland to start a new life and I show up. But you can't outrun your past, man. Trust me, I've tried. These folks in Louisiana must be close to the woman you killed and to them your long prison term will not suffice. They want you to pay the ultimate price. You understand what I'm saying?"

Duplantis doesn't look at me, stares at the carpet in front of him. Then he looks up at Kate. She blinks and slides her eyes sideways toward me, nervously, then back to Duplantis. She sits in the rocking chair, trying not to rock, her gun pointed at his head.

"I'm a professional hit man, Nolan. This is what I do. I've been doing it for a long time." Such bullshit. It's another lie but I want to intimidate him. I want to change his hatred back into fear. I deepen my voice as I speak faster.

"But this is your lucky night, Nolan. You ran into a hit man who's on his last job – the boss is cutting me loose after I kill you. Which means I have a decision to make. What to do with you. We're going to decide that tonight – we meaning you and I. In fact, it's more you. You can decide your fate tonight, Nolan – whether you live or die. Pretty sweet, huh?"

Duplantis sits motionless. Same with Kate. Having the floor to myself, I talk on.

"I don't know if you believe in God or not, Nolan. I don't. Heaven or hell either. But I admit I could be wrong. There's a chance I'm going to hell for what I've done. You too. But the real thing holding me back is my conscience. Mine is weighing in heavily on this. For some reason, it prefers I not kill you – or anyone, ever again. But it all depends on you."

I'm talking way too much but I can't stop. It happens when I get rolling. I need an editor. Or a hook from off stage.

Kate tilts her body toward me and makes a reeling motion with her non-gun hand, like turning a fishing reel. It's a signal we use, meaning faster, get to the point. She's always been a good editor and alert to my verbosity.

"So Nolan, I have a proposal for you. A plan." I stop talking as Duplantis begins shaking his head vigorously. He wants to say something. I hear garbled, unintelligible sounds – two syllables it seems like.

I step forward and take the duct tape off his mouth. He breathes hard and looks up at me.

"Leroy," he says. "I know it's Leroy." It catches me by surprise.

"Leroy? Leroy who?" I say.

"Leroy Dupree. I know all about Leroy. Knew him growing up. And I know what he does, and what you do." I'm intrigued. Just how much does this guy know.

Duplantis goes on, "He set me up. He and his partners in crime, on the police force."

"I don't know any Leroy and you don't know what you're talking about," I say.

"Yeah, you do. You're a lousy liar and a lousy detective." Kate looks at me and I detect a smirk. I frown back at her.

"I didn't kill her," Duplantis says. "I loved her and yes I know she was pregnant, with our child, a boy. I think Leroy himself killed her, but I'm not sure. Doesn't matter. I was framed for it and there was no way out of it. His cops testified, I was convicted, then locked away for murdering my girlfriend and unborn child, a crime I didn't commit. Not only did I lose them, I lost my freedom – for 37 long years. And that's the god's honest truth."

He has one of the saddest looks I've ever seen. I can feel the pain coming out from his soul through his skin. I believe him. It's something Leroy would do. Sounds just like him.

"I don't believe you," I lie. "You're just trying to save yourself. You're making it up."

"No. It's true. And if you know Leroy you know it's true."

He's right. It's obvious we both know Leroy. He goes on, "I made the mistake of falling in love with a woman he also loved – or not so much loved, a woman he craved for himself. He's had it in for me ever since we were in high school. He was a big stud on the football team – played quarterback. I was the team manager. We made it to the state championship and lost by one point."

"Wait, you went to Lafayette High? Leroy told me you guys won it all."

"No. We lost and he was the reason. He told you we won that game?"

"Yeah, we met a couple times when I lived in New Orleans. He told me about the game."

"Did he tell you he fumbled on the five-yard line with 28 seconds left that cost us the game? We lost to Booker T Shreveport on our home field 33-32."

"He told me you won and he scored the winning touchdown."

"He's a liar. After we lost the final there was a big party on the bayou. We all got drunk. As I was going to take a leak in the woods I saw Leroy making it with someone who wasn't his girlfriend. He saw me see them. Someone else saw them too I guess because his girl found out and broke up with him. He was mad as hell. Always thought it was me who ratted him out. It wasn't me. I'm not sure who else saw them. But he's sure it was me who told his girlfriend and she dumped him. And he's hated me ever since."

"He has it in for you because of that? A drunken high school incident?"

"Yeah, and I'm innocent of that, too. I've been innocent my whole life for all the good it's done me. I didn't know it at the time but he also had a thing for Violet. She was in high school with us. Once he found out Violet and I were gonna be married he set me up."

"And just how did he set you up?" I ask, curious to hear specifics.

"He had someone call me and say I needed to come to her house right then, she was hurt. I tried calling her and got no answer so I went there – the door was open and I went inside. I went through the house then found her in her bedroom – lying face down in a pool of blood. Dead. I think she'd been stabbed. I don't know. Then two guys grabbed me from behind and pushed me down on top of her, forcing my hands into her blood. Then they put a knife in my hand and I dropped it. They had gloves and masks on."

"You think one of them was Leroy?" I ask.

"Yeah, I think so. Then they ran out. I called 911 and some cops pulled up almost immediately. They arrested me and I was charged for the murder. They testified against me and with the evidence they had that was that. Violet and my son were dead and my life was over. And now here we are, 38 years later."

I don't do the math but he seems to know the score.

Chapter 32 Plan S

I don't say a word. It all rings true. Exactly how Leroy and the Agency operate. Kate I can tell believes him, too. I sense sympathy behind the mask.

Duplantis goes on, "So, yeah, I did my time. But I'm an innocent man who has been wrongly convicted his whole life."

"You're telling me you served 37 years behind bars for the murder of your fiancée and unborn child – and didn't even do it?"

"Yeah, life is a bitch. I'm writing a book about it." That catches my attention.

"Book? What kinda book?"

"It's a memoir – of the crime and time. Leroy may know about it. My cellmate may have told people. That may be why Leroy wants me dead. He doesn't want me telling the true story."

I'm interested. "Is the book done? Do ya have an agent?" I'm always eager to talk to other writers and wannabe authors.

"I'm working on it – it's up to 180 pages or so. No agent."

"First person point-of-view I assume?"

"Yeah, of course."

"That's great, man. I like first person – it's more engaging I think. You should finish it. Maybe it'll be a movie. Shawshank Redemption – the sequel."

"I plan to finish it. Unless I'm dead."

"Keep working on it. You never know. Might be a hit. But even if it becomes a blockbuster, you got screwed buddy. Fate and injustice have kicked your lily-white ass for 38 years. That's cold."

"Longer than that. That's how life works. It ain't fair, but I accept it. Gotta live through it."

"You're nuts. I would've hung myself in my cell."

"Oh I thought of that, believe me. But I tried to stay positive. Optimistic. It wasn't easy."

"I'm sorry you had to go through that. Really. But it doesn't change where we are now, and what I need to do."

"That's right. I'm wondering why you haven't killed me...yet. And why you're not wearing a mask."

"You're not dead yet because your luck has changed – for the moment. And I'm not wearing a mask because I don't care if you see my face. It doesn't matter."

"Then why does she have a mask on?" He points his chin toward Kate. I glare back at him.

"What do you mean she? Don't make him mad."

"It's obvious she's a woman. Look how she sits and holds that gun in her lap, like it's a cat, or her knitting." Kate looks at me, scared again.

"Shut the hell up! We're talking about you, not him. He's a he! And he will cut your throat believe me! He's killed more people than I have!"

I'm getting mad now. I never like getting caught in a lie. Kate blinks and raises the gun off her lap, hands outstretched holding it in front of her. But Duplantis is right, she looks like a she. I should've worked with her more.

"You're right, I'm working for Leroy," I say. "And he'll kill both of us if I don't take you out tonight. Don't make me. My conscience is your get out of death free card."

"So what do you plan to do?" he asks.

"Fake it. I plan to make it look like I've killed you. So Leroy will believe it. I'll show him you're dead, but make it look to the cops like you committed suicide."

"What?" he asks, eyebrow raised. "Why suicide?"

"Because then there won't be an investigation, there won't be a homicide to solve. You got something against suicide?"

"I got nothin' against suicide. Just wanted to know my motive." He starts laughing and I can't help but join him. Kindred spirits. Then I get serious again.

"If your death is ruled a suicide, the story ends. No more press. No investigation. No reason for Leroy or anyone else to check the news. Suicides don't get much coverage. All we need is one initial story calling it a suicide – that Leroy can see – and the story ends."

"And what, I skip town and leave this shitbag house behind?"

"That is correct. Plans are already in motion."

"What plans? Where would I supposedly go?" Duplantis asks.

"I have the means and you're going to Canada – Edmonton for starters."

"What? It's freezing up there. Why Edmonton, Canada?"

"What, you don't like Canada?"

"Hell no, it's cold as shit!"

"It's also out of the country and a long way from here for one thing. You're better off there. Canada is cool and I don't mean cold. They have national health care, jobs are plentiful, and Edmonton is a big city so it's easy to blend in. Leroy and his cronies will never track you there. And that's where your ID says you live."

"What ID?" he says. I'm slowly reeling him in.

I walk over and pull the Go Bag out of the backpack, then dump the bag with all the cash and fake ID on the floor in front of him. Kate's eyes go wide.

"What the...are you serious?" Duplantis says.

"Yeah, I am."

"This is... this is an escape bag. Your go pack - isn't it."

"You've heard of a go pack?"

"Sure. You learn a lot in prison."

Kate I now notice is looking straight at me. I can see through the eyeholes in her mask that her brow is bent sharp in a V. She doesn't appear to like this idea of a go pack – and the fact that I have one. I smile at her and try to wink.

"You can count it later, but there's a little over $22,000 there, plus a Canadian driver's license with the name Addison Thompson. Hope you like that name. It's yours now. The photo is of me but if you grow a beard and start wearing a hat it'll work in a pinch. I have a connection who can make you your own ID once you get settled in Edmonton. That other card is your Canadian Social Insurance card. It's like a U.S. Social Security card. You can get a job with it. And health care. Don't lose it."

"Why are you doing this? You obviously had plans to use it. Why aren't you using it yourself?"

I look at Kate as I reply. "Because I'm not running, I'm not moving to Canada, I'm not changing my name, and I'm not deserting my family."

Kate gives me a look I can't decipher, hidden behind her mask. I think of Jasmine in a motel room nearby. Again I ask myself, can I pull this off?

"Tell me more about this plan," Duplantis says.

I pull the printout of the news story from my back pocket and open it in front of his face. He reads it through and looks at me, incredulous.

"Now I know you're crazy. This is my death notice in the newspaper?"

"Not a death notice exactly, but yeah, it's a news story of your death, your suicide. It's too late for changes. It's already at the publication."

"Well, you spelled my name right. That's good. Where'd you get the photo?"

"Your driver's license."

"Gotta admit this looks pretty legit. How'd you pull this off?"

"It's not hard – if you know how. It's called counterfeit reality in intelligence circles. Fake news is just one part of it. This news story will appear tomorrow morning on the Oregonian website – just long enough for Leroy to see it when I tell him it's posted. But tonight we gotta create the scene and send photos to Leroy."

"Why do it in a park? Why not just stage it here in the house? Going to a park, out in public, is stupid."

"Who would find you if we did it here?" I yell back. "Who would report it to the news and police? We need this to be in the news tomorrow morning – we need this over and done fast! And Leroy has to believe the news story. That's why it's written the way it is, at a park, where someone can find you early in the morning and report it. Quit trying to change the plan!"

I'm steaming the more I stammer on. It's another thing that has always rankled me – clients who want to make changes or offer suggestions when it's too late – after production is in motion.

"We're going with what the news story says, everyone got it?" I say.

Nolan pipes up, "You're the writer. So tell me, how do I get to Canada?"

"You take the train. You leave tomorrow morning for Whitefish, Montana. Then a colleague of mine will meet you and drive you to a spot near Eureka. It's a little town near the Canadian border. From there he'll take you on a trail across the border – a hike of about 15 miles – to a dirt road that will connect with Highway 93. You hitch or walk to a town called Fernie and take a bus to Edmonton. The rest is up to you."

"And if I don't do it?"

"Well, I kill you and you don't get the $22,000. Or I tell Leroy I'm not doing it and he'll send someone else to kill you. Someone not as friendly as I. He'll have them here quick. They're probably already in Portland. You might live another day or two. That's it. Run and you'll be caught by his trackers. On the other hand, escape to Canada with 22 grand and your future is wide open. Edmonton. About a thousand miles north. That's where I'd go. In fact, I had it all set to go myself."

Damn, why did I say that. One sentence too many. I don't look at Kate but feel a chill in the air. I'll need to do some fast chin-waggin' later to explain this Canada escape I'd mentioned.

"You'll get used to Canada," I say. "If you get cold, buy some goddamn longjohns."

"I've never worn longjohns in my life."

"You want my advice? Become a hockey fan. Go to a few games and sit down close so you can see the action. Edmonton has a good team this year – the Oilers. I like basketball myself, but if I could skate, hockey would be my game."

Again, I think I see Kate roll her eyes. She must be getting tired. I look around for a magazine or book she can read.

"Okay, let's get back to this plan," Duplantis says. "What about my car? What happens to that?"

"It's a piece of shit. Leave it. Once we walk out this door we don't come back. Leave everything."

"It is a piece of shit. Doesn't run half the time so I have to ride a stupid bike like every other loser in this town. So, what happens next?"

"We sit here and wait. After midnight, we make our move."

I go on and explain every step of Plan S. Duplantis listens with interest. Kate not so much, she's heard it. She leans back in her rocker and stretches her legs. I can tell she's waning, tired of holding the gun.

Duplantis doesn't like the idea of Canada at first. But he starts coming around when we discuss Portland. He tells me he hates it here – the weather, the traffic, the hip attitude, the whole town thinks it's hot shit he says. But to leave his country for weak-ass Canada? I suggest he make a T diagram to come to a decision.

"I don't need any goddamn T diagram. I can see what I gotta do. Bye, bye apple pie. Canada here I come."

I'm not sure if he's telling the truth or just stringing me along, looking for a different escape.

Then Duplantis starts laughing. I glare at him, "What's so funny?" He laughs harder and leans back on his hands against the wall.

"Life is amazing, ya know? Leroy came to visit me in prison once. He said he just wanted me to know that when I got out he was gonna hunt me down and kill me. He said to count on it. And now it's come true. And you two wackos are the ones he sends. Life is so absurd."

"Absurd is an understatement," I say.

Chapter 33 Unmasked

Talk eventually turns into silence. We take a break with some TV, killing time. I try to rest and even close my eyes a bit. A micro power nap. By now it's midnight.

Then I flinch as my phone vibrates in my pocket. I fumble it out and it lands on the floor. Grabbing it, I see it's a text from Leroy. It says: FINISHED? LET ME KNOW.

"Message from Leroy?" Duplantis asks. "What's he have to say?"

"Nothing of interest to you."

"Yeah, right. Liar." The smirk on his face didn't sit well with me and I felt an urge to kick it off. Instead, my legs carry me into the kitchen.

"You got any weapons in the house?" I ask, voice edging up in volume.

"As a parolee I can't possess weapons, sir," he says. "I have not a weapon to my name, your honor."

I throw open kitchen cabinet doors and drawers ostensibly looking for a weapon, but not really. I'm looking for a bottle. Any booze at all. My nerves are getting fried and I need, for lack of a better word, a fix. A way to escape for a minute, or two. My plan to avoid liquor all day is stupid I now realize. I can't function well sober. What was I thinking?

The fridge is my last resort. Please god let there be beer. I fling it open and see a garden of greenery, sprouts, grapes, yogurt and other health foods that almost make me gag. No leftover pizza or chicken tenders or beef pot pies – and not one single solitary beer.

What kind of idiot lives like this. The fact he had not a drop of alcohol in the entire house was an affront to me. Who the hell does this guy think he is? Is he too good to drink? Another holier-than-shit health nut whose body is a goddamn temple or something.

"So, this the first day of the rest of your life or something?" I say, staring into the fridge.

"Whaddaya mean, detective?"

"You got nothing but health shit in the house – as if you've turned over a new goddamn leaf or something. Is that true? Starting a brand new sober life here in the Rose City are ya?"

"No, sir. I think a drink would be good. To celebrate the occasion of me moving to Canada." I'm stunned for a moment, and try to show disinterest while shooting a glance at Kate. Her eyes have that serious look I've seen so many times before.

Duplantis sits forward, "There's a bottle of Southern Comfort in my bottom dresser drawer in my bedroom. Take these cuffs off and I'll get it."

"I guess we could have one," I say, not looking at Kate but feeling heat coming from her direction. "Stay where you are. I'll get it." I find the bottle and pour two stiff drinks. I don't offer one to Kate.

Time flows better and faster once the booze goes down. We sip our drinks and talk about a range of subjects. The Allman Brothers, Little Feat – the Tom Petty album Southern Accents.

Duplantis goes into detail on how to make "toilet wine" in a prison cell.

The talk keeps me engaged. I begin to pontificate on the differences between college football in the PAC 12 and SEC and that's when Kate comes unglued.

"Shut up! Shut up, stop babbling both of you!" She yells behind her mask as she stands up.

"I knew it," Duplantis says. "She's a chick."

"She's not a chick!" I say. "Shut up, Duplantis!" Then turning to Kate I say, "And you shut your yap too ... man!"

"I can't stand this stupid mask any longer," Kate says, reaching her hand up and pulling off the Mexican wrestling mask.

"Told ya so," says Duplantis. "That, my friend, is a female. Sorry to inform you."

"What are you doing?" I yell, stepping toward Kate and reaching for her mask to put it back on.

She's irate. "You two idiots are sitting here drinking and talking like frat boys at a party – get serious! What about tonight! Do you even know what you're doing? Have you forgotten what's at stake? This is unbelievable! I can't take it!"

She's shaking and for a sec I think she's gonna lose it. I step closer to catch her if she falls, but she remains steady on her feet. Not a tear falls. I marvel at her and think to myself, she's tougher than I.

"She's right," I say. "We gotta get focused. You got a suitcase?"

Duplantis nods and leads me into his room, hands still cuffed, and gestures toward the closet. "There's a suitcase in there." He points out the clothes he wants and I pack them.

"I have money in the top drawer of my desk. It's all I have here but I have some in an account at US Bank." I grab his money from the drawer – about $800 – and put it in a zipper pocket of the suitcase.

"You got a winter jacket or warm coat?"

"No, just a windbreaker. One sweatshirt."

"Bring 'em. You'll need both." I pull them out of the closet.

By now it's after 2:00 am. I check my phones – no messages. Then Nolan and I go back into the living room where Kate is back in the rocking chair, eyes glazed as if she's the one who's been drinking. I grab the go bag and stick it in the suitcase.

From my backpack I take out the spool of rope and begin wrapping it around Nolan binding his arms.

"My hands are cuffed, what're you doing?" he asks.

"This is for Leroy, to show him we have you – for real. He likes rope. And I need to put the tape back on. Just for some photos." I retape his mouth, then stand back and turn to Kate.

"Okay, we're about ready. Are you up for this?" I ask her. She looks up at me, listless, unresponsive. I go on, "We have one more thing to do. Stand up." She doesn't move.

"Come on, get up." I reach out and help her slowly rise, her mask in her hand.

"Put your mask back on."

"Why? I don't want to."

"Do it. We need a photo. Please put the mask back on. Nolan, come over here and stand between us."

He does so and I pull out my phone and take a selfie of the three of us, Kate with her mask on. I take four shots to make sure I have a good one. I then untape Duplantis and he sputters, "Are you serious! You took a selfie?" Kate is mystified as well.

"It's for Leroy. Precaution and protection. I want him to know I have an accomplice – someone he doesn't know. He'll recognize me and when he sees your butt-ugly face he'll know it's you. But he won't know her. Quit asking so goddamn many questions! Everyone shut up and lemme work! I've got this handled."

I hate it when people interrupt me when I'm concentrating on something – like writing. Writing is hard – it takes intense focus. I can't be distracted or questioned in the process.

Kate and Nolan are silent while I select the best selfie and write a message to Leroy. The pic, showing Nolan roped and taped standing between me and Kate reminds me of the swamp party photo Leroy took that first night we met – Mario on one side and me on the other with the dead vic Leroy strangled in the middle.

It'll be obvious to Leroy that tonight's photo is a retake of that picture he took long ago on the bayou. The night he threw a rope around that guy's neck, crushed his windpipe, dragged him to the swamp, and fed him to the gators.

Along with the photo I text Leroy the following message: Yep, got him. And duh, I got another guy too. You don't know him. But he knows everything about you and the Agency. If anything happens to me, or anyone in my family, he'll give you up. Fast. With evidence. Ya like his mask? Thought you would.

Sixty seconds later Leroy gets back to me: AT LEAST YOU GOT THE RIGHT ADDRESS THIS TIME. THAT'S HIM. NEXT PHOTO HE BETTER BE DEAD. NEED TO DO A BACKGROUND CHECK ON YOUR PARTNER. WHAT'S HIS NAME?"

I don't respond and put my phone away.

"Okay, we ready?" Nolan and Kate look at me and nod. "Once we leave here, no sounds until we get in my vehicle. I'll carry your suitcase. Kate, you carry the backpack." She looks at me with quick anger.

"Kate?" says Duplantis. "Your name's Kate? I like that name. I had an English teacher in high school named Kate. She encouraged my writing."

I cut him off, "Forget I said that and never say her name again! No names!"

Duplantis mocks me, "Do as you say, not as you do? Okay... Les."

"Shut up! After we do this I'll take you downtown to catch the first train. Say goodbye to your humble abode, Nolan. You won't be coming back."

"So I have to walk all tied up in this rope?"

"Yeah, the rope stays on until this is over. And we're putting the tape back on once we get to the park. More photos. We have to make it look real."

"Okay, boss. Let's get on with it."

And with that I pick up his suitcase, Kate puts on the backpack, and we walk out the door. When we get to the Escape I help Duplantis get in the front seat. Ben stares him down, unblinking, and tries to climb over the seat to sniff him up. It's obvious the dog is suspicious. I can tell he suspects something bad is afoot. Dogs can sense trouble.

Kate is shocked to see Ben.

"Oh my god, you didn't take Ben home? You're taking him with us?"

"I didn't have time to take him back. He'll be fine." I don't tell her I'd forgotten he was still in the car.

"What is wrong with you," she says. It doesn't seem phrased as a question so I don't answer. Instead, I turn the keys and start out for Frazer Park. The wheels are turning. I pray they don't come off.

Chapter 34 Frazer Park

Sunday night

It's soul-crushingly sad on these dark streets in the middle of the night, especially when you're on your way to a hanging. We ride in quiet and I feel a deep despair.

What in god's name am I doing? How did I get to this point? How did I turn into a stark raving maniac – driving to a neighborhood park with wife and dog in the middle of the night to hang a guy from a tree and take pictures of it. Who does that? I do, apparently.

I switch on the radio. The oldies station is playing "Do You Know The Way To San Jose" by Dionne Warwick. It wrecks me. The idea of heading for San Jose, for a new start. Old favorite tunes are dopamine that take me back to better times. To days when I had numerous paths open in front of me.

In ten minutes, we arrive at Frazer Park. I slowly drive by to check it out. Not seeing anyone around, I pull up to the curb a half block away. Ben gets up and looks out the window, excited. He knows this park. But he can't get out which will make him mad.

"Okay, let's go. Kate, put on your mask. And keep it on until I tell you it's okay." She and I get out of the car and I open the trunk. I take out the chair I'd brought and the rope with the noose I'd tied. I put the noose in the backpack.

"You take the chair, I got the backpack."

Still sitting in the front seat, roped tight and cuffed, is Duplantis.

I open his door and help him get out. With him shuffling his feet like a penguin, we all walk to the park and head toward the trees in the center. I smell dew on the grass.

The only sound is the soft hum of vehicles on I-84, which I can see just a quarter mile away. White lights going one way, red lights the other. In the distance, I hear a police siren. Somebody else is up to no good tonight.

When we get close to the hanging tree I stop. It's even more menacing and monstrous than I remember. I look up in the tree and see something strange that makes me gasp. It's the boy whose father I'd killed a couple nights before. He's wearing a t-shirt and underwear, sitting on a branch high in the tree. He looks down at me, no expression on his face. I'm struck dumb. I shake my head and blink my eyes to focus. The boy is suddenly gone.

From the backpack I take out the duct tape and step up to Duplantis.

"We're putting this on now, for photos. It says on until we're done. Understand?"

"Okayyy, this is it. I'm trusting you... Les. What's your real name by the way?"

I pause then say, "Teddy," too tired to think of something else.

"Okay, Teddy. I hope these aren't my last words. Don't kill me."

He looks at Kate as he finishes speaking. I instantly wonder why. A final plea and he looks at her? What, does he think she has the ultimate power here, the final call? It pisses me off.

"She's not the one who decides things here dumbass," I say. "You'd better be addressing me, not her." I'm whispering but there's rising anger in my voice. I can tell he doesn't trust me at all. Thinks I'm a fool.

I tear off a stretch of tape and stick it over his mouth, then take the chair from Kate and position it below the branch sticking out 12 feet above.

"Okay, we gotta get you up on the chair, but first we need to put one more thing on."

Reaching into the backpack I pull out the noose and rope. Next, I take out the gun with silencer and give it to Kate. I close her fingers around the gun grip. She's shaking a little. She may be crying, I can't tell.

"Okay," I say to Duplantis. "Gotta put this noose around your neck. It'll make sense to Leroy. He always said hanging is one of the best ways to kill someone."

He rolls his eyes, then bends down as I slip the noose around his neck and cinch it up.

"Lean back, I'll pick you up." He leans back and I reach down and pick up his legs and lift him up to stand on the chair. Kate moves forward, wearing her blackhawk Mexican wrestling mask, watching as if she's in the front row of a play. I wish I could read her mind – but as much as I've tried, I can't.

"Stand like I taught you and hold your arms out with the gun on him." She does it and I take the phone out and snap her pic. The flash lights her up, but then is gone. She looks like she's in a horror film, wearing an eerie, animalistic mask, legs spread, arms straight out, pointing a gun at Duplantis.

I take the other end of the rope, coil it all up like a lasso, and throw it up and over the branch. It lands twenty feet away in the grass.

To Kate, "Get that rope." She retrieves it and brings it to me.

"Okay, I want you to stand a few feet over there and pull on the rope, take out all the slack and tighten it up so the noose pulls on his neck."

Kate pulls back on the rope and I take several closeup shots of Duplantis, showing the noose around his neck. His mouth is taped, but his eyes are open. He has a flat affect, almost looking bored.

"Act scared," I say. "Make your eyes big. Look like you're scared shitless. You're about to be hung. Show fear." I keep giving directions as I shoot.

I get closeups and move back for midrange shots, showing as much of his body as possible without showing the chair he stands on. But it's not right. Not real enough.

"Pull harder on the rope," I say to Kate. "Make it really tight." She leans back and yanks on the rope. To Duplantis, "Try rolling your eyes back as far as you can." I shoot a few more shots from different angles.

"Okay, take a break. I'll check these." I examine the pics. No good. Our fake looks fake. I delete all the shots except one – a closeup with his head hanging sharply down. You can't see the face though, which is a problem.

Then I remember the white facial cream I have in the backpack. I reach in the pack and pull it out.

"Let up on the rope," I say to Kate. Then to Duplantis, "Get down off the chair." He hops off, landing on his feet but toppling over on the ground. I hear a moan from behind the tape and step forward to help him up.

Opening the cream container, I dip a couple fingers in and wipe a smudge across his cheeks and rub the cream lightly all over his face. It makes him a little more pale. Not dead, but better than before. It'll help.

But I realize there's another problem. The chair isn't tall enough. He needs to be higher. I look around and spot a picnic table under a different tree not far away.

I run over and drag the table back across the wet grass to the hanging tree. I remove the chair and push the table in its place, so one end is under the branch.

"Okay, get on the table. I'll help ya up." He doesn't move. He acts like Ben when he refuses my commands.

I sharpen my tone. "Listen to me! We need you higher up, so it looks like you're high off the ground!"

He sighs then bunny hops over to the table and I lift him up on it. He stands near the edge and turns his pale face toward me. I motion to Kate to yank on the rope. The noose tightens. I go in below him and take photos of his face showing the noose and branch above.

Checking the photos, it still doesn't look real enough. I start pacing and almost throw the phone on the ground. My mind prowls like a caged cat. What do I do? I'll never get away with this. What were you thinking you fool, you idiot, you can't fake out anybody – Leroy, god, the universe.

Anyone else in my place would just dispose of the guy. Right? Of course! It's the only move. It'd be over in a snap. Jasmine saved. Leroy satisfied. No $22,000 of my money gone. Why don't I just do the goddamn job! Step up, be a man!

I look at Duplantis. He's standing on the table, noose around his neck, tape over his mouth, his eyes boring deep into my psyche. He knows I'm pondering something and tries to probe into my mind. I'm not sure myself what I'm going to do.

Chapter 35 The Hanging

This whole ordeal is making me furious – why do I have to decide this guy's fate? I just killed two people two nights ago. Why do I have to do it again?

But then, what's it matter if I kill three people instead of two. Is there a penalty per death – is god keeping score? Three strikes and you're out?

And then I get an idea. There's only one thing to do.

"We gotta reshoot and make this right," I say. "Kate, come give me the rope." She walks over and hands it to me. I take the rope and keep it taut as I move to the tree. I walk around the tree twice, then tie the rope securely to the trunk. Duplantis is standing on the table, rope stretched tight above him. He looks down at me trying to gauge my next move.

"Tilt your head back, roll your eyes back too," He doesn't do it. "Do it! The sooner we get this right the sooner we get outta here." He's nervous as hell. But he tilts his head back as I walk around behind him to the opposite end of the table. I motion to Kate to stand back, then pull the phone from my pocket.

"Tilt your head farther back – as far as you can." Duplantis sighs, then his head slowly rolls back, like a bobblehead in slow-mo. Then, he turns his head toward me and realizes what I'm about to do.

What I do is grip the wood table with both hands and yank hard, stepping backwards and pulling the table across the grass a good five feet. The roped, shadowy figure swings down, body wrenching back and forth, legs trying to kick out, torso rotating back and forth, neck gripped in a noose, veins bulging, face straining, eyes frantic with fear.

The figure makes a muffled sound, smothered by duct tape. I can tell it's a one-syllable word repeated in a series. Like no, no, no...

When you're hung or strangled, oxygen is cut off to your brain. Your brain can't function long without it and will eventually shut down. If your neck snaps, you die fast. If you're strangled, it can take a few minutes.

In the hanging tonight the body hasn't dropped far enough for the neck to snap. Duplantis is still alive, but I have just a couple minutes to get the shots I need before it's lights out.

I look up in the darkness at the full moon hanging high in the sky. It casts a wicked shadow from the tree – a devilish shape with a bony, skeletal arm from which dangles a twisting figure.

The only sound I hear is the rubbing of rope on the branch above, the wood softly creaking.

Looking up I see a power line where several crows are perched. A murder. That's what you call a group of crows. It makes me laugh out loud. What is this murder of crows thinking I wonder. Are they aghast at what this dumb human is doing? Disapprove? Or are they cheering me on – wanting me to kill one of my own species.

They look down at me and sound off, cawing in a high-pitched mocking tone that irks me. I sneer up at them and then suddenly feel a sharp sting on my cheek and hear the piercing sound of a slap. Pain focuses my mind. The slap is from Kate who yells, "Move!" She shoves me aside then leans over and starts pushing the picnic table toward the hanging figure.

Furious, I rush forward and throw my shoulder into her and knock her to the ground. I grab the phone off the table and start shooting photos of the no longer squirming figure hanging in the air, dangling between life and death. It looks real as hell.

I shoot fast, the flash lighting up the scene like a strobe. I zoom in on his head and widen out to show the whole body. It's a rush.

The crows stop cawing and peer down at me. I can feel their judgment. I drop the phone on the grass and sprint to the tree, past the figure hanging motionless in the air.

I untie the rope and drop Duplantis to the ground. I'm on him in a second, tearing the duct tape off and putting my ear to his mouth to check for breathing. Nothing. I loosen the noose and pull it off over his head, then straddle the body and start CPR, pushing down to the beat of "Stayin' Alive" – a song I've always hated.

"Stay alive, stay alive, stay alive you asshole," I repeat, trying to think of a different, but suitable tune. I continue CPR, trying to pump air back into his lungs, breathing hard myself. The crows don't interrupt.

Still no sign of life and I look behind me for Kate for help. But don't see her.

"Kate!" I whisper, then louder, "Kate! Where are you?" I hear not a sound. "Kate!"

Then I spy something on the ground about 30 feet away. Lying face up in the grass is the Mexican wrestling mask, the eyes now just two empty holes. Next to it is the Beretta and silencer. Kate's fled.

Turning back to Duplantis, I feel for a pulse in his neck. Nothing. Jesus Christ, have I killed this guy? A man who just served almost 40 years in prison for a murder he didn't commit? An innocent man – and I've just taken his life? Just like two nights ago? Can that really be? Not yet, not yet. He can't be brain dead yet.

"Nolan!" I yell in his ear. "Nolan! You're not dead yet! Your brain is still working – you can hear me, I know! Breathe, man! Breathe! Breathe! Tell your heart to beat!"

I pause and listen for breath. Nothing. His eyes are closed and his face is the color of flour. It's been a couple minutes now since his oxygen was cut off. He's on the edge. I again press down on his chest – faster, harder, and raise my voice.

"Listen, don't do this to me – you sorry piece of Louisiana trash!" I start beating on his chest, sweating bullets.

And then I receive mercy. He suddenly coughs. Spit forms on his lips.

I shake his shoulders, "Keep breathing, keep breathing, you're alive." His eyelids slowly rise, like shutters over a window. He coughs more then finally catches his breath enough to say something.

"You... you tried to kill me."

"Man, that was close," I say. "You scared me, dude."

"You killed me."

"No, I didn't. I saved you."

"No, I saw. You killed me. I watched."

"I saved your ass."

He rolls over and coughs hard. I go on explaining. "We need to get realistic photos and we did. Look." I show him the photos I've just taken. Tears fill his eyes as he sees just how real the last few minutes have been.

"Leroy will believe these," I say. "Anyone would. You look dead – this is great." I'm trying to cheer him up. "We're done – it's over. You're good to go. Let's get outta here!"

He's still cuffed and roped. I help him up, then pull the rope down from the tree, curl it up, and put it in the backpack, along with the wrestling mask and gun. I pocket the phone, then pick up the chair and scan the ground to see if we've left anything. The only thing that's out of place is the picnic table, which I leave as is.

"Let's go!" I whisper, and we start off across the grass, leaving the hanging tree and its shadow behind us. The crows, like Kate, have disappeared.

When we get to my vehicle, I help Duplantis get in. He groans as he leans down into the car and I give him a shove to speed things up. Backpack tossed in back, I jump behind the wheel feeling exhilarated from the adrenaline surging through me.

Ben sits up and leans forward, looking directly at Duplantis in front and trying to sniff the top of his head, then glares at me as if I'm doing something stupid. I don't like his attitude. So judgmental.

We drive west down Halsey. Nobody is on the street. I pull in to the parking lot at the Northeast Community Center where I've played hoops for almost 30 years.

"Get me outta this rope," Duplantis says. "Take off these cuffs. My arms are killing me!"

"Okay, hang tight. I need to pick a few photos to send to Leroy."

"Well hurry up! Where's Kate?"

"She left, shut up a minute!"

I look through the photos, examining each closely and deleting the obvious bad ones. Those remaining I show to Nolan – both closeups of his face and full body shots.

He points his shoulder at the phone, "This one."

"Yeah, that's good. I also like this one – really shows you're in agony."

"I was." I see a flash of something in his eye – could be anger. Maybe it's a memory, of seeing his life pass before his eyes twenty minutes ago.

I end up with four pics. Two head closeups and two body shots. All taken in the final moments when his life hung in the balance. The pics are killer and look authentic.

I send them along with a text to Leroy. The message: He's gone for good. You'll love the pics. Since this is my last job I did it old school, your favorite way – rope a dope. Left him swinging near a picnic table so it looks like suicide. Took off duct tape and rope around his body. Made anonymous 911 call. News story could be online soon. Will send link. NOW I want my daughter! That's the deal! Let her go!

The fake is in the ether, fate in the air. This harebrained scheme better work.

Chapter 36 News Story

My mind flashes to the photo of Jasmine they sent earlier – sitting on a bed watching TV in some motel room. I can't imagine she's sleeping – with kidnappers in the same room. I try to perish the thought.

Wrenching my focus from Jasmine, I conjure Kate. Where'd she go? Is she at home? I gotta reach her and tell her I'm close to getting Jasmine, so she won't call the cops. I send her a text: Where are you?! I'm getting Jasmine! Duplantis is alive – the plan is still on! DO NOT call police!

Sitting in my Escape, I close my eyes. What I need is sleep. Not now. I wrench my eyes open and look at my phone, hoping by staring at it that a message will arrive from Leroy or Kate. Nothing. I start to get nervous.

"Those assholes had better let her go," I hear myself say.

"What assholes?" Duplantis says. "Who ya talkin' about?"

"None of your damn business."

"Let who go?" he says. I decide I might as well tell him. Lying is exhausting.

"They have my daughter. They kidnapped her to make me kill you. That's why we're doing this."

"Wait, you mean they kidnapped her to make you kill me?" I nod my head, too tired to obfuscate.

He goes on, "Wow, even with her kidnapped you wouldn't kill me? I can't believe you. Why didn't you do it? Why didn't you just leave me hang from that tree? I would've." He shut up and shook his head.

"I almost did. But something made me save you. It's like I woulda been killing myself in some strange way. You're an innocent man who didn't deserve to die, neither did I. And I didn't deserve to have you on my conscience, like a crow mocking me the rest of my life, shitting on me."

"A crow?"

"Yeah, you and others. A murder of crows."

"You're losing it, man."

"The other thing is, I thought I could get away with it – faking your death. I liked coming up with a plan where everyone lives – not necessarily happily ever after. I'm not a sap."

"When are you gonna put up the fake news story?"

"Soon. Have to give time for the Oregonian to write the story and post it on their site. It'd normally take about an hour this early in the day."

We sit in the Escape and Ben lies down in back. Duplantis tries to stretch, "Jesus Christ, man – take off these ropes. I'm not goin' anywhere. I'm on board with the plan! I wanna make that train! C'mon, Les!"

"Alright. I guess I trust ya, man."

I unwrap the rope and remove the cuffs and throw them in the trunk with the kitchen chair, backpack, and suitcase. As I close the tailgate, a phone buzzes. It's a text from Leroy: HOLY HOLY GOD ALMIGHTY – YOU DID IT WELL T! LOVE THE ROPE AND SUICIDE. SEND ME NEWS STORY WHEN IT APPEARS. JASMINE HOME SOON.

I slapped my hand on the steering wheel. "Yes, Leroy bought it! The photos worked. He's happy."

"What about your daughter?"

"They say she'll be released."

"You trust 'em?"

"Leroy's a bastard but he has principles. He'll keep his end." I try to sound as if I believe it.

In seconds I get another text – this one from Kate. She's at the end of her rope, so to speak. She says: You have 1 hr. If you can't PROVE you have her by then I'm calling police!

I respond back: Getting her soon!

But these things can never be easy – at least in my life. I hear nothing from Leroy or the kidnappers. I text them again and again but they remain silent. I play the radio, trying to steady my nerves. I'm frantic, getting desperate.

What have I done, where is Jasmine, what do I tell Kate? Duplantis sees it all and piles on telling me I should never have trusted Leroy. Calls me a fool. I feel like strangling him, for real this time.

Ben has a mocking look and I yell at him, "Stop it! I'm sick of your negative vibes!"

"What're you talking about?" Duplantis says. "I don't have any negative vibes. I've been on your-" I cut him off. "I'm not talkin' to you! Keep your goddamn mouth shut! This is between me and him."

I glare at Ben who stares back, steely eyes auguring into my soul. He's tired of sitting in the car – wants me to let him out. He saw me unleash Duplantis and now he wants loose too – so he can sniff up this stranger in the front seat. He doesn't like him I can tell. He's hungry as hell no doubt so I cut him some slack.

"Sit! Just a little longer. I'm sorry you had to go through this but it'll be over soon. I'll get you something to eat."

"Good, I'm hungry," Duplantis says.

"I'm talking to Ben! Shut up!"

"What about me? How about feeding me?"

I start the engine and head toward home. It's begun to rain again and fog hangs low in the dark, dank streets. It takes just a few minutes to get to our place. Nobody is around when I pull into the driveway – no sign of Kate, her Subaru gone. No lights on in the neighborhood.

"Come inside," I say to Duplantis. "I don't want you runnin' off somewhere." I unleash Ben from the seatbelt and take him inside.

Entering the kitchen, I grab Ben's bowl and fill it. Duplantis walks into our living room, checking out the family photos on our walls.

"Pretty homey place ya got, Teddy," he says.

"We've lived here a long time, since Jasmine was born." Saying her name makes me queasy and I feel like I might puke.

I text Leroy and the kidnappers again demanding Jasmine, then go to the closet where I had stashed Mario's backpack with the manila envelope full of money. I pull out all the cash and count it - $14,000. I figure it's mostly my take of the RIP job I was to do with Mario. He's in no position to dispute it, so I slip the money into the inside pocket of my jacket.

It's been 45 minutes since I've heard from Kate, 15 minutes to the deadline she'd given me. Still no message back from Leroy or the kidnappers. I feel pressure on all sides, like my body's in a vise, my oxygen slowly being cut off. It's earlier than I planned to have Lex post the news story but I panic. In desperation I grab my cell phone and text Lex: Go! Post it, now!"

The only sound is the clock on our mantle, ticking off the seconds. I cover my ears and look out the window. It's the darkest time of the night, an hour before dawn. The moon is distant now, a small orb above the house across the street.

My cell vibrates. It's a text from Lex: Affirm – story up in 2 min.

In less time than that, he sends me a link to the news story on the Oregonian's Oregon Live website. I click it and up pops the story, appearing exactly as it should, a page in the Local News section, third story down. It reads as follows:

Man found hung in NE Portland park

Police were alerted early this morning that a body was seen hanging from a tree in a park in NE Portland. According to a Portland Police officer on the scene, the body was discovered by an anonymous 911 caller who was out walking his dog before work. Police found ID on the deceased that identify him as Nolan Duplantis, a resident of Northeast Portland.

Police report it appears to be a suicide. No other injuries or signs of a struggle were evident. The Police officer reported that suicides are on the rise this year. He commented, "People are stressed out these days for many reasons. Layoffs and tough times are devastating."

In the left upper corner of the news story is a picture of Duplantis. The caption reads: Man dies of apparent suicide.

I send the news story to Leroy as well as the kidnappers. My message: Oregonian has posted the news story – see for yourself. I want Jasmine NOW! Where is she???

"The news story is up. I just sent them the link."

"Good. I hope it works," Duplantis says.

"You wanna see the story?"

"No, I've had enough dying for one night."

Chapter 37 Kidnapper

I walk into the living room and collapse on the couch. Ben sits on his haunches on the hardwood floor and stares at Duplantis. Normally he would climb onto the couch next to me. Not now. It's clear he doesn't like this stranger being in our house. He looks at me as if to say this guy is bad, something is off. Get him out of here.

"No!" I hear myself say. "You're not the boss here, I am!" I can't stop myself. "You don't know what the hell is going on! So just sit there and don't say anything!"

Duplantis gives me a wary eye but keeps silent. My momentary madness is interrupted by a text – from Kate: You have 10 min before I call 911.

My desperation deepens and I feel a pain in my heart, like somebody hit me in the chest with a sledgehammer. Dear god, don't give me a heart attack now I pray. Kill me later once Jasmine is safe.

Realizing I have no choice, I text Kate and lie: I have her! She's okay. Come home. My battery dying.

It's the only way to stop her from calling the police. One more lie in the mounting pile of lies my life is built on, a funeral pyre. But it may buy me a little time.

Kate texts me: Where is she?

I don't respond. Instead, I walk into the kitchen and take down a bottle of vodka from the liquor cabinet. I unscrew the cap and pull out two small glasses from the cupboard. As I'm about to fill them

I get a text from Leroy: SAW NEWS STORY. THEY BOUGHT THE SUICIDE – YOU PULLED IT OFF. WILL KEEP MY WORD. YOU'RE OUTTA THE AGENCY. ADIOS, MY FRIEND.

What about Jasmine? I start to text him back when I get a message on my burner phone – from the kidnappers. It says: The park on Halsey. Now. Go to baseball field and wait. Alone.

"They got back to me!" I yell. "I need to go!"

Duplantis runs into the kitchen. "Where is she?"

"A park, not far. You stay here. I'm turning off the lights. Go downstairs and stay outta sight."

"Can I take that vodka with me?"

I pause, "Alright. But leave me some. No, go ahead and drink it, I don't care."

Grabbing my keys, I jump in the Escape and head for Normandale Park. It's less than five minutes away. When I arrive I drive to the baseball field.

I'm waiting when suddenly my back door opens and a figure jumps in. He has a ski mask on and is wearing dark jeans and a black denim coat with a high collar.

"Drive," he says, in a low, strange voice. "Go straight and turn left. Don't turn around."

"Where's my daughter?" I ask. He doesn't respond. "Where are we going?" Silence. I assume he's taking me to Jasmine.

I drive down the road and check my rearview. The kidnapper looks behind us to see if we're being followed. Nobody is around. He's nervous, but cool. No doubt has a weapon in his pocket but I can't see it. We drive on for several blocks, then he tells me to pull over in front of a church. There's a Cadillac across the street with Louisiana plates. The windows are tinted so I can't see if anyone is inside.

"Is my daughter in the Caddy?" I hear the crunch of gravel as my tires roll to a stop by the curb. To see better I roll down my window. The air is soggy, heavy with dew and despair, making it hard to see clearly.

"I want my daughter now! Where is she?"

"She's a pretty girl," the man in the mask says. The tone now higher. There's something familiar about it.

I look closely at him and he says, "She's not in the Caddy."

"Where is she?" I yell. I'm ready to climb over the seat and grab the guy by the neck.

"Home, by now. I dropped her off a few blocks from your house. Call her." I take out my cell phone and punch in the numbers. It rings once and I hear Jasmine's voice.

"Dad? Is that you?"

"Yes! It's me. Are you alright – where are you?"

"Yes," she whimpers, sobbing softly. "I'm okay, at home. Come home!"

"I'll be there in a sec. Call your mom right away. Now! Tell her you're okay!" She says she will and hangs up.

"She's a lovely lady," the guy in back says. "We got to know each other a bit. She can tell you about it." His voice still throws me and I lean back to listen closer – like I do when driving Uber and want to eavesdrop on passengers.

He goes on, "I'm glad you killed that asshole. Duplantis deserved all that – and more. I wasn't sure you'd actually do it. You being such a decent man and all – at least that's how I remember you."

I whip my head around to look at him – he's thin, angular, and has a certain manner I can't place.

"Don't look at me," he says, and I do as told as he goes on. "It's been a long time since we last saw each other. But I still remember you. You've raised a strong girl. I'm sure her mother had something to do with it. Tell your wife I'm sorry about that picture we left for her on your porch. They wanted to put some pressure on you. Mess with you."

"I don't know who you are," I say. "But your voice is familiar. Take off your mask why don't ya."

The man slowly takes off his ski mask and I see a smooth, olive-skin face with expressive, brown eyes framed by thin eyebrows. It dawns on me. This is no guy. And then I know.

"Ho-ly shit... I don't believe it – Lulu? Is that really you? Leroy's little girl, in the flesh?"

"Good memory," she says.

I turn around further to look at her. She has the same lively face and engaging smile I remember when she sat on my lap at Leroy's party that first day we met near 40 years ago. She must be in her mid 40s now.

"Lulu, don't tell me you work for your dad. Are you part of the Agency? I thought you were a school teacher."

"How'd ya know that?" she says. "Doesn't matter, I'm doing this for daddy. You don't know what's going on."

"I sure as hell DO know what's going on! I've been a part of it as no doubt know. But I'm done. I'm out of the Agency. Taking out Duplantis was my last job."

"The Agency hasn't had a job in five years," she stammers. "Everybody left except Mario. And now he's gone. I was his backup. I came because I wanted to see Portland. Then I hear from daddy that you guys went to the wrong house and Mario got killed. And you threw his body in the river and then refused to kill the real guy daddy wanted dead – Duplantis. Well, daddy freaked. Went crazy and said if I didn't kidnap Jasmine he'd come up here and grab her himself. He has a history with Duplantis and with his girlfriend, Violet McRae."

"I know, Duplantis told me about it. They all went to Lafayette High together."

"He's a bad man. Killed that poor woman and child she was carryin'. People like him need to die, it's justice."

"Assuming he did it," I say. "You sound like your old man."

"Oh, he did it," she responds.

"Leroy's all about justice. A hanging judge."

"Was," she says. I detect a break in her voice. She turns her head to look out the window into the night.

I change the subject, "Who's this guy Bobby Lee? Leroy texted me twice by mistake, asking if I knew where Bobby Lee was. Who is he? You don't have a brother do you? I thought you were an only child."

She turns to me with tears in her eyes, "Daddy asked you about Bobby Lee?"

"Yeah. I didn't answer at first but then I just told him he was with me."

"Great," she sighs. "No wonder he's been all over me."

"So is this Bobby guy in Portland? Do I have to worry about him?" I see a tear run down her cheek as she responds.

"Yeah, you're right. I am an only child. And no, you don't have to worry about Bobby Lee."

"Who is he?"

She choked up. "He's not a guy... he's not in the Agency. He's daddy's blue heeler. His dog. Was his dog. He's dead – we had to put him down three months ago. And daddy can't remember it – or refuses to. He thinks Bobby Lee is still alive but lost, or that I have him. He asks me almost every day where Bobby Lee is and every time I tell him the truth he gets mad and accuses me of lying. I feel so bad for him. He had that dog so long. Now he's gone. And Mario's gone too. Daddy will be alone now."

It starts to make sense. Leroy's world is crumbling, kinda like mine. I don't know what to say.

Lulu goes on, "You're right, I am a teacher. I live in Lafayette. Soon, I'll have to move daddy from the ranch to an assisted living center near me. He'll hate me for it – maybe kill himself. I don't know what to do."

The news of Leroy's demise and approaching dementia is a shock. I keep seeing him as I remember him – vigorous and violent. Not a quiet soul in soft pajamas and alligator slippers watching Wheel of Fortune, sitting in a recliner close to senility.

"Aging sucks," is all I can muster up. "Time is a mother that just won't quit. I'm right there with Leroy. I'm losing it, too. Tell him that, maybe it'll make him feel better."

"I'll do that. But it won't be long before he doesn't even remember your name."

"Likewise. But this is getting depressing."

"Yeah, you'd better get home to Jasmine. And I need some sleep. I'm driving out to the coast to Astoria later. I want to see where the Columbia River hits the Pacific Ocean. They say the waters off Astoria are the graveyard of the Pacific. I love graveyards."

"That's funny, me too. I gotta go, Lulu. I wish it was different circumstances but I'm glad to see you again. Tell Leroy I hope he's well and to never ever contact me again. And to not kill himself." My attempt at levity, always pushing it, falls flat as Lulu drops more tears. I feel bad.

Reaching for the door handle she says, "Tell Jasmine to stay in touch. I gave her my number and email."

"You did what? You're kidding."

"No, I hope we stay in touch. She's a sweetie. It was great seeing you, Ted. I'm sorry you had to do this last job – but don't feel bad about it. The world's a better place without that monster, Duplantis, on the loose."

She honestly believes that Duplantis is guilty – that he's the one who killed Violet, not Leroy or Leroy's crew. I decide not to tell her the truth. She doesn't need to know the real story. It's better for children to think their parents are good and decent, even if they aren't.

I start the car and Lulu opens the door and climbs out. She smiles weakly and waves bye, then crosses the street to her Caddy and disappears inside. I drive off and don't look back.

Chapter 38 Jasmine

I walked in the door two minutes after I left Lulu. Jasmine was sitting on the couch with Ben, his tail wagging incessantly. She jumped up and we hugged as never before.

"I'm so sorry, so glad you're okay. Did you call your mom?"

"Yeah, she's on her way. I'm not sure where she was."

"She didn't call the police?"

"No, I don't think so. Where were you?"

"I met with...your kidnapper."

"She dropped me off a few blocks away," Jasmine said. "She said you had to do something for her dad. And once you did it I'd be set free. What did you do?"

"Just a job. I'll tell you about it later. How'd she get in here? Where'd she take you?"

Jasmine went on to explain how Lulu had busted through the back door and found her hiding in the furnace room downstairs, then tied her and gagged her and hustled her outside into a car and drove to a motel. Jasmine thought it was near the airport. She heard planes overhead. She didn't ask me any questions and I could tell she was in a state of shock.

She went on to explain how Lulu calmed her and assured her she wouldn't be harmed. How they watched TV all evening and talked into the night – how they shared similar experiences of growing up with crazy fathers and wanting to get away – to see the world.

At that moment the door flew open and Kate came in, breathless. "Oh thank god, you're okay!" she said to Jasmine. "I was so scared for you!"

They hugged as Ben jumped up on both of them, happy to have the family unit together at home. He looked at me and I could tell he was pleased. I was too. My plan had worked, amazingly enough.

"Are you sure we're okay?" Kate asked me, still nervous.

"Don't worry. It's all over. We're in the clear." I sat down, so tired I was trembling. "I'm so sorry I got you two into this. It'll never happen again."

Jasmine looked at me, "Are you okay, dad? I mean, you're not totally crazy are you?"

"No, not totally. I'm fine. We'll talk about it later."

"What now?" Jasmine asked. "I was set to fly to Ecuador today for my Amigos job."

"What do you wanna do?" I asked.

"I don't want to stay here, I want to go. The flight is around 11. I think I should go."

"Are you sure?" Kate asked. "You can cancel and stay home. You just went through a traumatic…"

"I'd feel better going. I don't want to stay home the next three months."

We discussed it and decided Jasmine would leave as scheduled later that morning. Kate and I'd take her to the airport and see her off. Then, we'd come home and I'd try to mend our fraying marriage.

Jasmine went into her room to pack and closed the door. Kate turned her focus to me, spitting like a cobra.

"I don't like you right now. I may never like you again."

I was too tired to mount a defense. She went on, "You knocked me down, almost broke my arm! How could you do that!" It wasn't phrased as a question, but I answered.

"I didn't mean to hurt you, but I had to stop you until I could get the photos I needed. They had to look real and that was the only way. I'm sorry! I'd never hurt you!"

"I thought you were going to kill me. You scared me to death!" Kate gets her first FOG, I thought. I can't help myself.

"I'm sorry, really. I don't want to live without you." I'm surprised when I say it. And I know it's not a lie.

"You may have no choice. So, where is he?"

I suddenly remembered Duplantis and ran downstairs, Kate on my heels. He was flat on his back in our guest room, snoring softly, an empty vodka bottle by his side. My immediate reaction was jealousy. I roused him and he opened his eyes, blinking wildly in confusion.

"What happened?" he said. "Where am I?"

"You're in our basement. Get up, we're leaving."

"Kate, you're back," he said. "Where'd you go? Last I remember you were watching him hang me. Thanks for nothing."

"I tried to help you, it doesn't matter," Kate said.

"I could've died then and there."

"So could I," she said. Duplantis didn't understand but moved on. "Did you get your daughter back?"

"Yeah, we have her," I said. "She's okay. You don't need to see her and she sure doesn't need to see you. Get up, you've got a train to catch."

Chapter 39 Departure

Monday morning

I looked at my phone. It was 5:45 a.m. The train to Montana left in 45 minutes. The three of us went upstairs – all silent. I took Duplantis out to my car and said, "Stay here, I'll be right back." I went back inside and apologized again to Kate and told her I'd be right back so we could take Jasmine to the airport.

"Your plan has worked so far, somehow," she said. "Don't screw it up now." Ben sat on the floor behind her and seemed to say the same thing. I promised them both I wouldn't. The plan was indeed working. Getting Duplantis out of town and on track toward Canada was the next step.

As we drove to the train station we talked so I could keep awake. He told me how he was raised on a former slave plantation west of New Orleans and went to college at Tulane. How he wanted to be a famous author. How he and Violet had fallen in love and made plans to marry and had a child on the way. How everything was grand and glorious until the night Leroy put her in a grave.

I felt truly sorry for him. Sorry for all those years he spent in prison for the crime of falling in love with the wrong person at the wrong time. Fate is a cruel mother.

"Your life is about to get a whole lot better," I said. "And that $22,000 of mine stashed in your suitcase will help you get started in Canada. Don't blow it."

"Don't worry. I'll put it to good use. I'm gonna buy a winter coat first thing and gloves and hat. Maybe watch some hockey. But I can't promise I'll like it. Really man, I don't know how to thank you. I can't believe you're doing this. I'm not used to people being nice to me, and giving me their get out of town escape bag to boot."

"Don't mention it. To anyone. But you gotta promise me you'll stay on that train all the way to Whitefish. If you don't show up there, the man who is set to pick you up will let me know and we'll track you down like a dog. He's a bounty hunter you don't want to cross. He's going to be well paid to get you across the border and if you don't show, he don't get paid. I warn ya, do not get off that train anywhere but Whitefish, Montana. You're no longer Nolan Duplantis – you have no US driver's license or ID. Police will be looking for you. Your best bet is Canada, and you already have a Canadian identity. You're Addison Thompson now."

"I suppose people call me Add."

"That's what I'd call you. But it's up to you."

"What's the name of this guy meeting me in Whitefish?"

"You don't need to know his name. Just make sure you get off there. He'll find you."

"Where do I sleep tonight?"

"At his hunting camp or at the trailhead. He'll know. Then tomorrow morning he'll take you on the game trail to cross the border – it's about 15 miles. Can you walk that far?"

"I guess I'll have to."

"You'll be in Canada tomorrow night. Just do what my man says."

"Wait, what about my suitcase. I can't pull it on the damn trail!"

"Hell no, you gotta move all your stuff to a backpack. My buddy is bringing an extra pack for you."

I parked on the street two blocks from the train station. Reaching under my seat, I pulled out the curly black wig and sunglasses I kept there.

"I'm wearing this in case they have security cameras in the station – I don't want to be seen with you." Duplantis rolled his eyes and kept quiet. We walked into Union Station, a church-like place with a vaulted ceiling, polished wooden pews, and hushed tones. Five minutes later came the boarding call.

We shook hands and I looked him in the eye, "Listen, you still have a chance to live a decent life. Don't look back or think about how you got screwed in Louisiana in prison all those years. Look ahead. And keep working on your book. You're a new man – with a new name and a wide open future."

He responded, "You shoulda kept the money and used the go bag yourself."

"I don't want it. You deserve it more than me. You're innocent, I'm not. Besides, I have a family here and a life I can live with."

He looked at me and smiled. "I guess it would be impolite of me not to thank you for not killing me. Your fake hanging may have saved my life. Who'd a thought?"

"I thought! I thought of the whole thing – and executed it! And never mention that story again. Or I'll find you and hang you for real." He laughed. I didn't.

As he started off through the gate I said, "Don't stay in touch." He gave me a thumb's up and walked away pulling his suitcase behind him. I watched and stood by the gate until the train left the station. I then walked back to my car.

I felt wonderfully free. Duplantis, now Addison Thompson, was on his way to a new life in Canada. I was headed home to restore my marriage and reclaim my family. I almost felt...happy. But it may have been exhaustion.

As I got in my car I thought of all that had happened the night before. Then I remembered the news story – Leroy had seen it and was satisfied it was real. I knew his fear of being online would mean he wouldn't come back to check the story again or see how other news media covered it.

I texted Lex: We're done. Take it down.

Less than a minute later I got online and checked out the Oregonian site. The news story of the hung body found in a Portland park was gone. It was as if they decided to pull it – the media hates suicide stories. It was as if it'd never happened.

Weariness seeped through my bones. My mind and memory began to shut down. Pulling out my little notebook, I wrote: Addison Thompson on train – arrive Whitefish 8:06 pm Monday.

Then I texted Kate: All good. He's gone. Home soon. Love you!!!!

Finally, energy sapped, I sent one final text – to my associate in Montana. It said: Delivery on the way. Train arrives Whitefish 8:06 tonight. Name Addison Thompson. Has ID and cash. Needs a backpack so bring one. He's no danger, unarmed, ready for Canada. Take him across – same plan we had for me.

The whole ordeal was over, or at least it was now in someone else's hands. Sitting back in my Escape, I felt a wave of emotion wash through every pore of my body. A pure rush of relief I hadn't felt in a long time.

Then, I thought of the murders I'd committed a couple nights earlier. The boy who saw me after I'd strangled his father haunted me. I'll never forget his blank expression – how his eyes just stared right through me. I'd taken his daddy away forever.

My eyelids were heavy, impossible to hold up. Just a ten-minute power nap I thought. Then I gotta get home. That was my last thought before sleep took hold.

Chapter 40 Sammy

The story I'd told Duplantis/Thompson about my associate in Montana being a bounty hunter was a lie. I know, big surprise. He's actually a fill-in bartender in Butte at the Silver Dollar.

Before that he was a trucker, insurance salesman, substitute teacher, underground tour guide, and Montana Highway Patrolman. He didn't handle authority well, even when he was the authority. His name is Sammy O'Shea.

Sammy is an oddball character, like most people from Butte. He's six-two, about 230, with Popeye biceps and a laugh that shakes the earth. If you're from Butte, you might recognize the last name. He's the son of Sonny O'Shea, the great welterweight boxer who fought in many big time bouts a generation ago.

I met Sammy in Butte during Evel Knievel Days one summer. Evel Knievel grew up in Butte and the proud burg celebrates that fact in high spirits every year. Or used to anyway.

I was standing by a cannon that was going to blast a woman called the CannonLady high in the air down Granite Street. Sammy was working security. I snapped a photo an instant after the cannon blew and got a great shot of white smoke emerging from the barrel and the CannonLady soaring into the blue sky.

We were both impressed with the cannon shot and got to talking. I kept running into him after that – as if we were in synchronous orbits.

Sammy O'Shea was now just bartending, hunting, fishing, volunteering at the Butte archives, and enjoying his fair share of Jameson's. He often hunts up near Eureka in the far Northwest corner of Montana, near Canada, where animals are thick and people are scarce he'd say. He didn't like people all that much. One of many things we had in common.

On one of his hunting trips he found a game trail across the border into Canada. He took me on it a few times. I'm no hunter and don't care for it. The only shooting I'd do on these ventures was on the pool table at Trappers Saloon in Eureka before and after the hunt.

I liked going out in the backcountry with Sammy. I'd bring along my camera and take photos of a landscape not many humans have laid eyes on. Always keeping my eye out for animals that could swallow me.

Chapter 41 Ronan

Three hours after dropping off Duplantis/Thompson at Union Station and falling asleep in my Escape I was awakened by a sharp rapping on my driver's side window. It was a cop who said to move my vehicle or pay the parking. I noticed I already had a yellow parking ticket on my windshield.

I was dazed. What the... where am I? What time is it? I started the car and saw on the dash that it was 10:25 a.m. My mind started engaging as I pulled out and wheeled down the street. I slept too long. What time does Jasmine go to the airport? I couldn't remember. Was I late? After driving a few blocks I pulled over to see if I had any messages.

I had two texts and one voicemail. One text from Kate said: Where are you? Need to take Jas to airport!

Before calling her I checked the other text. It was from Ronan Duecker: Call me. Now!

What could that be? I checked the voicemail message. It was also from Ronan. All he said was, "We need to talk. Right away. About this Nolan Duplantis guy. Call me." I deleted the message and punched in his number, nerves heating up.

Ronan answered, "Jesus man, it's about time. Where are you?"

"I was asleep. Sorry – so what's up?"

"Where's Duplantis? You following him?"

I started feeling a twist in my gut. "Duplantis? Why?"

"He's missing and wanted."

"For what? I don't know where he is." I had a bad feeling and it got worse.

"Portland detectives are looking for him. So are the Feds and folks in Florida, but they can't locate him. They all want him."

"Why? He did his time – he's on parole." By now I'm thinking as fast as I can, trying to stay ahead of Ronan and anticipating his questions.

"They're at his house – he's gone. Not at work. He's wanted, Teddy."

"What?" I tried frantically to clear my mind. "Wanted for what?" I didn't want to know.

"Looks like he did more than kill the woman in Louisiana. He did a double homicide in Pensacola, Florida and three murders around Jacksonville in the 70s before he did the Louisiana vic. They retested some evidence and were able to get the DNA – it's a done deal, it's your man. They think he could be a serial who's got a powerful urge to kill somebody now he's outta prison. He hasn't killed someone since that woman Violet McRae in the 70s."

The ceiling in my mind started to crack, walls were caving in. I said, "Oh, no, no, no way, that can't..."

He cut in, "Yeah, man, I'm telling you he's solid for these."

"But the Violet McRae murder was a setup – Leroy Dupree or one of his gang did it."

"Wrong. It was Duplantis. His DNA was there and nobody else's was. His prints were all over her throat. Dupree proved he wasn't there – he was at a Fireman's Social in Baton Rouge. A ton of witnesses. Duplantis did it and he did those five other homicides in Florida. In my math, that's six killings. And he may have more – the Feds are looking at his history. Earlier than Florida he was in Morocco and they say he may be linked to two murders there."

My brain caved in at hearing it. I immediately thought of Jasmine. She'd been on study abroad in Morocco and had been followed once she told me. I was dizzy and had trouble breathing.

Ronan went on, "There's more. You hear about the local murder the other night where a guy was strangled with a rope in his bedroom?"

My heart sank. "Yeah? What about it?"

"It was just ten blocks from Duplantis. He lives exactly ten streets away, same house number. Smells funny to me. He's #1 on the hit parade for that homicide now – especially now he's missing. Where is he?"

I couldn't believe it. It rocked me. Nolan was not the type to do that. I'd spent time with the man, got to know him. I can read people. It's my business. Nolan Duplantis was no serial killer. He couldn't be!

Or could he? It threw a wrench in the gears of my mind. My Duplantis plan lurched to a stop. It had to be true. Nolan Duplantis aka Addison Thompson was most likely a serial killer. And I'm now an accomplice to what he does.

All I could fumble out was, "I don't know where he is." If I hadn't been sitting in my car I would've fallen to the ground.

"Listen, I don't know how deep you're in here," Ronan said, "But you gotta let the Feds take over. It's not worth it, whatever you're up to. This is not one of your client surveillance gigs." I didn't say anything. But my mind was making a racket. Gears were shifting.

Ronan went on, "You're playing with fire my friend, you know that right?"

"I know what I'm doin'. Thanks, though. But, I gotta go."

"Teddy, why are you involved with this guy?" Ronan asked.

"I'm not involved with him – anymore. And I don't know where he is."

"You're a lousy liar. You know something about this guy."

"I'm not in a position to comment."

"Do not get yourself killed, man. This dude is bad. Dangerous. Potentially insane. More insane than you."

That insane line irked me but I just said, "Thanks for telling me. I'm good."

"Tell me where he is, T."

"I don't know, seriously. I'll let you know if I find out."

It was true, I didn't know where he was. He could be on the train hurtling through the Palouse of eastern Washington toward Whitefish, or off the train in Pasco stalking around in search of a victim. A thrill. A fix. An addict having a relapse. I know the feeling.

Ronan said, "Don't go near him. Hear me?"

"I hear ya. I'll be in touch."

A long sigh was followed by, "You are crazy. Watch yourself."

We hung up and I thought, I'm getting sick and tired of people saying I'm crazy, or stupid, or disrespecting me in some way.

"I AM NOT CRAZY!" I yelled, inside my car. And then an eruption of anger blew from my lungs and an unintelligible word screamed out sounding something like "NOOOO!" I beat my fists on the steering wheel and then applied them to my head. How could I have been so stupid!! To fall for the lies! Believe his shit! Get lured in by his sad-sack story!

He'd killed Violet McRae as Leroy and Lulu said. Not only Violet, but her unborn child, which he probably sired. And he had murdered several others in Florida before that and maybe others in Morocco. And if he's a serial killer, more victims may be down the road. Starting with my good friend, Sammy. This won't do.

I calmed down and realized what I had to do. Taking Jasmine to the airport with Kate was not it. And I couldn't tell either of them what I had in mind. So I dissembled once again in a quick text to Kate.

The text said: I'm fine. Please see Jas off. Tell her I love her and sorry I can't be there. But I need to get away and think. Will explain later. SORRY! Will be in touch. Love you. Please wait for me."

The rain had let up and the sky was a pale blue with just a few clouds that looked like pieces of gauze. I gazed at the sun for energy and thought about what I had to do. Then started the engine and drove home. When I arrived I saw Kate's Subaru was gone, meaning she'd taken Jasmine to the airport. I pulled into the driveway and ran inside.

Grabbing a duffel bag, I stuffed a few shirts and jeans into it as well as the cash I had left that was from Mario. I took the bag outside, opened the trunk and tossed it in. Then checked through my backpack left there from the night before. There was something wrong. The rope, duct tape, and handcuffs were there, but the Beretta and silencer were gone. I checked the whole car. They weren't there.

Could I have left them at the park? I didn't see how. I wasn't that stupid. Thinking hard, I tried to figure out who could've taken them. Kate? No. She wanted nothing more to do with them. Duplantis? How?

Then I remembered taking him out to the car earlier that morning and going back inside to talk to Kate. Did he get in the trunk and take the gun out of my pack and stick it in his suitcase?

I pulled out my phone and tried to call Sammy in Montana. No answer. He was no doubt on his way to Whitefish, taking the Swan highway on the east side of the Mission Mountains, out of cell coverage.

Knowing it was a long shot I checked to see if Southwest or Alaska had a flight going to Kalispell, just ten miles from Whitefish. That would get me there before the train arrived. No such luck. The only way was to drive.

The clock on the stove said 10:47 a.m. That gave me about 9 hours to get to Whitefish and meet the train. It's a little over 600 miles if you cut off from I-90 in Montana at St. Regis. I figured if I averaged about 85 mph I could get there in time to meet the train, counting for 2 gas stops. It'd be close. But it was possible. And I knew the fastest route to take.

I raced downstairs to my gun cabinet and pulled out the only other gun I had – a Remington shotgun I'd bought at a gun sale in Reno. A weapon that didn't mess around. I grabbed a box of shells, locked the cabinet, and ran back upstairs.

In the kitchen, I threw a box of Triscuits and a few bananas in a sack, opened the fridge and pulled out a bottle of water.

I tried to think of what else to take. Music. I'd need a bunch of CDs for the drive. What do you listen to when you're chasing a train to kill someone? Death metal? I didn't have time to ponder it, so grabbed a handful of CDs from the shelf.

I took it all out to my car, then grabbed a sleeping bag, shovel, and flashlight from the garage and threw them in the trunk.

Just then I got a text on my cell. It was Kate: I don't know what you're doing but don't count on me being there when you get back. I may be gone. We may be done.

I ran back inside and quickly scribbled a note to her on the back of an envelope: *I'm so so sorry but I need to get away and think. This is something I have to do. I know I'm acting crazy but I'm not. Please don't leave. I'll be back soon. I promise! Love you!!!*

I ended it with three exclamation points which I felt were needed. She knew I only used them in rare instances when I felt they were called for. Leaving the note on the dining room table I looked over to see Ben sitting quietly on his haunches eyeing me. He knew I was going somewhere and wanted to go along. I put food in his bowl but he didn't move. He kept looking at me with disapproving eyes. Like always.

"What? No, I can't take you. Forget it." He didn't move. Sat mute, his tail motionless.

"Why you looking at me like that?" He didn't blink, just kept staring at me. It was unnerving and I didn't like it a bit.

"Yes, I'm leaving. But you can't go! You gotta stay here with Kate." I walked over to the window to check the weather. Ben kept his eyes on me, unblinking.

"Stop pouting," I said. And then it dawned on me that he could see what I was about to do, even though it'd hardly become clear in my own mind. It got heated after that.

"Stop accusing me! Quit looking at me like that! You got something to say to me – say it!" I glared at him. He finally turned his gaze out the window and yawned. As if he'd heard it all before.

And then he looked back at me and spoke.

"You don't know what you're doing," Ben said. "You're lost. And you're getting deeper into the woods by the minute."

"Shut the hell up! I am NOT lost! I know what I'm doing – you don't know the whole story."

"I know enough. And what you're doing is wrong."

"I can't let this guy live! You're the one who's crazy! He's a killer and the only reason he's loose is cause I faked his death!"

"Another dumb move," Ben said.

"And you're just a rescue mutt, so how would you know? Stop looking at me like that!"

"You can't just kill someone. You don't have the right to do that. Even if you are the alpha."

"That's right! I am the goddamn alpha! So quit questioning me! You are part of the pack, get in line, you eat after I do!"

"Of course, I do. I know my place. But that doesn't mean I can't try to stop you from doing something really, really stupid." He put a mocking emphasis on the word stupid. That pissed me off.

"It is NOT stupid! I can't just let this guy leave the country – he's a freaking serial killer! Can't you get that through your thick head? He could kill more people. More dogs, too."

"Yeah, and he might not. Maybe he'll never kill anyone – or anything – ever again."

"I can't take that chance. Besides, he made a fool of me, and I want my money back!"

"Oh, that's right, you hate being made a fool of. How pathetic."

"Would you please just shut up and act like a dog for once?"

"There's no real justification for killing him, you know that."

"I do NOT know that. Stop telling me what I know! You can't read my mind."

"Yeah, I can." He still stared straight at me and I knew he was right. He went on, "You should take me with you, I can help."

"How the hell would you help – all you do is sleep, you don't even bark!"

"I can bark if I want to. I've just never needed to. Take me with you."

"Shut up! You're not going. Keep an eye on the house."

Ten seconds later I was behind the wheel backing out. I had almost a full tank of gas. I didn't need a map, I knew the way. East on I-84 to Umatilla, then across the Columbia River into Washington and north to the Tri Cities, then up to Ritzville to I-90 and east again through Spokane and Idaho into Montana to St. Regis, where I'd cut off north on a two-lane to Hot Springs and then get onto Highway 93 to Whitefish. Eureka was another 50 miles up the road from there, in the remote northwest corner of the state, about a dozen miles from the Canadian border.

I had to catch up with the train and be there when Duplantis got off in Whitefish. The idea of helping a serial killer escape the country and giving him $22,000 of my money was not something I could live with. He'd fooled me big time. And I don't like being made a fool. I won't stand for it. I have my pride.

This was my state of mind as I drove down the ramp onto I-84 eastbound. I needed music to kick the trip in gear. I grabbed a CD from the pile I'd brought. Earth, Wind and Fire. Good, but not now. I tossed it on the passenger side floor and grabbed another. Led Zeppelin. Now we're talking. I cranked it up as I put my foot down, pedal to the floor.

I was bound for Montana with vengeance and justice on my mind. Nolan Duplantis was not going to become Addison Thompson, he was not going to Canada, and he was not going to take my money and self-respect. Make a fool of me? Over my dead body.

Chapter 42 Train Chase

MONDAY MORNING

Led Zeppelin and my pique of anger carried me through The Dalles and on. I gambled I could get to Umatilla before needing to fill up.

As I drove, cruising at 95 and keeping an eye out for Highway Patrol, I thought of what could happen in the next 24 hours.

It seemed likely that Duplantis had my gun hidden in his suitcase. What he planned to do with it was unknown. I thought about making a list of the options but didn't. I couldn't imagine Sammy getting killed by this guy I'd sent to him – a presumed serial killer. I'd have to shoot myself. Two more deaths to be responsible for – Sammy's and my own.

I kept checking my phone for messages from Sammy. Nothing came. No messages from Kate either. Or Ronan.

I took out my charger and plugged in my phone, then changed CDs to Muddy Waters. Good sounds for the dusty terrain that rises out of the Columbia River gorge and ripples across eastern Oregon.

My mind kept wandering off topic as I drove. I thought about Jasmine now on a plane to Ecuador and made a mental note to text her when I next stopped. I remembered an argument we'd had. She'd mentioned that my Uber driving days were numbered with the advent of self-driving cars. She said robots are gonna be the only ones driving. I said they'd have to pry my keys from my cold, dead hands before I gave up driving. I'm never giving up my wheels.

I had a similar argument with a client who thought copywriters would be extinct in a few years. Artificial intelligence would do all the writing – in journalism, advertising, everything. The client said an automated writing program would win the Pulitzer Prize within ten years. That got me riled and I ended up suggesting he shut his trap, and then cranked up my line of attack and told him he was an idiot. He yelled back saying I was an old hack. It was totally unprofessional. I flipped him off and walked out the door. We never talked again, but he did pay my bill. I'm just glad I didn't have to hit the bastard.

Around 1:30 I pulled into Umatilla and gassed up. A couple blocks down I could see the sign for the liquor store and for a second I thought I might grab a bottle for the road. I could do it in minutes. But I decided no – stay sober. I drove on across the Columbia River bridge before my mind could make a rebuttal.

Getting through the Tri-Cities is tricky. You gotta pay attention. I hunkered over the wheel and navigated through as fast as possible, then turned north on Hwy. 395 to connect with I-90 at Ritzville and head east for Spokane.

To keep from getting drowsy, I lowered all the windows and focused on the world around me – waves of brown, green and yellow with the agri-aroma of manure and rootsy earth.

On our trips to Montana, we'd always stop at the park in Ritzville to stretch and let the dog out. No stopping this time. I had enough gas to make it to Wallace and kept the wheels spinning fast.

Changing music kept me awake. It gave me something to do rather than think bad thoughts. JJ Cale sang me on through Spokane and up the passes out of Coeur d'Alene. He has a sly sound that hides in the background. Good for creative thinking. Which is what I needed.

All the way from Portland I'd been pondering my options, going through multiple scenarios, and still I did not have a decision, a plan, a way out. I turned off the music.

Looking down the freeway ahead I said out loud what I kept thinking, "So, genius, what're you gonna do?" The sound of my voice startled me.

Louder this time, "What're you gonna do with this guy when you catch him? This Nolan Duplantis serial killer. What exactly are your plans, genius? Kill him? Add one more to your murder rap? Take the money and start a new life in Canada yourself? Or bring him back and make him face justice for the other murders he committed? And then what, turn yourself in? You gonna face your own truth – do your own time? Leave your family and go to prison? Time's running out – better decide, asshole!"

I started laughing hard – my default response when I don't know what else to do. I thought about Duplantis, sitting on the train, probably in the bar car, blasting through the north woods of Idaho by now, hurtling east toward Whitefish. Did he know what he was going to do? Did he have a plan? No doubt he did.

Around 5:30 I pulled off the freeway at Wallace for gas. Right then my phone rang. It was Ronan. I didn't answer. Driving into Wallace I turned on a side street and pulled over in front of the Oasis Brothel Museum. I'd taken a tour there a few years ago and bought a coffee mug, but it was closed now. Jumping out of the car, I stretched my legs and did squats while I checked my phone. No texts. One voicemail, from Ronan. I played it back.

"Where are you? Teddy! Answer the damn phone! Jesus Christ, man! I got more news for ya. Your guy Duplantis is ID'd for the murders in Morocco – DNA from the Marrakech PD matches what they have from the scenes in Florida. And there may be more. Teddy!

Talk to me, bro. Pick up! C'mon, I know you know where this freak is!" His emphasis on freak surprised me. It was a word I'd never heard him use. Or maybe I forgot.

Ronan paused. I could hear him breathing...thinking. After several seconds he erupted, "Are you SERIOUS? REALLY? You're not gonna answer – I know you're listening! Ted!" Another pause, then a sigh and a low growl, "Get back to me. Now."

I deleted the message and got back in the Escape. What could I tell him? That I'd been conned by a serial killer who I gave $22,000 and helped escape to Canada, and that a few days ago I killed an innocent man, the father of a kid who saw me, who will haunt me, for the rest of my sorry life? Could I actually say that? Admit to that? Confess to that? No. I couldn't.

Ten minutes later I had a full tank of gas and was gunning it up the ramp back onto I-90, heading east up Lookout Pass and down the other side into Montana. It was 47 miles to St. Regis where I'd turn north on Hwy. 135 and cut across the Flathead Indian Reservation to Flathead Lake where I'd turn north on Hwy. 93 to Whitefish.

As I barreled down the freeway, speedometer pegged at 105, I felt energized. Pine-flavored air rushed through the windows as if I was in a forest wind tunnel. The road stretched out in front of me, void of other vehicles, an open path to the future.

As the roadside blurred by, I was transported back in time – to when I'd arrived back in Montana on this same road from Louisiana in 1979. I wondered how I got from there to here.

Chapter 43 Montana 1979

After escaping New Orleans and returning to Montana in spring of '79, I lay low at my friend Dana's pad in Missoula. But if I thought I'd left my past behind I was mistaken.

One month after arriving I got in a fight. Three friends and I took on a couple guys from Butte. Four vs. two. Being a former math major, I figured the odds were in our favor. But our strength in numbers didn't add up to much and we took the worst of it.

One thing I remember from the fight is wishing I had my brass knuckles. When I got home I took them out of my footlocker and stashed them in my glove compartment. They stayed there until one night about a year later.

A month after arriving back in Montana, I applied for a job selling advertising for a new radio station in Whitefish and surprisingly was hired. The station was KTXX – the Mellow Mountain Sound they called it, a pathetic little tagline. Whitefish is a small railroad-logging-tourist town in the upper northwest corner of Montana, north of Flathead Lake, west of Glacier National Park, south of Canada.

It was a Canuck that caused me to bring out the knucks. I was with a date, bellied up at the bar in the Great Northern. While I was ordering drinks a pasty-faced Canadian derelict sidled up to my date and began hustling her. She laughed uncomfortably and I told him to take a hike. He kept at it, ignoring me. When I stood up and confronted him, he slowly walked off.

She and I drank at the bar awhile longer and I excused myself to hit the can. When I came back the same drunk Canuck was sitting on my stool. I told him to move his ass and he just ignored me. And that's when I thought of the knucks.

I told my date I'd be right back and went to my car and grabbed the brass knuckles and took a good grip. I remembered what Leroy told me – how to use a glancing blow, not straight on. I flexed my fist and walked back into the bar.

The Canuck was still sitting on my stool, leaning toward my date. I went up to him and said, "Hey, I know you." He turned his head toward me and I swung my brass-knuckled fist upward at an angle into his nose, turning my fist as I'd been taught. I heard and felt bone crunch.

He tried to cover up but I got in another two shots to his face. He fell back against the bar and dropped to the hardwood floor. I bent over him and slugged him once more, aiming straight for his right eye and connecting. He didn't make a sound, not even a Canadian "eh". Hardly anyone took notice. Fights happen a lot in this corner of the universe.

I took the arm of my date and we headed for the door. When I looked back the Canuck was lying on his side, one hand covering his gashed face, blood seeping through his fingers. It gave me a warm glow of satisfaction I can't deny. I thought about taking her home and coming back to hit him again. It may have been the testosterone, or the tequila.

From the beginning, the radio station job and I didn't get along. I was a terrible salesman and hated the job. I gravitated to the sound booth where DJs seemed to have fun.

When I expressed an interest in changing from the sales department to the on-air department, the manager scoffed and said forget it. But a week later they had to fire a DJ on the spot and I was asked if I thought I could take over the guy's afternoon shift.

It turned out to be a sweet gig once I got over the "dead air" dreams I had every night. Until one day I came to work and they had changed formats – from Album Rock to Top 40 Country. No more Van. No Dylan. No Dead.

In short order, my attitude dropped a country mile. I could feel I was about to be canned so started applying at other stations in Montana.

And that's how I ended up back in Billings, working at KOOK. I didn't want to go back to the Magic City as it's called (some say Tragic), but it was my only route out of Whitefish, the only job that called.

Using money from my Agency work in Louisiana, I traded in my Mustang for a used Ford Elite with an extended front end and red velvet seats that folded way back. At night I'd cruise from bar to bar in Billings, listening to Billie Jean and Billy Idol and getting belligerent often.

I didn't think much about New Orleans, or Leroy, or Mario. Frankly, I didn't like talking about my time there. I didn't want to think about what I'd seen and done and could be convicted of with the Agency.

When people would ask about New Orleans, I'd answer in vague terms, "Yeah man, crazy place, what a party, I don't remember much," then change the subject. The less I thought about those times, those people, the more it seemed I'd escaped them. Fat chance.

Chapter 44 Kate

While covering a rape trial for KOOK News, I met a Gazette reporter named Joanne who I liked a lot. Not in a romantic sense. We just got along well. She had an impish grin and ingratiating sense of humor. We often met for drinks after work – usually at the Monte Carlo. She introduced me to her brother, Scout, who worked at Bert & Ernie's and was the wittiest waiter I ever met. He could have you on the floor before you finished your order.

They both said I should meet their sister who lived in Portland. They said we were a lot alike and would get along great. I said, "Well, get her over here."

It took over a year but it happened. One day Joanne called and said, "Kate's coming to Billings!"

I said, "Who's Kate?"

"My sister! I told you about her, remember?"

"Oh yeah, let's have a drink."

We made plans to meet Friday after work at 5:00 at Bert & Ernie's downtown. When the time came, I showed up early. As I waited, I tried to think of some good lines. But by 5:30 they hadn't shown and I wondered if I'd been stood up. I was about to leave when they walked in.

Kate was like nobody I'd ever met – a combustive mix of class, brains, independence, and attitude. She was a study in contrasts. She wore a dressy-for-Billings red blazer and sported a punk haircut.

Knew how to cuss like a miner and speak formal French – in the same sentence. Played duplicate bridge and loved bowling. Was brassy and bold but also had a vulnerable sensitivity she tried to hide.

I quickly became smitten and asked her out for the following night for a test-worthy date – bowling and bingo. I figured if she could enjoy herself with a bunch of old farts without turning her nose up, she had legs for a potential relationship.

She passed with flying colors. I proposed that she pack her stuff in Portland and move to Billings, which surprisingly she did. I'm not as bad a salesman as I thought.

Newly arrived in Billings, Kate jumped from job to job faster than anyone I'd ever seen. If she didn't like one job, she'd find another. She had high standards and was particular about her work.

I changed jobs as well and left KOOK in the dust. Through a hole in the fence, I bolted into the exciting field of advertising and got hired by a local ad agency. It was my second agency job – if you count Leroy's Louisiana outfit as the first.

One of our clients was an automotive supply dealer with locations throughout Montana. Its name was Valley Motor Supply. We ran a TV campaign for them featuring a spokesman in a Valley Motor Supply shirt announcing the sales specials for the week – spark plugs, windshield wipers, beaded seat covers.

I was cajoled into being the spokesman due to my background as a radio DJ. I filled the role, and shirt, poorly. There was a name above the front pocket: Les. Friends would call me Les and make fun of my Valley Motor alter ego. Ask for deals on motor oil and shit.

Appearing on TV in these cheesy ads was one of the biggest mistakes I ever made. It led to some serious problems that continue today. You could say it's how I got discovered.

One Friday after work I drove to the Monte Carlo to meet Kate and Joanne for a drink. We had a couple gin and tonics, then Joanne said she had to take off.

I asked Kate if she wanted to stay for one more and without a beat she said of course. I loved her for that. Not so much the liking to drink (which indeed was a fetching attribute), it was more the devilish spirit of living life with why-not gusto which turned me on.

Then she caught me with an uppercut. "I can't live in Billings," she said. "I don't like it. I might move back to Portland."

My jaw hit the floor. I had no inkling. I thought how could she just up and leave? What about us? The bowling, the bingo? Our future?

All I could say was I thought we should give it more time. I had a good life going and I wasn't ready to pull the plug on it yet. But she said straight out, "Stay if you want, I want to go back to Portland and pretty soon."

I didn't like it one bit and got in her face. It was the disrespect, as if I was nothing to her. A dalliance. Not worth sticking around for.

Lashing out in whip-like fashion, my passive aggression kicked in and I said some not so nice things to strike back. Tears began falling and I knew I was a dead man. This argument was over. There was no talking to her now.

She said she wanted to go home and would walk. I heaved a deep sigh, drained my drink, and said I'd drive her. It was a cold, silent ride. I dropped her off and left without saying a word.

After that, to drown my sorrows, I went to the Western Bar, wondering what to do with the rest of my life. I was clueless. With just one drink down I went into the can to relieve myself. Standing at the urinal, I'd just started streaming when I heard someone come in behind me.

A strange voice said, "So who's ya squaw, T?" The voice cut me like a rusty saw, a serrated edge cutting into my chest. I knew the voice, although it had a bit more of a southern drawl than I recalled. I froze and almost stopped pissing, even though my bladder was full.

It was, of course, Mario. "What's yer dog's name? I got her address. What's her name?"

I went on peeing, no need to turn around. I knew it was him. It was a long pee and I let it flow slowly so I could think of what to do. Mario put the time to use.

"Well T, I told ya you can't run. We'll find ya. But it's a funnnaaayyy story cher how we did that. I'll tell y'all later. For now, here's what we gonna do. You're gonna walk outta here without saying a howdy, or yeehaw, or whatever you hicks say to each other. You go straight outside and get in the truck across the street. And you don't do nothin' else."

I finished peeing and was shaking as I said, "And what if I don't?" I tried to make my voice calm and steady – my radio announcer voice. But I was never much of a radio announcer and it came out shaky. A weak signal.

He'd called Kate a dog and that I didn't like. I stood up straighter and slowly zipped up my jeans, getting ready to face him.

"I don't gotta know her name, peckerhead," he said. "I've got her address." He reached into his shirt pocket and took out a notepad. He flipped a few pages then read to me Kate's address, on the button.

"You know the drill, little T. If ya don't do it yo Indian Princess will disappeah – soon. No big loss. Looks like there are a lotta dogs in this town. You always liked dogs." He laughed and walked out the door and left the bar. My heart was pumping. I washed my hands and looked in the mirror and quickly turned my head.

Chapter 45 Mario

Outside, I zipped up my jacket and crossed Minnesota Avenue and headed toward a Ford F-250 Extended Cab truck. It had Louisiana plates. Mario at the wheel. I got in the passenger side and he fired up the engine and drove a few blocks away and parked on a quiet southside street.

I looked at him. The creases in his face had become ravines and his skin was more leathery than ever. Like snakeskin cowboy boots. He had the same pointed Tony Lamas he always liked to wear, with tight black jeans. He looked like a rodeo bronc rider, or a Hutterite from Roundup.

Mario stayed silent so I took the reins.

"What're you doing in Billings, my long-lost friend? I thought you hated Montana." He didn't say anything and I kept on. "Musta been a long drive for you, amigo. Louisiana to Montana, did ya get lost? How long it take ya?"

"For goddamn ever," he spit out. "I hate this dirtbag place and can't wait to get the hell outta this backass shithole."

"Don't let me stop ya," I said.

He looked over and grinned. "Still the smart ass. Don't ya wanna know how we found ya, cher?"

"Not really. But enlighten me."

"The wife of one of Leroy's associates was at a reunion, some town called Harvey or something, and she seen you on TV." He meant Havre I realized, which many people mispronounce. It's where Kate grew up as a tot.

"On TV? When?"

"A few weeks ago. She said you worked for some place called Valley Motor Supply – but you'd changed your name to Les."

I wanted to kick myself. I knew playing Les the Valley Motor Supply guy on TV was a bad idea. They were terrible ads.

"I don't work for Valley Motor Supply," I said.

"I know. We checked. Called them up and asked for Les, the guy on TV. They say no Les works there and that you work for their ad agency. I said got a name of this agency? They say sure: Sage Advertising. So I called this Sage Advertising and spoke with some chick named Kelly and she confirm you work there."

Kelly never mentioned his call, which pissed me off. She should have told me. He could have been a new account as far as she knew.

"So I follow ya from work tonight to the Monte Carlo – kind of a dive, buddy... but good for you and your dog, right?" If he'd called her a dog one more time I would have come unleashed. I wished I had my brass knuckles, now in the glove compartment of my Saab, which I'd traded my Ford Elite for a month back.

He went on, "Then I seen ya drop your little sweetheart off and I follow ya to this cowboy shit-hole Western Bar. And here we are. Just like old times."

"Where exactly are we?" I said. I looked out at the empty street, moon reflecting off a tin corrugated shed across the road. "What're your plans, Mario? Sightseeing? Going to Jellystone Park to see Yogi and Boo-Boo? They're not real you know."

"No, I'm here on a job. May throw someone off a cliff." That stopped me cold. "And you're gonna help me."

I didn't say a word. He went on, "Still got your camera? How about a video camera?"

Over the next few minutes, Mario filled me in on the Agency assignment. It was a Fear of God job – scaring the holy shit out of somebody. I was to again be the photographer, and if possible shoot video as well. I'd be paid $1,500 for a night's work.

The guy we were after was a horse trainer who lived in a trailer near Lockwood, across the Yellowstone River from Billings. He was in town for the Fair – the Yellowstone Exhibition horseracing season. He was trainer for a couple horses running in the races.

"What'd he do?" I asked.

"He torched a barn and stables at a horse ranch outside Lake Charles. For the insurance money."

"That's it?" I said. "Anybody get hurt?"

"No humans. But six quarterhorses, and one colt, got burnt to a crisp."

"Six horses burned to death?" I said.

"Seven. Locked them in their stalls and set it all ablaze. I woulda hated to hear the sound of those ponies kicking their stalls down to get out. He had insurance on them. He was in Florida at the time, partying in Key West. Cooked up a nice alibi. We found the guy he hired for the arson and he talked. But they couldn't use him as a witness. He was an ex-con nobody believed. So the bastard never got charged. He take the insurance payout, then skipped town and vanished. He stopped paying child support to his ex and left his kids with nothin.'"

Mario went on to say someone had spotted the trainer's name in a race program in Sheridan, Wyoming and he was eventually tracked to a trailer outside Billings, where he was now.

I love horses and the thought of this dude burning seven to their death incensed me. He was also a lousy dad. He deserved retribution. And I needed the money. I'd warped the head on my Saab, overheating it while driving over Beartooth Pass to Cooke City. Now the engine overheated whenever I drove anywhere. I needed a new ride.

But most important was Kate. I dug her big time. I had high hopes for her, for us. And I couldn't put her in danger. We'd only known each other a few months.

Mario told me to pick a place to meet him the next day at noon. He said we needed to scope out a location for the Fear of God job, which would happen the next night.

I chose a place to meet I knew none of my friends ever went – the Rainbow Bar on the tail end of Montana Avenue. I told him where it was and he wrote it down. Then he took me back to my car at the Western. I didn't go back in for a drink.

Chapter 46 Cliff Jump

The next day we met at noon. I don't know what fleabag Mario stayed in but he looked bad. His hair was like sagebrush, sticking out all over, and his eyes were as watery as fish bowls. I assumed he was hung over. I wasn't.

Mario started us off. "You know what something called a buffalo jump is?"

"Yeah, I know what a buffalo jump is. Do you?"

"Hell no, but Leroy does. He read about it in some history book. Said they have 'em here. He wants to run this guy off one, on a rope, and pull him back up. Make him piss his cowboy pants."

"There's a few in Montana. But the closest is Madison and that's past Bozeman, 180 miles or so from here."

"Too far, need something closer."

I told him about Sacrifice Cliff, a few miles south of Billings. Prehistoric people lived in the area 2,000 years ago and drew pictographs on the walls of caves.

Sacrifice Cliff is named after a legend in which two Indian braves returned to their tribe after hunting for weeks. They found everyone in the tribe dead or dying – most likely from smallpox. The braves were so bereft they tore off their leggings and used them to blindfold one of their horses. Then rode the horse together as it galloped straight off the cliff – now called Sacrifice Cliff. I don't like the story. I can see killing themselves but why take the horse down with you?

243

I recounted the tribal legend to Mario and he didn't bat an eye.

"Dumb Injuns," he said. "But this Sacrifice Cliff sounds perfect. We could scare this guy to death up there."

"Well, it's not easy to get to. We'd have to walk a ways. And there are a lot of TV station antennas up there, so people might be around."

"No good. Leroy hates TV towers. Says they can listen in on ya. What else ya got? Leroy wondered about Custer Battlefield."

"No, that's an hour drive and you don't want Indians after ya."

Then I thought of a place I knew well. Close in. But tucked away from people enough that we wouldn't be spotted. We drove to it and scouted the area. Mario liked it. We were on. On the way back we stopped at a used electronics place and I rented a video camera. Then we went back to the Rainbow Bar.

Before we split up, Mario gave me a piece of paper. "Leroy wanted me to give this to you. We need you to write a message for this guy – to read to him tonight when we videotape him. For the vic's family. Here are some notes to use. Bring it with you tonight."

We made plans to meet back at the Rainbow at 8:00.

At home, I called Kate and lied to her for the first time. I told her I was going to a poker game at Parker's so I wouldn't be seeing her that night. I didn't bring up the argument we'd had the evening before.

Downstairs I had a Smith-Corona typewriter and I plugged it in and inserted a sheet of paper. In the envelope Mario had given me was info for the message I was to write. Also included was a handwritten note from Leroy.

It read: "T – been too long. The Agency misses you. So does Lulu. But now you work for a different Agency out in Montana. Remember that time we left a baby crocodile in that guy's bed who was cheating on his wife? You wrote him a note. I still remember, it said "Congrats on your new baby". I still laugh. I like the idea of writing a message to go with the justice we dispense, like a judge's sentence. We could call it Last Writes! Like last rites. I want you to write out the last writes for this job – background info is enclosed. And videotape the guy when you read it to him. Then, come down and have some more of Evangeline's voodoo punch."

I had to admit his idea of "last writes" was funny. And so I wrote them out for our perp and typed them up for delivery that night.

At 8:00, I met Mario at the Rainbow and we both had beers. We discussed the plan. Mario had tailed the perp for two days and knew his schedule. He always came home from the Exhibition fairgrounds at 7:00 and ate supper and watched TV. A loner. Hiding out. He'd be there now.

Mario said he needed to call Leroy before we moved on the FOG. I said I wanted to talk to him. Mario said no way, Leroy only talks to him, no one else. He's paranoid as hell.

He went to a pay phone and made the call. I wasn't sure what I'd have said to Leroy anyway, other than I'm never doing this again and I resign from the Agency. Maybe I'd put it in writing and mail it to him. Get it notarized. He'd respect that.

After Mario hung up he came back with a big smile and said everything is go. We then left. He'd given me the rough location of the perp's trailer and I knew how to get there so I led the way.

I drove south toward Lockwood, past the Planet Lockwood Gentlemen's Club, a popular strip bar. Mario followed me in his big truck. Five miles out of town we turned north and drove up into the dusty hills.

We rounded a bend and drove up a dirt road to the perp's trailer. I stayed in the car while Mario went up to the door. I was surprised how easy it was. He knocked and I saw the door start to open. Then he shoved his way in and I saw him pull a pistol out of his leather jacket pocket. I sat in the car and waited – my camera and video camera at my side.

A curtain parted and I saw a hand wave me in. I ran up to the door with camera and video camera and stepped inside the trailer. Mario had his gun pointed at the man's head. He said, "Cuff him." I set the cameras down and took the cuffs Mario gave me and snapped them around the perp's wrists. Then stood back and took a couple photos. The perp was short with slumped shoulders and a paunch that hung over his belt. The top three snaps of his shirt were unbuttoned and a few gray hairs stuck out as if to get some air.

"We found ya, mon," Mario said. "You thought you had us all beat. Could just disappeah up here in the sticks. Wrong! What'd ya do with all the insurance money? I know ya wife and kids never saw it." The man didn't say a word. I think he knew who Mario was.

"And now we gonna take some photos for the folks back in Louisiana. They've missed you. Smile!" Mario motioned to me and I started taking pictures. He pointed to the video camera and I lifted it to my shoulder and started shooting as Mario asked more questions.

"So, did you or did you not torch ya place?"

"I don't know what you're talkin' about." His voice matched his appearance. Weak and sniveling – pitched like an electric lawnmower. You wouldn't want to listen to it long.

"Look at the camera when ya talk! I ask you again, did you burn your place and seven horses to the ground? Answer me!"

"No! I wasn't even there. I was in Flor-"

"Shut up! We know where ya were, and we know what ya did."

"I want a lawyer."

"Oh, let me call one for ya! 1-800-YOU DEAD. You may have hired it out, but you did it. Got anything to say to ya friends in Louisiana?" The perp looked down and kept his mouth shut. I moved around him, shooting video from different angles. Like an MTV music video. Lots of motion. I can't help myself.

"Okay, let's go," Mario said. He looked out the window. Nobody was around. Mario tied a blindfold on the man and we led him to

Mario's truck. We got him into the passenger seat and they took off, with me following in my Saab.

I passed them on the road and led the way up on the rims, which is what they call the sandstone cliffs that jut up from the earth, creating a high stone ledge over 100 feet tall along the north side of Billings.

I knew a place on the rims called Fence Line where we'd had bonfires and keggers in high school. Since then, kids had moved on to other spots for their parties, but I still knew Fence Line well. The end of the street on which I grew up was right below the cliff at Fence Line. We used to climb up there and shoot rabbits. I shot one once that fell right off the cliff. No lie.

Chapter 47 FOG

I knew Fence Line would work for the Fear of God plan Mario had in mind. I led them down a dirt road and parked under some pine trees not far from the edge of the cliff. Mario pulled up behind me and we got the perp out, still blindfolded. He had no idea where we were. No idea a 100-foot cliff was a stone's throw away.

Mario pulled out a roll of duct tape from his coat pocket and tore off a piece and stuck it over the perp's mouth. Then he got a rope from the toolbox in the truck and tied it around the man's waist, wrapping him several times.

Holding the rope, he walked the perp toward the cliff. The guy stumbled along, feeling his way, and they stopped about 20 feet from the edge. I followed close behind. I noticed the remnants of old bonfires with burnt crushed beer cans in the dirt and dark smudges on stones, like pictographs from ancient times.

As we'd worked out, I tied the loose end of the rope to a tree a short distance from the cliff, leaving about 30 feet of lag between the tree and the perp.

I could hear sounds of vehicles down on Rimrock Road, and birds flitting through the pine trees and sky above. Clouds were moving fast, as if trying to get home before a storm.

The sky had gone prune, like a huge bruise. It was turning to dusk and I could see the twinkling lights of Billings starting to pop on below me.

I took more photos and Mario piped up.

"I know ya got money hidden in yo trailer. Nod ya head and I'll take the tape off if you tell me where ya stashed it – and we'll get ya back home." The perp didn't nod, didn't grunt a word. Mario motioned to me to read the message I'd written earlier that afternoon.

I pulled the typewritten paper out and placed the video camera on my shoulder and pointed it at the perp and hit Record. Then I began reading the "last writes."

"It's a fact that in the fall of 1980 you hired a man named Jack Hershay to burn your ranch to the ground, including a stable with six quarter horses and one colt who died in the flames, and then you took the insurance money and disappeared and haven't paid a dime of family support since. And now your past has caught up with you, way up here in Montana, where justice comes true and swift. You are guilty as charged. May the lord have mercy on your soul."

The last line I threw in because it sounded good. I don't believe in a lord, but I do believe in a soul. But it doesn't matter what I believe. In writing, the focus should always be on the audience. In this case, the "last writes" were written for the perp – to scare the holy hell out of him and make him fork over the money he'd stolen.

The "last writes" were also written for his struggling family he'd left behind in Louisiana. They could at least see some revenge on video if they didn't see any financial retribution. I assumed they were good god-fearing Southern folk who would gather, perhaps over a table of crawfish, and view the videotape while they cracked and sucked crawfish heads.

The perp showed absolutely no response to the message. It irked me that my writing had not elicited some reaction. I'd covered all the key points, with emotion, but it was to no avail. I agree I didn't have a call to action. Perhaps that was a mistake. The man was unmoved and stayed silent.

Then I heard a click. I turned to Mario and saw he had my camera and had taken a photo of the perp and me.

"No! No pictures of me!" I shouted.

"All right, don't worry. Stand aside." I stepped away and he took a few more shots of the perp. Then handed me back the camera.

"Okay, let's move," Mario said. "Turn around and start walkin'," he said to the perp.

Mario smiled at me as he pushed the guy forward. The guy took a step. Mario pushed him again and the perp walked on haltingly towards the cliff, reaching each foot out carefully, one after another, to feel the ground in front of him.

When they got near the cliff edge the perp paused. No doubt he could feel the air change, the open space in front of him. Birds were all silent, as if dismayed. I was a few steps behind and felt a breeze in my face.

Suddenly the perp turned, sensing where he was, but it was too late. Mario pushed him, sending him off into the sharp night air, falling backwards, his arms pinned behind him, his legs kicking frantically into space.

I saw him drop straight down along the face of the cliff. He fell for seconds until the rope tied to the tree went taut, and he came to an abrupt stop, swinging back and forth 30 feet below us. I tried to take a photo but it was hard to see him dangling below and I didn't want to drop my camera.

After a minute, we pulled him back up, scraping the skin and blindfold off his face along the sandpaper stone cliff. The skin on his cheeks was pulled back in rough patches, making his face look like a strawberry. He was bleeding from his nose and forehead as Mario took the duct tape off his mouth.

"Jesus, you mother, you... okay...okay," the perp sputtered, gasping for breath.

"Where's the money?" Mario said, quiet and firm.

"In a toolbox... buried... under tree... behind...my trailer."

"So we take ya there now it'll be there?" Mario asked.

"Yeah...it's there."

"How much ya got?"

"40 grand. Maybe 50."

"If ya lying to me we have a much higher cliff in mind."

The perp (now that I think about it I never did catch his name) was still trying to catch his breath, and wits. "It's there...I swear...you can have it." If it was a lie, it was the best lie I've ever heard. But I knew it wasn't.

"Let's go." Mario motioned to me and I untied the rope from the tree and coiled it up.

"Give it to me," he said. I handed him the rope and he threw it over his shoulder and started pulling the perp by the rope towards the car, away from the cliff. But after a couple steps he dropped the lariat coil from his shoulder and gripped the rope with both hands and whipped the perp around and began swinging him in an arc back toward the cliff, causing the perp to stumble and almost fall.

Mario pulled him forward, yanking hard, and as he got near the edge he yelled something sounding ancient, then bent his knees and swung his arms in a wide sweep and flung the perp off over the cliff. The guy screamed as he fell but the sound was muffled by the bluff and the breeze.

As he dropped, the rope uncoiled like a viper and followed him over the edge. I remembered how the ball and chain had slithered off that bridge into the Louisiana swamp years ago. Deja vu.

The fall took a couple seconds then I heard a crack, like kindling being broken for a fire, followed by a rustling of bushes and rocks rolling down hill. Then stillness.

This was not part of the plan.

"What're you doing?" I yelled. "You weren't supposed to kill him! This was supposed to be a Fear of God!"

"Leroy change it when I call him."

"I told you – I am NOT doing any RIPs! Nobody gets killed. You guys lied to me!"

"It's what the family wanted."

"You coulda just taken his money and left him broke!"

"He is broke!" Mario laughed. "Didn't ya hear it?"

"No, no, no, I'm not doing this!"

"You just did. It's done. The family came up with more dough and decided they wanted him dead. You know he deserved it."

"I do NOT know that!"

"Ya think he's dead down there?"

"Goddamn right he's dead. What do ya think, moron?"

"How do we get down there?"

We jumped into Mario's truck and I directed him to Zimmerman Trail, a paved road that winds from the top of the rims to the bottom, not far from where we were at Fence Line.

At the bottom of Zimmerman, we turned right on Rimrock and drove to the street where I once lived, then turned and drove up toward the cliffs, passing our old house. I looked at our split-level with deck and remembered how simple life was back then. Sledding down the street in winter, sneaking out in summer, shooting water spiders with a BB gun in the ditch. How the hell did I get here? Where'd I go wrong?

At the top of our street Mario parked the truck and we climbed up through boulders and sagebrush to the base of the cliff. There was no sign of our prey. But I knew we were in the right spot. I'd been up there many times as a kid and I knew we were directly below Fence Line. He had to be there.

We looked for five minutes, then I found him. His body was all busted, legs bent in ways they're not meant to bend, his nose smashed to the side like a cubist figure in a Picasso painting. His face was still bleeding. There was no pulse. Dead.

Mario said to wait by the body and he ran to the truck and got the camera and video camera. He came back and we took photos and video of the perp. Mario turned the man's broken neck so he faced the camera. Then we carried the body down and put it in the bed of the truck.

We drove back up Zimmerman to Fence Line to get my Saab. Along the way I asked Mario what he intended to do with the body.

He looked at me and grinned, but didn't say anything. We pulled up to my Saab and he said to open my trunk, he had the money and something else he wanted to give me. In a hurry to get out of there, I opened it and watched as he took a manila envelope from his truck cab and tossed it in my trunk.

Then he lifted the body out of his truck bed and threw it in my trunk on top of the envelope.

"No way," I said walking forward. "No way, Mario!"

"He's yours now," Mario said. "Make sure he's not found. I gotta go."

"No! You can't leave! You take him!"

"Your money's in the envelope, and a couple pictures for ya."

"Wait a minute, I'm not taking him!" I was furious. "Mario! Where you think you're goin'?"

"I'm goin' to dig up his money box of course, and get the hell outta this sorry state. Sheeit, ya stupid." He then ejected the VHS tape from the video camera and tossed the camera in my trunk.

"Gimme the film," he said. I popped the roll out of my camera. Mario took it and climbed into his truck. I started thinking maybe it was better that I disposed of the body. Who knew what Mario might do with it. Drop it off another cliff and leave it? Leave it in a dumpster at West Fork Plaza?

"Which way is Custer Battlefield? Leroy wants pictures of it." I thought about giving him the wrong directions, sending him north toward Harlowton, but I wanted him gone so I told him how to head south towards Hardin and watch for signs for Little Big Horn Battlefield.

"Little Big Horn? I hearda that. Custer opened a can a whoop-ass on some savages there."

"Yeah, exactly, Custer's big moment in the sun." Mario had no clue about Custer and couldn't have cared less.

"It's a shame it's way out here in the sticks in this dead-end state," he said. I felt my anger rise and I jammed my hand over my mouth to not respond.

"See ya, cracker," he said, and with a cackle he started his engine. As he began to pull out he rolled down his window, "We may be doin' more business up here. Don't go far, hick! Oh, and by the way, I'm gonna kill ya someday. Count on it." And he hit the gas and spun dirt all over the hood of my Saab as he roared off. I wished I had a gun.

Turning to the trunk, I reached under the dead body and pulled out the envelope Mario had left me. Inside was fifteen hundred dollars in cash plus two pictures. One was a photo of me and Lulu, Leroy's daughter, at one of his parties. I was swinging her on a tall tree swing. The other was a color copy of a photo I'd seen before – of myself, Mario, and the guy Leroy had strangled that first night I met him in Louisiana – at the swamp party. I turned it over and on the back was written: You may be in Montana, but you're not far from prison.

I threw the envelope in the front seat and pondered what to do next. I didn't have a lot of options. After some careful thought I chose the path that seemed most prudent. I drove home and got a shovel. It was all I could come up with. Bury the guy, bury the memory, and vamoose.

Chapter 48 Westward Ho

With the body and shovel in my trunk, I drove west out of Billings past the Yellowstone Country Club toward Molt looking for a remote place where no keg drinkers or deer hunters or fossil diggers would find a grave.

The radio stations at that time of night were mostly airing public service programs so I turned to KGHL, the local country station. I had started to like country. Merle Haggard, Buck Owens, Tom T. Hall and others took me down the blacktop road. Down and out tunes for a down and out time.

About 20 miles out of town, I turned off on a dirt road and followed an irrigation ditch along the edge of a sugar beet field. I parked my car – no lights or farm or ranch in sight.

My thinking was that no hunters or drinkers would venture out into a big, open sugar beet field. Years back, I'd spent part of one teenage summer hoeing sugar beets for a farmer. I spent most of the time sweating under a bandanna and wiping the dust outta my eyes, and then resting in the shade of the only tree around. I didn't make squat. Got paid a total of $39 for six weeks work. I never hoed beets again. Until now.

I figured if I dug deep and buried the guy, then covered him up and replanted the sugar beets, nobody would notice.

I carefully unearthed an eight-foot by three-foot section of beet plants. Setting the plants aside, I dug down five feet, then dropped the body in the hole and covered him up. Then I filled the hole, replanted the sugar beets, and smoothed over the ground. It was totally silent. Even the birds were asleep. The smell of sugar and soil, mixed with a lemon moon and a sky of sparkling ice, created a cocktail that made me dizzy. I felt drunk.

It took me two hours total. By the time I got home the sun was peeking unaware over the horizon. I collapsed into bed, hoping I'd wake up and realize I'd dreamt it all.

After a few hours sleep I got up, ate two eggs over easy, then left to return the video camera I'd rented. Coming back home, I got my typewriter out of the closet and typed a letter to my landlord giving him notice that I was moving out. Then I called Kate.

"I've been thinking," I said, but she cut me off.

"I don't want to talk to you." Her tone was so cold I shivered. But I plowed on.

"We should move to Portland. Soon. How soon can you go?"

"What?" Her tone changed. "I thought you were against that. Do you even remember what you last said to me? You were really mean."

"You like Portland. So do I. Portland's advertising scene is taking off. I'm ready to get outta Billings. We could have a lot of fun in Portland and see where this relationship goes. We should do it. Now. Why wait?"

"Wait a minute, what is with you?" She was stunned.

"Nothing is with me! You know who I am, you know I like you, you know everything you need to know!" I paced back and forth in the living room, a caged cat.

"We need to talk this over," she said. I could tell she was trying to calm me down. I wasn't having it.

"We are! Talking and deciding. And acting. Now!"

"Really? You're sure?"

"YES, I'm sure!"

"I don't know about you. Who are you?"

"Yeah, you do. You know me. You go to Portland next week and find us a place to live. I'm giving notice on my job Monday. We're outta here."

"Are you drunk? It's only noon."

"Sober as a judge. Will ya do it? Let's go to Portland!" I was never more sure of anything in my life.

We did exactly as I said we should. I didn't mention anything to Kate about tossing a guy off a cliff and burying him in a beet field the night before. Told her nothing about my past, and my running from it as fast as possible.

I traded in my used Saab for a used Audi 5000, then loaded up my stuff in a U-Haul and hauled ass to Portland where Kate had secured us an apartment.

Suggesting the move to Portland was the second best proposal I ever made. The first was my proposal of marriage to Kate on April Fools Day 1987. She was furious and I thought I was gonna get hit with a fireplace poker, but once she realized it wasn't a joke, and waited a few hours to leave me twisting in the wind, she finally accepted and we were married six months later.

Life was fine for many years and I heard no more from Mario, Leroy, or the Agency. I began to forget about my past. But it's a fact, the past doesn't just vanish. It's right behind you.

Chapter 49 Whitefish 2018

Monday evening
As I floored it down I-90, crossing from Idaho over the mountains into Montana, my mind raced. I kept the windows down, wind and music blasting through my skin. I turned on the AC to make it cold and keep from getting drowsy.

Trying to stamp out bad thoughts, like sparks from a wildfire, I kept tapping my phone to check for messages. Nothing. No word from Sammy who'd now be getting close to Whitefish on the back roads through Swan Valley. No message from Kate either.

At St. Regis I exited the freeway and turned north on Hwy. 135 to Plains, then turned northeast and headed for Flathead Lake to catch Hwy. 93 to Whitefish. I couldn't remember what time the train would arrive there. From my pocket I pulled out my little notebook and was relieved to see I'd written: Addison Thompson on train – arrive Whitefish 8:06 pm Monday.

I didn't remember writing the words. Was today Monday? I felt sure it was. But my memory was as threadbare as worn jeans.

It was now about 6:30 p.m. and I was still over a hundred miles from Whitefish. I had trouble remembering what had happened over the last few days and couldn't recall the last time I'd eaten or slept. Didn't matter. I gripped the steering wheel hard and shook my head vigorously, trying to clear it. In the distance I thought I heard a train horn blast.

The clock on the dash kept my attention and I watched each minute change. It was gonna be close.

I blew through Kalispell at 8:01, still 13 miles from Whitefish, and realized I wasn't gonna make it – I'd be late. I drove on, no longer tired. The end was in sight and I was ramped up.

Entering Whitefish I drove past the location of KTXX, the radio station where I used to work years ago. The building had been torn down and was now a Holiday Inn Express. My past recorded over.

I drove through downtown, past the Great Northern Bar where I'd brass-knuckled the Canuck in 1980, and pulled up at the train station. It was 8:22. I was 16 minutes late. The train was already there, idling while it caught its breath before rumbling east toward Glacier National Park and on across the plains to Chicago. I put on the black curly wig and sunglasses kept under my seat and ran into the depot.

People were talking, hugging, happy to be home. There was no sign of Sammy or Duplantis. I asked an Amtrak ticket agent if everyone had disembarked. He said yes, as far as he knew – the train was early. Of course it was.

I took one last look around and checked the men's room, then came back into the depot and collapsed on a wood bench. It was either sit down or fall down. Exhaustion took over and I closed my eyes for a moment – digging my fingernails into my wrist to not fall asleep.

In a minute, I opened my eyes and forgot for a second where I was. Then I saw the boy, in his underwear and t-shirt. The one whose father I'd mistakenly killed. I blinked and he didn't move – just stared back. As I slowly stood up he disappeared like smoke. An apparition.

I ran back outside to my Escape. Before driving off, I tried to call Sammy but got no answer. He must be on the road to Eureka with Duplantis – about 30 minutes ahead of me. Beyond cell service. Then I took out my little notebook and wrote a new message: Addison Thompson is aka Nolan Duplantis – serial killer. Sammy taking ND to Canada on game trail – stop him!

It was a message to myself, in case I forgot what I was doing. Know thyself, as they say.

I changed the music. Put in Steve Earle, hoping to summon some outlaw energy. "Mama says a pistol is the devil's right hand," he sang. Ain't it the truth. The pistol in my case being my Beretta that Duplantis must have hidden in his suitcase. The one I'd used in his abduction and fake hanging the night before. Did he plan to use it? Add another murder to his rap sheet?

This story is coming to an end I thought as I roared north on 93, heading into the remote northwest corner of Montana, a place where people hunker down and wear guns on the hip, outnumbered by beasts that are hungrier than them.

It was still light out. The sun goes down late in northern Montana. It wouldn't get dark until after 10:00 and I still didn't know how the day would end.

A little way out of Whitefish I drove past Grouse Mountain Lodge. Kate and I had stayed there on our honeymoon for a night. I got an idea. I looked up their number on my phone and called and made a reservation for that night.

The sky was lavender as I drove the two-lane road north toward Eureka, the last Montana town this side of Canada. I knew the route well. I'd driven it many times while living in Whitefish – sometimes trailing along with Sammy into the backwoods, he bow-hunting for elk or moose, me looking for antlers to sell to antique dealers and chandelier-makers.

There was no one else on the road. Every few miles I could see a trailer or small shack back in the trees, with rusted vehicles and junk out front. I heard a dog barking in the distance. It sounded hoarse. My mind wandered as the goose-bump air flew through the windows.

What am I doing? How did I end up on this path? How do I get that damn kid outta my head?

I yelled out, "Mario you asshole! If you had the goddamn address right I wouldn't be here! Duplantis would be dead like he's supposed to be! And I wouldn't have killed someone, the father of some poor little kid!" I slammed my hands down on the wheel.

"A goddamn typo! Wrong address! One number off!" I was livid but it felt good to get it out, outshouting Steve Earle.

Forcing myself back to the present, I tried to focus on where Sammy and Duplantis would be. By now they were probably on the turnoff heading north toward Bald Mountain, outside Eureka.

I remembered it'd be about 11 miles on a gravel road, then a right turn at the broken green sign and up along a ridge on a dirt logging fork for another few miles until you reached the end of the road. That's where Sammy would camp for the night, on a rise with a view of the mountains, valleys, and any predators approaching. We'd camped there before. His plan would be to guide Duplantis over the border into Canada tomorrow.

Twenty minutes later I took the same turn they did. The sky was still plum, although the clouds had turned darker. I kept my eyes on the road, my energy waning. Pulled out Steve Earle and put in Howlin' Wolf. It seemed fitting. With the windows down I howled myself, straining my lungs, trying to stay strong, or at least awake.

There wasn't a soul around. No trailers. No shacks. No cell coverage either. Checking the odometer, I slowed down when I reached the 11-mile mark on the gravel road and almost missed the broken sign marking the logging road turnoff. The sign was semi-hidden by a large, leafy bush that almost consumed it.

I turned right on the dirt logging road and kept going, slower now. My intention was to park well below their campsite and take a backpack with gear and guns and sneak up to see what was happening. I had a rough plan in mind. I knew I needed to neutralize Duplantis. After that, I wasn't sure what I'd do.

The road brought back memories and I remembered every turn. When I got higher on the ridge, I knew I was getting close, so pulled over and parked a few feet off the road. The air felt heavy and breath didn't come easy.

I checked my phone out of habit and saw I had no coverage. My battery was 75% charged. From the trunk I grabbed my backpack and started filling it with gear: Glock pistol, rope, duct tape, handcuffs, flashlight, and crackers. I was hungry. Before I shut the tailgate, I took out the Remington shotgun and loaded it.

I wondered if I should bring my brass knuckles. Why not. Maybe I'll punch a man, or animal, in the face. I grabbed 'em and thought, who the hell do I think I am? What am I doing?

The questions unanswered, I set off up the road, backpack shouldered and shotgun in hand, walking fast.

Chapter 50 Catching Up

It was silent all around other than the hum of a light breeze, as if nature was softly snoring. I looked into the woods on either side of the road, trying to spot any movement, of humans or animals. Nothing.

Then, after walking 15 minutes I saw something through the trees – a figure moving, then a voice. It sounded like Sammy. I moved off the road into the trees, creeping forward.

When I got within 200 feet, I hid behind a big tree and watched them. Sammy was talking about the game trail they'd take. I'd last seen him two summers ago. His hair was more silver than gray now and it was longer. He wore a camo hunting jacket and had a large gun in a holster on his hip.

"...and that's where you reach the road," I heard him say. "You're on your own from there. Just head north. We get up at 7:00 and start hiking. It'll take about 12 hours. That gives ya another couple hours of light to hitchhike north."

"Sounds good. No sweat." said Duplantis, who was wearing a purple LSU sweatshirt.

He gave Sammy a friendly look, disarming. "As our friend Teddy says, Canada's cool if ya like hockey. I'm ready for a new start. So, did he tell ya much about me?"

"Nothing," Sammy said. "And I don't need to know nothin'. I'm just doing what I said I'd do – get you to Canada. I don't want to know anything about you, so no need to make small talk."

They stood silent for a minute then Sammy said, "I got a backpack for ya, by my truck. Why don't you go move your stuff from your suitcase to the backpack. I got a sleeping bag for you."

Sammy started clearing off a sleeping area, kicking pinecones and rocks to the side. Duplantis shuffled off toward Sammy's truck, his hands buried in the front pocket of his sweatshirt. His face was noncommittal.

At Sammy's truck, Duplantis pulled out his suitcase, opened it, and began stuffing his clothes into the backpack. He kept peering over at Sammy while filling the pack. I saw him pull out the envelope that had my money and the fake Canadian ID. He shoved it inside the pack, then reached deep into his suitcase and brought out something black – my Beretta.

He quickly looked up again at Sammy who was still clearing the site. Sammy didn't see him. Duplantis ducked down and checked the gun to see if it was loaded. He may have switched off the safety, I couldn't tell. He slid it inside the pocket of his sweatshirt, stood up, and tossed his suitcase in Sammy's truck. Then he started walking towards Sammy as if he had something in mind. I ascertained what it was.

Acting as if on primal instinct, I opened my mouth and from deep in my soul emerged a low guttural growl that grew louder in volume with a raspy sound, like that of an animal. I've never heard a grizzly roar but that was my aim.

In a word, it sounded like this: "Ohhrrrrrrraaaaawwwwwww!"

Duplantis stopped dead and turned his face, suddenly ashen, my way. His eyes were wide, his mouth agape. He stumbled backward a few steps. Sammy stared directly at me, but I was still hidden behind the tree. He pulled his gun from his holster and pointed it in my direction.

"Howdy boys," I yelled out as I stepped out into the open. I had my shotgun to my shoulder, pointed at Duplantis. "Don't worry, I'm no griz."

"Teddy, that you?" Sammy yelled. "What the hell you doin'?"

"Duplantis, put your hands behind your head," I yelled. "Now! Do it, or I will blow you away I swear!" Sammy now trained his gun on Duplantis, unsure what was up.

"What's going on, man?" Sammy said.

"Yeah, what's going on, Teddy?" Duplantis said, speaking as if we were friends. He slowly moved his hands up over his head.

"Shut up and stay where you are! Sammy, keep your gun on him. I'll explain in a minute." Duplantis looked at me, his eyes now smaller, squinting, trying to determine what I was up to.

I walked up to him. With one hand pointing the shotgun at his head, I reached into his sweatshirt pocket and pulled out the gun. It was my Beretta. The safety was off. I switched the safety on and stuck it in my pack.

"I thought you said he was unarmed," Sammy said.

"Yeah, I apologize for that. He stole my gun. I tried to reach you."

Duplantis saw an opening and responded with a flurry. "Okay, yeah, I took your gun. But I thought I'd need it. You have guns!" He pointed an elbow at Sammy. "He's got one, why shouldn't I have one? I mean there are grizzlies out here - grizzlies. I gotta defend myself!"

"You took the safety off though," I said. "You planned to use it on Sammy, not some bear!"

"No, I swear! I didn't know the safety was off! I thought I switched it on. I'm an idiot about guns, you know that. I'm scared man, gimme a break, you'd have done the same thing!" I could tell he was talking as fast as he could think, trying to win Sammy over to his side. Sammy looked at him, then me, his gun still pointed at Duplantis.

I threw my pack over toward Sammy and said, "There's cuffs and rope in there. Cuff him and tie the rope around his waist, good and tight. Then tie him to that tree there." Sammy got the cuffs and rope from my pack and tied Duplantis to the tree.

"You don't have to tie me up! I'm not going anywhere!"

"Shut the hell up! We'll talk about where you're going in a minute."

"Let's talk," I said to Sammy. I motioned for him to follow me and we walked away from Duplantis, out of earshot.

"What's going on?" Sammy said. I thought about how much to tell him and decided to keep it short.

"I can't say right now. But I need you to get in your truck and leave. I don't want you involved in this. I made a reservation for you at Grouse Mountain Lodge. Stay there tonight and head home tomorrow. I'll be in touch soon and tell you the story. I don't have time now. Trust me, I know what I'm doing."

"Do you? You didn't know he'd be armed."

"Yeah, sorry about that. He stole my gun."

"Lemme stay and help."

"No, if you want to help leave now and let me finish this. I'm not sure what I'm going to do, but you don't need to know."

I motioned for him to follow me and we walked to his truck where Duplantis had left Sammy's backpack. I reached in and pulled out the envelope that contained my $22,000. I took out ten $100 bills and gave them to Sammy, then stuffed the envelope in my backpack.

"That's for your time. I gotta get going. The trail to get into Canada – remind me again how it goes." Sammy leaned forward and looked me in the eye. I surmised it was to see if I was drunk.

"You go straight up the hill from here about 200 yards to the game trail. Then take it north along the ridge above the tree line, follow it down into the woods and it winds west around the mountain. Stay on the trail for about 8 miles then you'll come to a fork heading north – take that and you'll connect with a logging road which takes you to Canada Highway 3. From there it's about 20 miles to Fernie, the first town. Is he going... or you?" I didn't answer.

"You got anything to eat?" I said. I was famished.

"Venison steaks. I was gonna cook 'em up." He reached into the cooler in the backseat of his rig and pulled out a vacuum-sealed pouch with two marinated deer steaks inside. I stuck them in my backpack. Sammy then pulled a flask from inside his jacket.

"Here you go. You may need this more than I." I looked at the flask and wanted to grab it from his hand. But I already felt drunk – the world was spinning.

"No thanks."

"You never turn down a taste. This must be serious." He grinned and I almost laughed.

"If only you knew."

"Who's this guy, Teddy? What are you doin'?"

"I'll tell ya later. You gotta go, Sam. Don't be surprised if you see a Ford Escape down the road. That's me."

Sammy stared at me, then shook his head and sighed. "Okay, whatever you say, boss. Call me tomorrow."

"You got it."

"You're lucky as hell I didn't shoot ya – that bear growl you made sounded pretty damn creepy. You're a piece of work, Teddy." I didn't know what he meant by that but I let it pass.

As he climbed up behind the wheel he said, "Guess I won't get a chance to show your man the claw tree. I was looking forward to it. I haven't seen it in a few years."

My mind brought up a faint misty memory. "Claw tree?"

"You remember the claw tree don't ya? That tree where animals rub their backs and scratch with their claws? With the antlers and moose hair all around?" I remembered then. It was a tree off the game trail where animals would come back year after year and leave marks. A territorial thing, dominant animals leaving their sign.

"Oh yeah, I remember that tree." It amazed me that I'd forgotten it – I'd been there twice, hunting with Sammy, and had always been fascinated. Sammy discovered it with one of his hounds years ago.

I was thinking now, wheels turning faster. "Where is that tree?" I said.

"You had a code for it, remember?"

I paused. "Rock... rock red something?"

"Rock right 250. You came up with that. Don't ya remember?"

"Sounds familiar. Rock right 250 – yeah, I remember. But I forgot what it means. What's it mean?" I tried to concentrate on his answer.

"You go about 3 miles up the game trail and you come to a big rock the trail goes around. You turn right at the rock and head downhill into the forest for 250 steps – to a small clearing where the claw tree is."

And just like that, I felt a big weight take wing from my shoulders. I didn't have to decide what to do with Duplantis. I could let the universe decide. If it wanted him dead, it could let nature (or wild animals) take its course. I was rejuvenated. I picked up the backpack for Duplantis and said, "Maybe I'll stop and see it."

"Take a picture if you do. I want to see the latest claw marks." Then he put his rig in gear and drove off.

I took out my notebook and wrote: Rock right 250. Then I carried Sammy's backpack up to where Duplantis was tied to the tree. As the sound of Sammy's engine faded a hawk circled overhead, searching for prey.

Chapter 51 Claw Tree

I went up to Duplantis. His head was down, but he sat up when I approached.

"You ever been to Africa?" I asked.

"Africa?" He looked at me curiously. "No, I've never been to Africa. What are you talking about? What are you doing here, man? How'd you get here?" He was tired, irked, like me.

"I decided I wanted to go to Canada. Maybe we both will."

"You're not serious. You're crazy."

"You sure you've never been to Africa?" He didn't answer so I went on. "You know Morocco is in Africa, right? Morocco? Ever heard of it?"

"Morocco is in Africa?"

"Yes, Morocco is in Africa you moron! Do I need to draw you a goddamn map?" It reminded me of living in New Orleans when we'd draw a map of the continental U.S. on a bar napkin and ask locals to draw where Montana was. Nobody had a clue. What was worse was nobody cared. It was disrespectful as hell. Totally pissed me off.

He looked at me closely, trying to decide where I was going with my line of inquiry.

"I ask again, have you ever been to Morocco?" He paused, then replied with a sigh.

"No, I've never been to Morocco. I've never been to Africa. I've never been to Montana until now. I don't think I like it."

"Lie. I maintain that yes you have been to Morocco. Not only that, you have killed people in Morocco. You've also killed people in Florida, and you did kill Violet McRae in Louisiana! You may have killed more people than that, am I right?"

"Shut up, Teddy. I've never killed a soul in my life, as I've told you. I went to prison for a crime I did not commit. I did not kill Violet! Leroy framed me! You know that!"

"I thought that, but I don't anymore. I think you're a lying, thieving serial killer is what I think now."

"What?! You've lost it, man!"

"I may have lost it before, but I'm not lost now. You committed those murders didn't you, admit it!"

"I've never killed anyone in my life!" Tied to the tree, he did his best to look sad and innocent. He was a decent thespian – acted the part well. But I knew the truth.

"Here's what's going to happen," I said. "We're gonna hit the trail now toward Canada. And if you don't tell me the truth, I can't guarantee you'll make it across the border."

"Now? It's gonna be dark soon!"

"We've got some time. You carry Sammy's backpack."

"Where are we gonna sleep?" he asked. I didn't answer. "Well, untie me then and let's go."

I took out my phone and snapped a photo of Duplantis tied to the tree. Then untied the rope from the trunk. I wrapped the rope around my waist and kept the other end tied around Duplantis. I took off his handcuffs and put them in my pack. Duplantis rubbed his wrists, then put on Sammy's backpack.

"Déjà vu, huh?" he said. "We were doing almost the same thing 24 hours ago in Portland." Were we? I didn't think about it, just pointed him up the hill toward the game trail.

"That way," I said.

He led the way, the rope between us taut. We climbed through the trees up to timberline and found the trail. A game trail is a path made by animals, not people. It's not as worn in as a hiking trail, but you can follow it once you know what to look for.

Following the game trail we headed north along the ridge. I had my shotgun in hand and the Glock and Beretta in my pack. My blood was up. I was ready for bear – I thought.

Duplantis started asking questions – trying to find out what I knew about him and what may have happened to bring me driving like a maniac to Montana. I stayed silent.

While we hiked the trail, I thought about my situation. I knew what to do with Duplantis, but what about myself? What about my own murder I'd committed? Didn't I need to do penance, like Duplantis? What would the universe do with me given a chance? Should I run to Canada, start a new life, avoid prison?

Or, I could catch the train in Whitefish and head east for Chicago. I'd be there in two days. I could hide out for a while, get my head together. Get my head together? I bristled at the cliché. Idiot. Stop thinking, I thought.

Suddenly I blurted out, "What's the worst thing about prison?"

Duplantis turned and looked at me, "Why would you give a shit about prison?"

"Just curious," I said. I looked up at the sky. Streaks of gold crossed through purple clouds, sun setting in the west. The smell of pine was all around, but also a scent of, for lack of a better word, wildness. It smelled ... raw, rootsy, ancient.

"It's not like Folsom Prison Blues I'll tell ya that much. I never heard a train a comin' the whole time I was there. It's bullshit. You never hear a peep from the outside. Johnny Cash made it sound lonely. But it's worse than that."

"How do ya mean? Free bed, free food, what's not to like?" He glared at me and I stared back deadpan.

"The worst thing is hearing the same lies and crap from the same fools day after day. Everyone has a story – everyone is innocent. Everyone is gettin' out. Everyone wants you to listen to them rant all damn day. You get so tired of hearing it you wanna kill someone."

"I can imagine," I said. And I could.

He laughed, "Prison is like Canada. It helps to like hockey. Prison guards love watching and talking hockey." He went on talking, trying to get on my good side. I stopped listening and focused on the hawk in the sky to the north. Was it the same one I saw earlier?

We walked on and then came to a huge rock the trail circled around. Rock right 250 I thought. Was that it? I dug my notebook out of my pocket and read my last note: Rock right 250. I read the note before that: Addison Thompson is aka Nolan Duplantis – serial killer Sammy taking to Canada on game trail – stop him!

"Hold up," I said. Duplantis stopped and turned around. "What's up?"

"I want to show you something. That way, off trail, down through those trees." Duplantis didn't move. "Start walking, I'll tell you when to stop."

He looked at me, frustrated. "Where are we going now?" I didn't say anything, just pointed the way.

As we left the game trail and headed downhill I began counting steps. We had to cross over fallen trees and through thick brush but kept our direction straight. When we reached 250 steps, I still didn't see the tree. We walked another 20 steps, then I saw a clearing to the left, and there it stood, gnarly and scarred – the claw tree. A scratch post for grizzlies. A gathering spot for creatures of the wild. Animals that could eat you alive. You could smell wildness in the air. We were unwelcome.

"Stopping here," I said. "Take off your pack."

"Here? Why here? Shit, man. What'd you want to show me?" Duplantis dropped his pack on the ground. He was tired. Irritated.

"Go stand by that tree over there," I said, pointing to the claw tree.

"Why? What's with the tree?"

"I'll show ya," I said. He walked over and looked up at it. He was still tied to me by rope. I set my pack and shotgun down and walked over to Duplantis.

"Stand up close to it," I said. He didn't move. I yanked the rope and pulled him up against the tree. "Don't move. I'm just gonna tie you up for a sec." I uncoiled the rope from my waist and wrapped it around the trunk several times and tied him down tight to the bark.

"Come on, Teddy! I'm not going anywhere. I'm no threat!"

"Yeah, you are. That's the problem."

I took out my phone and took a photo of him. Then walked around the tree and took photos of the claw gouges and tooth marks – old scars that had weathered and new marks that cut deep into the trunk.

"The thing I wanted to show you is right there. You're tied to it. It's called the claw tree."

He looked straight up at the tree rising above him. It was starting to sink in what I had in mind.

"It's where grizzlies and cougars and moose and other wild animals leave their mark. A claw mark. Or a bite. Dogs piss on trees, bigger animals claw them and chew on the bark. It's their way of saying they are the alpha in this area."

I showed him the claw mark photos I'd taken and went on, "Animals are territorial and they don't like it when their land is encroached upon. Like we've just done. On top of that they're extremely hungry this time of year."

"Untie me, now!" The timbre of his voice changed. "Let's get outta here!"

"I intend to do that, shortly. But one last thing." I reached into my pack and pulled out the two venison steaks. With a knife I cut the package open and poured out the bloody marinade on the ground in front of Duplantis. Then I grabbed one steak and threw it at his feet.

The other steak I impaled on a short branch a foot above his head. I wanted to make sure the world knew that Nolan was now available. Like advertising – building awareness.

I said, "With this breeze, every wild animal within five miles is going to smell this venison in a matter of minutes. Did ya know there are about 800 grizzlies in the Yaak? That's what they call this remote corner of Montana. The Yaak. And they say there are at least three packs of wolves up here, with about seven wolves per pack. Add mountain lions and moose and you have a lot of large animals in the area. I read once where two grizzlies near Eureka were so hungry they dug up a dead horse buried behind some guy's shed and ate half of it. Dug the whole animal up."

Duplantis hit the panic button. "No, man, no, no, no..."

"You better talk fast," I said. "Did you kill Violet McRae? And how many others have you killed? Confess now – while you can."

"I swear. I swear! I've never killed anyone! Not Violet. Not anyone in Morocco. Not anyone in Pensacola. Nobody! You know that! You know me!"

"Pensacola? I never said anything about Pensacola. I said Florida." But I actually couldn't remember if I did or not. I was consumed with making him confess. Couldn't stand him continuing to con me.

"I don't have time to mess around," I said. From my pack I pulled out the duct tape. I tore off a foot long piece. "Do you want me to tape your eyes?" I asked, looking him in the eye.

"What? Hell no, I don't want you to tape my eyes! Untie me and let's get outta here!"

"You're okay with watching what happens to you? Seeing a grizzly or wolf come up and eat those steaks, then sniff you up and rake you with their claws, sink their fangs into your neck? Stick their drooling snout in your face and bite off your nose and swallow it right in front of you? You're okay with that?"

He gasped, "You're sick. You're sick."

"Sicker than you? I don't think so. I'm leaving your fate up to the universe. You didn't do that to those people you killed. You're the sick one here, not me."

I put the duct tape back in my pack and looked up at the sky. The light was fading. I had a half hour at most before dark set in. I went through the pack Duplantis had set down. All it contained was his clothes, nothing with Sammy's name on it. I then grabbed my own pack and put it on.

Duplantis yelled out. "Okay, okay, I did it! I killed Violet and those others. I confess. I admit it. I'm sorrrrry! But I did my time and I've changed, man! Honest! All those years in prison changed me. I've accepted the lord as my savior." There it was. Getting religion is always the last resort of a dying man. So cliche. I knew he was lying. He could give a shit about the lord.

"Well, your savior won't save you out here," I said. "Won't keep a grizzly from ripping your face apart, from tearing into your heart, no matter how much you pray. You're the prey out here. Get it? That's a pun. Your last one. You're in the animal world now. Who knows what they'll do." I stopped, short of breath.

It would be so easy to just shoot him, or strangle him. But I couldn't. I was done killing people. Forever. This is what I told myself. To lessen my guilt. Of course, leaving him tied to a tree to die is as much a murder as shooting him in the head.

I took a step closer to the tree. "I know one thing. You were gonna kill my friend, Sammy, back there. I saw ya grab my gun – you were gonna shoot him dead."

"No, man." His voice was trembling.

"Yeah, mannnn! You were. Well, you're through lyin'. But I'll tell ya what, I'll give you a chance. I'll let nature decide what to do with you. I'm gonna hike back to my car, fold down the back seat and get some sleep, then drive down to Whitefish tomorrow, have a big breakfast, drink a Bloody Mary or a dozen at the Great Northern Bar, and decide whether to make an anonymous call to 911 and tell them where you are. I figure that'll give the universe enough time to swallow you up if it wants."

I stepped up closer to him and looked him in the eye. "If you survive tonight and tomorrow, you may get rescued. If not, well, good luck in the afterlife."

He stared back, slack-jawed. Then his eyes turned hard and he spat in my face. "I'm gonna get you, man," he snarled. I smiled and wiped off the spit, then turned around and started walking.

"Wait. Stop! Don't do it, don't do it! You can't leave me here! Teddy! Ted! Ted!! I'm gonna get you! You're a dead man! Don't leave me!" He yelled as loud as he could, "Helllp! Hellllllllp!"

As I left the clearing, I turned and yelled back, "The nearest human other than me is more than ten miles away. Go ahead and yell. Only animals are gonna hear ya. And the more scared you sound, the more appetizing you become. They can sense it. So you may wanna keep your trap shut. Nice knowin' ya."

I never looked back. Climbing uphill through the trees I came to the game trail. I looked up the trail and down it and tried to focus. Which way do I go? Then I remembered, north was right, south left. I pondered it for a minute. Should I go to Canada? A new life with a new identity? I had my escape bag. I could get some freelance writing gigs and start following hockey. But I knew I was lying to myself. I could never follow hockey.

No, I needed to go back the way I'd come. I'd decide what to do tomorrow.

I reached into my pocket and pulled out my pen and notebook and wrote: D tied claw tree. But it didn't appear. It said "D tied" and that's all, the other words didn't show. I pressed down harder and tried to finish the words, but no ink emerged. The pen had run empty. I burst out laughing uproariously, rolling my head back.

"Of course," I said out loud as I put the pen and notebook back in my pocket. Then I heard a sound. An echo of my voice? It was human. But not mine. I realized with a jolt it was Duplantis. He was...growling in a deep tone.

He suddenly shouted, "Get away! Get away! Shoo! Get away from here! Get away! Teddy!! Teddy!! Help!! Get away! Get away from me!" Then he started roaring like an animal, but in a high-pitched, terrified voice.

I reached for my shotgun and got another jolt – the realization I'd left it at the claw tree. Shit! I wanted to kick myself. No going back. I pulled the Glock handgun from my pack and took off running down the game trail. Light was fading fast.

Chapter 52 Red Eyes

Monday Night
You can't outrun a grizzly. You can't outrun a mountain lion. You certainly can't outrun a wolf. And you can't outrun your past. These are the things that crossed my mind as I sprinted down the trail.

The moon hung in the trees, shining through the pine branches like a Christmas ornament. It wasn't long before it got dark and hard to see the trail, so I pulled my flashlight from my pack and turned it on.

With the Glock in one hand and flashlight in the other I ran on. The light bounced up and down and I focused straight ahead on the thin path. It felt like driving home from a high school kegger outside Billings when I would focus on the headlights and centerline so we all wouldn't tragically die in a flaming wreck. I was in the same zone.

The rhythm of running made me sleepy and it was hard to keep my eyes open, so I stopped for a break. I tried to stretch, and as I did my light flashed into the trees. Wait. I saw a figure. Someone was there. Two people. I kept my light on them and tried to focus. Then I saw, it was the kid whose dad I'd killed. The kid I'd seen at the train station in Whitefish. Was he tracking me?

"Stop following me!" I yelled. I looked at the figure next to him. I knew the face but it took a second to realize who it was – Mario. Oh yeah, I'd also killed him. He turned his palms out as if to say, "Why ya do it, cher?"

I turned away and blinked hard, took a deep breath and looked back toward the figures. They were gone. Ghosts. My mind – or the universe – playing tricks on me.

Turning back to the trail, I walked on, too tired to run anymore. My legs carried me but my eyelids became heavy. I used my gun hand to hold my eyes open, telling myself not to accidentally shoot myself in the head. That would be dumb, I thought. I tried to make myself laugh. Anything to stay awake.

Another mile and I'm thinking I must be getting close to the cutoff down to the logging road. But it was really dark now. I stopped to think about where I was. You are looking for the logging road I said to myself several times. Looking for your Escape.

A rustle in the woods – a stick cracked. I sensed something moving and froze. Then heard another series of sounds, like paws on pine needles, running. I flashed my light into the trees and yelled out, "Hey! Who's there?"

Two red dots appeared, like LED lights, right next to each other, and when they blinked in unison I knew what it was: wolf. Which meant it was probably a pack.

The red lights disappeared and I heard more rustling. I took the safety off my Glock and fired three shots into the trees, hoping to scare them off. I started down the trail, slowly at first, but within steps I began running – and yelling, nonsensically. I tried to sound like a crazy human who'd gone bad. As in bad meat, rotten to the bone, something to avoid. Animals would know, I hoped.

Fear took over and I couldn't help myself. I yelled out to the universe, "I confess! I confess! I killed two people! I admit it! I admit it! Just don't eat me! I've changed! Please god, don't let me die!" I was stark raving mad, grasping and gasping for life, on the edge of the void.

I ran, half stumbled down the trail, flashing my light into the trees, looking for wolves. I heard sounds in the dark, animals running, parallel to me. I could barely see the trail ahead.

Fear grabbed me by the throat and I had trouble breathing. Thoughts spun through my mind. Does the universe want justice? Am I to be sentenced, swallowed, exterminated? I was going to fight it I decided. I thought of my brass knuckles and pulled them from my pack as I ran, putting them on my right hand. I figured I'd get in one last punch.

And then, with the world closing in, running like a lunatic, I took my eye off the trail and tripped over a tree root. In an instant I was launched toward the moon, flying headfirst, flashlight flipping in the air, gun still gripped in one hand, brass knuckles in the other. And then came a thunderous crack and the gun and flashlight and wolves and woods and moon ceased to exist. I fell into a black hole.

SOMEWHERE, SOMEHOW, something is breathing on me. I feel it on the back of my neck. More than a breeze. Something cold pokes me, prods me, rolls me over on my back. Then my lungs contract, as if crushed by a powerful force.

I look up and it's a wolf, standing on my chest, drooling on my face. I feel the drops land on my nose. Then, the wolf's face changes and it's the boy. He leans down and frowns at me.

I shove the boywolf off and stagger to my feet and run. After three steps I fall. I can't move one leg – it's dragging something. I look down and see a rusted iron ball, attached by chain to my left ankle. The boywolf is watching me. Expressionless.

I pick up the iron ball and stumble on into the trees, dragging the chain with me. Someone puts on Howlin' Wolf and I hear it reverberate through the forest. His song "Smokestack Lightning," a soundtrack for a dreamscape. I fall again and get up. Running hard through the woods.

To my side, almost hidden in the trees, I see a dark shape. A grizzly. He hears me and turns his huge head my way. He sniffs the air and starts walking toward me. I speed up and he breaks into a trot, then into a dash, chasing me. I see a river in front of me and in seconds I am running into the water, surging forward, carrying the iron ball and chain, going out deeper to escape the griz which has stopped on the bank. The current takes me and I flow down river.

I drop the heavy ball and chain and use both arms to swim for shore where I now see two figures reaching out. It's Kate and Jasmine. They have waded into the river but I'm still too far out.

I stroke hard with my arms and kick furiously with one leg but I can't get there. My head goes under and I pull myself up and swim as hard as I can – arms reaching out for the shore. I go under again, and straining with every muscle in my body, I rise and my eyes break the surface for one final teary look at my family, and then I go under, too tired to fight anymore, the iron ball and chain pulling me down into the depths. I realize it's the end. The sadness is indescribable.

And then, my mind flashes on a funny but morbid thought: Thank god no gators around. That would be the worst. I open my mouth to laugh and water pours into my heart.

Chapter 53 Werewolf

Tuesday Afternoon

A thought formed. Am I dreaming? Am I alive? Is this real? My mind seemed to be working. I forced one eye open, then the other, and saw an aqua blue sky above me.

I sensed pain. In my chest, my head, my heart. Holy shit, I thought, if I feel pain then I might be alive. I wiggled fingers, put a hand down in the dirt, and sat up. I saw my hand had on brass knuckles. Why am I wearing knucks, I wondered. What happened to me?

My Glock was on the ground next to my left hand. I struggled to my feet and ran my hands over my face and body looking for blood or signs of injury. I had a pounding in my head, a pain in my chest, and a deep, gnawing hunger in my belly.

I took off the backpack I had on and checked for food. Nothing but a smashed-flat box of crackers. I grabbed a handful of crumbs and shoved them in my mouth, then stuffed the Glock and brass knuckles in my pack.

What the hell happened? Where am I? I looked out over the landscape of rolling forested terrain. It could be Oregon. Or Montana. Or... Canada? I had no idea where I was, no knowledge of how I got there, no memory of the past several days.

All around me were animal tracks, claw marks of various sizes, dug into the earth. Was I attacked by wolves, or did I dream that?

I pulled out my phone and saw the time: 1:25 pm. I had 20% battery left, but no cell service. Turning on the camera, I reversed the focus to get a look at myself. I saw a purplish gash across my forehead and a gnarly knot above my right eyebrow. My face was smudged with dirt and my glazed eyes seemed to have a crazed look. The word werewolf came to mind.

Switching to messages I saw my last text had been to Kate. It said: I'm fine. Please take Jasmine to airport. Tell her I love her and sorry I can't see her off. But I need to get away and think. Will explain later. SORRY! Will be in touch. Love you. Please wait for me.

Get away and think? Did I really write that? What bullshit. There was no message back from Kate so presumably she thought the same thing. Bullshit. I felt bad. Making it worse was I didn't even see my only child off on her trip to...Morocco? Paraguay? Ecuador? I had no clue.

I stuck the phone back in my pocket and looked around. I saw a game trail a dozen feet up the hill and began following it with one thing in mind. Eat. I didn't know how I got there but I had to get off that mountain and feed myself. I could eat a horse.

After walking a while, I came around a ridge and saw down through the trees to my left a logging road. I headed for it and then followed the road down the hill. In 20 minutes I saw a vehicle parked off near the trees. As I got closer I realized it was my own. Ford Escape. What was I doing out here? I couldn't conjure an answer.

I unlocked the car, fired it up, and turned around to head downhill. Like a horse that knows the way, the Escape found the way down the mountain to a highway. After pondering which way to go I turned left, east according to the compass on my dash, and motored on, unsure where the road led.

Less than an hour later I found out where I was as I passed the Grouse Mountain Lodge where Kate and I spent the first night of our honeymoon. I realized I was near Whitefish, in the northwest corner of Montana, and had been in the mountains close to the border the day before. I knew it had something to do with Canada.

I pulled over and got the backpack out of the trunk. At the bottom of the pack was a manila envelope in which I found a lot of cash and a Canadian ID in the name of Addison Thompson. The photo was me. I remembered when I had the fake ID made years ago. I'd buried it with the money in a graveyard in Portland – my escape pack. Had I dug it up? Was I really heading for Canada? Why? What about Kate and Jasmine? What the hell happened?

Parking in front of the Great Northern Bar in Whitefish, I went inside and ordered steak and eggs, a side of fries, a Bloody Mary, and double shot of R&R.

I pulled out my phone, now with cell coverage. There was a text from Ronan: Where is D?! I know you know. Call me asshole!

Wait, who's D? What's he mean? And why is he so pissed at me? There were no other messages. Switching to my photos, I opened my photo file and about threw up. The last couple pics were of a man tied to a tree – two different trees. Was this D?

I scrolled back further and saw the same man in several pictures hanging in a noose from a tree. He looked dead. But how could he be dead in that shot, then appear in two photos after that tied to other trees?

It made no sense. But whatever was up, it was bad. I was in deep shit. And what about Kate? Does she know where I am?

The last memory I had was of Kate and I sitting at the kitchen table. We were having an argument of some sort. I don't remember what it was about. It seemed long ago.

Finished eating and drinking, I pulled out some cash to pay and saw my little notebook. Why didn't I think to check it? I flipped it open and read the last hand-scratched entry: D tied … That's all it said. What did it mean? The scrawled message right above it said: Right rock 250. It sounded vaguely familiar.

But then it became clear as I read earlier messages to myself. I was trying to stop a serial killer named Nolan Duplantis from escaping to Canada. I had no memory of the man, no inkling of what happened.

I walked outside the Great Northern Bar and heard a train. The station was two blocks away and the afternoon Amtrak was just arriving. I felt a pull in that direction, but instead got in the Escape and drove past the station and crossed over the tracks.

In a few minutes I was on the edge of town on the shore of Whitefish Lake, near where I lived in a cabin when I worked at KTXX Radio. It was quiet. Clouds floated lazily. The air carried that unmistakable lake smell that I remembered so well from my youth.

The log cabin I lived in before was now gone, replaced by a large set of ho-hum condos joined together. I walked down on the wood dock where I once had tied up my 8-man rubber raft, to the chagrin of others who had their sleek sailboats and powerboats tied up there.

At the end of the dock I looked all around – mountains to the north where the ski area was, Glacier National Park to the east, forested shoreline across the lake to the west.

I took out my phone and checked to see if I had a message from Kate. Nothing. I wondered what she was doing right now.

I looked through photos of Kate and Jasmine. And Ben – our wise-ass dog. I quickly scanned back through pictures of birthday celebrations, vacations, and family occasions of all sorts. We looked so happy.

We had a good life, I thought. And I totally blew it. Ruined it. Recklessly destroyed it. What a colossal waste of an existence. I looked down at the deep blue water and thought, I could drown in this lake. It would be a good place to end it. Where's a ball and chain when ya need one?

But I decided not to fling myself into the lake. Instead, reaching my arm back as far as I could, I whipped it forward and hurled my phone as far out over the lake as I could. It made a small splash. I then took my notebook from my pocket and threw it in the lake, too.

The last thing I did was get back in my car, get a room at Grouse Mountain Lodge, and fall into a deep sleep.

Chapter 54 Driving On

Wednesday Morning
It's a funny thing about memories. Two people at the same event can have totally different memories of it. We remember what we want to remember, whatever matters to us for whatever reason, and forget the rest. Apparently I wanted to remember what I'd done. Because it all came back to me in my sleep – the whole story. Only this was like a movie.

It started with a close-up of the kid – in Spiderman shirt and underwear. The scene widened out and I saw him in a room watching as I strangled his father with a rope, the innocent man who lived at the wrong address – the victim of a typo. I saw myself shoot Mario and dump his body in the Willamette River. I saw the fake hanging and me knocking Kate to the ground and my train chase to Whitefish and tying Duplantis to the claw tree, letting the universe decide his fate.

My recall of the last four days meant something. My memory and conscience wanted to atone, even if I didn't. I now knew I'd left Duplantis tied to a tree in the remote wilderness of Montana, not knowing if he'd ever be found. And if he dies, it's first-degree murder.

But what about the fact that he was a serial killer? Don't I get a break for that? I decided I did. I was not gonna go back to save the guy, and I would not call the cops. My skin was more important than his.

I took a hot shower and stood under the nozzle and let the water pour off me. My chest still ached and it had a large bruise the shape of Russia. But I felt better. Hot showers are good for ideas and I conjured one up out of the steam. I made a plan and tried to convince myself it was a good one.

After breakfast in the hotel café, I got back in the Escape and hit the road south toward Missoula. It was sunny and I drove with the windows down, trying to blow away any bad energy around me.

Missoula is where my mother-in-law, JoJo, lives. I always stop when passing through, but not this time. At the I-90 junction I had a choice of west toward Portland, or east toward Butte and Billings. My plan called for east, and south.

I drove to Butte, then turned south on I-15 and continued on, arriving at my destination around 8:30 that evening – Salt Lake City, where my brothers, Stu and Jeff live. I rang Stu's bell and in a few seconds he opened the door with a shocked look.

"T.R.! What're you doin'? Another roadtrip?"

"Yeah, Stu. Sorry I didn't call. I'm on a little tour." We went inside and he got two Polygamy Porters from the fridge (tagline: Bring some home for the wives). We talked a few minutes and he asked what the hell happened to my head. I told him I fell getting into the shower and gashed my head on the towel rack.

"Musta hurt. You don't look too good."

"Yeah, now I scare people. More than I used to." Then I asked if I could use his phone to call Kate. I said I'd left mine in a casino in Winnemucca the day before. He laughed and said sure, then handed me his phone and walked away to give me privacy.

I called Kate's number, knowing she would think it was Stu calling. She liked him but she might not pick up. She didn't, so I left a message: "Hi, it's me. I'm in Salt Lake at Stu's house. I lost my phone – in Winnemucca on the way over here. Remember that casino we used to go to when we'd come through on the way to Salt Lake? Well,

I must have left it at the blackjack table. I went back and it's gone. So I'm calling you on Stu's phone. I'll get a new one when I get back – so if you can't reach me, that's why. Just want you to know I'm heading to the Utah parks – Bryce and Zion – maybe the Grand Canyon and Phoenix, then back up through Death Valley and Yosemite. You know how I always wanted to do that. A national park tour. I'll find the good spots and bring you next time."

I paused, gathering steam and forcing myself to say out loud how I felt. I hate getting emotional.

"Kate, I'm so sorry. So sorry to be like this. I know I've said it before but I promise I will change. I have to, I understand now. I swear honey." Another pause. "I miss the hell out of you and I'm sorry I took off. But I had to do it. I needed to think."

Then I went for the closer. "All I can say is, please be there when I get back. Please! I love you, honaayyy! Say hi to Ben." I threw in that last line because I knew it would tug at her heartstrings. But I did want her to say hi to Ben. I missed him. Not near as much as I missed her.

Stu walked back in the room a minute later and I told him I wanted to make one more call. But I wanted him to call the number and say who he was, then give me the phone. I had the number memorized from way back. I told Stu the guy's name was Ronan. Stu punched it in, then waited.

"Hi, is this Ronan?" Stu paused. "Hi. Teddy asked me to call you. I'm his brother, Stu. He lost his phone.... no, I live in Salt Lake City.... yeah, I do know where he is. He's sitting right next to me. Here you go." Stu handed me his phone.

"Hi, man," I said. "Stu's not quite right. I didn't lose my phone. I think it was stolen. At a casino in Winnemucca a couple nights ago."

Ronan sounded tired. "Winnemucca? What the hell were you doing in that jack-off town?"

"I'm on a road trip to the National Parks. Nevada, Utah, Arizona… You ever visited our National Parks, Ronan?"

"Shut up."

"I'll be back in a couple weeks, then I'll get a new phone."

"Where is he, Teddy?" He was in no mood to mess around.

"Where's who?"

"You know who. Your pal, Duplantis. They still haven't caught up with him. He's out there. You know where, don't ya?" I was on tricky ground now. Ronan had a sharp nose.

I walked into another room and spoke quietly. "He's still loose? Oh, shit! I was following him for Leroy Dupree. I saw a Cadillac with Louisiana plates on the street by his house. Dupree may have done something done to Duplantis – you may not find him."

"You have any idea where they might have taken him?" Ronan asked.

"No. I don't know those people. They're not my type." The attempt at humor fell short.

Ronan didn't say anything. I needed to cut this short.

"I gotta go, man. I'll get in touch when I get back to Portland."

"Okay, T. I'll let you know if something turns up on your man. You better watch yourself."

The next day I saw my brother, Jeff, and his family and then ventured south to Bryce National Park. It was nice not having a phone to keep checking. From there I drove down around the Grand Canyon to Phoenix and saw my brother John, and his wife Diane. I told them the same story. I was on a National Parks road trip.

It was great seeing all of them, but I felt the pull of Kate so after two days in Phoenix I drove to Las Vegas, on to Death Valley, and then north on Highway 395 along the beautiful Sierra Mountains. I was too focused on the road to enjoy it. I had a nose for home.

The next day, around happy hour, I pulled into Portland. I drove straight past several bars, never once slowing down. In the driveway,

I saw what I hoped to see – Kate's little red Subaru. I pumped my fist and yelled, "Yes!" I was ecstatic that she hadn't left.

I'd spent many hours thinking what to say. I went over my lines as I unlocked the front door. She wasn't there, nor was Ben. The house was eerily silent.

I went into the kitchen and instinctively looked to see if we had any booze. Nothing. No beer in the fridge either. Not a good sign. Was she changing things? I sat down and began to get nervous.

A sound on the porch broke the spell and I heard the key in the door. Then it opened and I saw her. Kate. Black windbreaker, black ball cap, brown eyes under dark eyebrows, same as before. I gave her a huge smile but it was not returned. She and Ben entered. Only Ben looked at me. She didn't say a word. Neither did he.

I started talking. "I've done a lot of stupid, reckless things in my life I know, but I've also done one very smart thing. I fell in love with you and married you. And I'm still in love with you. And I always will be. I'm done lying, I swear. While I was gone, I did a lot of thinking on how I can change and I'm asking you to trust me. I'm a different man than the one you saw last. I don't want to relive the past or talk about it. I want to look ahead, start fresh."

It sounded like complete bullshit but I meant it. It was about as sincere as I've ever been.

She took off her cap and looked out the window. I waited.

In a straight, quiet voice she said, "I thought you were in Montana, catching up with your buddy." I shook my head and looked at Ben. I could tell he wondered the same thing as Kate. Where had I been?

Kate went on in a voice so sharp I could shave with it, "I don't know what I'm going to do, whether you're worth it, or whether our marriage is worth saving, but I never want to hear his name or discuss that event ever again. Never. Do you understand me?"

I looked her in the eye, wiped the smile off my face, and nodded. I had just enough smarts not to say another word.

Looking back on it, I'm not sure why she didn't just boot me out and call a lawyer. But it may be as simple as this: I'm flawed. And vulnerable – at least, that's what she thinks. She sees through my bad guy façade and feels I'm struggling to be good, but just no good at it. And she can't resist trying to solve the puzzle that is me.

Chapter 55 One Month Later

In a dream last night I saw him again. The boy. Standing in his Spiderman shirt by my bedroom door. No expression, just staring at me. Then I saw Ben, sleeping at the bottom of our bed. He lifted his head and looked at the kid. He saw him, I'm sure of it. He raised his ears, then turned his head to me with a scowl. "What'd you do now?" I didn't answer.

In the morning I got up and checked my new phone. I'd replaced the one I tossed into Whitefish Lake. No messages. I decided to call Jasmine who was in Ecuador. I'd missed connecting with her a few times. When she answered, I immediately started in with questions. She told me she was doing well and talked about the projects she was working on with other students.

She asked how I was and I got the sense she was concerned about me. I didn't want to talk about me and steered the conversation back to her. We talked a minute more and she said she had to go. She hates talking on phones.

I told her I loved her and to be careful. She said, "Same to you, dad."

I decided I'd better check in with Sammy in Montana. He'd be wondering what happened on that game trail with Duplantis. I wasn't sure what to tell him. He picked up on the fifth ring and in a gruff voice said, "Yeah, who's this?"

"It is I, your buddy T. Haven't talked in awhile."

He brightened up, "Yeah, shit Teddy, I tried to reach you, what happened?"

"Lost my phone after I last saw you. Had to get a new one. This is my new number."

"So what happened after I left you guys up there? What'd you do with your man?"

I paused. "Let's just say the job was finished and leave it at that."

"C'mon man, you can tell me."

"Nah, it's better if I don't. Sorry, bud."

Sammy was silent a few seconds. "Okayyy compadre, I got ya. I don't need to know. But hell, someday you gotta tell me." We talked a bit more and hung up.

As the day wore on, skies turned dark and it began to rain. I felt like going to a bar. But I don't do that anymore – meaning drink. I've been sober ever since Kate and I had our little sit-down the day after I got back. She laid it on the line, said she was in control now. Everything I do she has to sign off on. She loves fixing things, always has. But I wonder, can I be fixed?

Frankly, sobriety sucks. I hate it, so far. Better for my marriage no doubt, but boring as all get out.

So, instead of hitting a tavern, I hit the Uber road for something to do – talk to folks and try to amuse myself. Maybe find that elusive killer story. I used to think everyone had one, buried deep inside. But lately I've begun to think most stories are bullshit. People will make up anything. You can't trust anybody these days.

My phone chirped as I dropped off a fare at Migration Brewing. It was Ronan. I'd given him my number after getting the new phone, so he wouldn't be suspicious of my whereabouts.

"Detective, que pasa?" I said.

"Didn't you used to live in Whitefish, Montana?" I leaned forward to turn down the radio, playing "Crossroads" by Cream.

"Yeah, back in the early 80s. Why?"

"Been there lately?" I didn't like the way this was heading.

"Uhhh, no. About 20 years ago I guess." I kicked my mind in gear. This was not good.

"They found him."

"Found...who?" I needed time to think. Am I nailed?

Ronan roared back, "Who do ya think! Don't be cute."

"Duplantis," I said. I had to tread carefully.

"Bingo. He was up north of Whitefish, out of some town called Eureka. Some hunters found him. You sure you didn't hit Montana on your recent tour of the National Parks? Glacier is close to Whitefish."

Be patient I told myself. "Thank god they found that bastard. Alive?"

"Give you one guess."

"I'll bet not."

"Dead right, dude. He was tied to a tree, on a mountain, a mile from Canada."

"What? No way!" I imagined the claw tree with Duplantis tied to it. I went on, couldn't stop myself. "What'd he die of ...animals eat him?" Ronan paused and I stopped breathing.

"There were animal tracks all around and signs of some venison left there as if someone wanted him to get eaten. But no creature ate him. He died of exposure, starved to death they figure." I knew what Ronan was thinking and I headed it off.

"I was nowhere near Whitefish, you know that."

"No, Ted, I don't know that. I wish I did. But the investigation is ongoing. I'll tell ya this much, if you had something to do with this I can't help you."

I scoffed back, "Of course it wasn't me. I'd never do something that stupid." Ronan stayed silent.

Trying to make my case I said, "Truth is, he disappeared on me. I was following him in Portland for Leroy Dupree. I think I told ya that. Dupree musta had him taken. Why to Montana I have no idea."

Ronan didn't say anything, allowing me more rope to hang myself. I knew I was on the edge of talking too much.

"So, who'd you say found him?" I asked, striving for nonchalant.

"Some local hunters. Probably poachers."

"Did they find anything else? Any... evidence?"

Ronan paused and I thought here it comes, my prison sentence. But to my relief he replied, "Nothing reported, as of yet."

My mind raced on. The Remington shotgun I left at the claw tree had not been turned in – so far. Or maybe it had and was now being traced to me as we spoke. I told Ronan I couldn't talk, I was driving Uber and just got pinged – a lie.

After we hung up, I saw a faint glint of hope, like the first sliver of light in the morning. It dawned on me that poachers in the remote back country of northwest Montana, living out in the woods among hungry animals larger than them, would love to get their hands on a good Remington shotgun. I'll bet the folks who found Duplantis stole it. I know I would.

Chapter 56 Run or Stay

Later after midnight, still Ubering around, I drive past Holman's and see the bar packed. Laughter spills out through the swinging double-entry door. Damn, I miss that bar. Their five-dollar "Special" – a 16 oz. Rainier and a shot of whisky – was a Les Overhead happy hour staple. But no more.

I ask myself, can I live like this the rest of my life – sober and one step from prison? I seriously don't know. It's only been a month since I got back and already I'm feeling itchy – with nothing to take the edge off.

It reminds me of a line from the poet, William Stafford: When the snake decided to go straight, he didn't get anywhere.

I wonder how long I can last, going straight. What if I just took off? Problems solved? But then, what about Kate? And all my talk about having changed? Will the real Teddy Murphy please stand up.

I continue on and turn right on Stark and drive a couple blocks, then turn left and park in front of a black, wrought iron fence. Behind it are trees, tombstones, cash. Lone Fir Cemetery. I turn off the engine and sit. Three crows are perched on the fence in front of me – defenders of the past.

I think of the escape bag I'd reburied in the cemetery shortly after getting back to Portland. It'd be easy to dig it up and vanish.

Pulling out my phone, I check Amtrak and see the next train leaves at 6:30 a.m. Same train Duplantis took.

Option A is to split. But not for Canada. I know I can't live in the great white frozen north, no matter how great they say it is. I'm no hockey fan and I hate Canadians – at least the drunk ones I came across in Whitefish.

What about Chicago? Still too cold. But I could change trains in Chicago and head south – down along the Mississippi River on the "City of New Orleans", back to the Big Easy. Go full circle. I could get a job there. Get a fake ID. Easy. Maybe resume my earlier career as a furniture store credit manager. Or try to write. Become a French Quarter drunk. Kate and Jasmine would slowly disappear into a fog. Can I live with that?

Option B is to stay. Face the judgment I may have coming. If my shotgun is traced to me, I'd be arrested and put on trial for murder. Convicted. Imprisoned. End of story.

My face would be plastered across the Oregonian and other news media. Former advertising clients would smirk. Friends would shrink. I'd have one last road trip – to the state prison.

Who knows, it might be good for me. Maybe I'd find a killer story from an inmate. But would Kate wait for me? She might pull the plug on us. I wouldn't blame her.

Then again, what if those Montana folks who found Duplantis also found my shotgun and kept it. What if there was no evidence, no arrest, no trial, no imprisonment, no atonement? What if I escape justice and get away with three murders. A serial killer, on the loose.

The more I think about it, the better I feel. A little positive thinking does wonders. Optimism is oxygen.

It reminds me of a friend, a motivational speaker, who likes to ask people what's going well. He does it to get you to focus on positive things in your life. Our natural instinct is to talk about negative things – health concerns, family problems, murder trials.

He says research in neuroscience shows that positive thinking has a profound impact on your attitude and wellbeing. It means not letting your old reptilian brain worry about danger and survival, and instead focus on the good in your life.

More bullshit? I hope not because it's all I have left. But in my case, my positive thinking is based on a partly negative view of human nature. There are some among us who are a lying, thieving, killing sort. If they want a shotgun bad enough, they'll steal it. And if they want to stay out of prison bad enough, they'll lie their asses off and leave loved ones behind to escape it. Judgment be damned.

Justice is relative I tell myself. It's based on a society's supposed ethics and values at a particular time. Does absolute truth and moral justice even exist? Who's to say whether I'm guilty or not guilty? God? Don't make me laugh.

It's stuffy in the car, and in my mind, so I roll down the windows. A misty fog flows in around me.

And right on cue as if she's received my reptilian brain waves, I get a text from Kate. It reads: How late are you driving? Going to bed. Be safe! Come home soon.

The pain in my chest comes back. I wonder, am I coming home at all? Can I possibly say these words to her again – sorry, I need to leave.

Moments later I text her back: Sleep well. Don't wait up.

Moving helps me think so I get out of the car and walk around the neighborhood. Streets are slick from rain, sidewalks empty of souls. A dog barks a block over. It reminds me of Ben.

I lose track of time as I walk, trying to gauge my feelings. I think of Kate, my wife of 30 plus years, and Jasmine. Can I live without them? Not very well. But can I live and behave the way Kate wants me to? Maybe for a while, but I know myself.

Head down thinking hard, I walk straight into a tree branch reaching across the sidewalk. It knocks my ball cap off and startles the shit out of me. I'm thinking someone hit me. Seeing the branch makes me bend over and laugh. It's a slap to the head I realize. Telling me something very important: Hey idiot, watch where you're going.

I turn it over in my mind, still laughing. That's good advice. And that's when I see where I am going.

Picking up my cap, I turn around and walk back to my car, eyes wide open. I feel a bird lift off my shoulder.

Twenty minutes later I enter a dark room and see red numbers on a digital clock. It's 3:26. I feel a ping in my heart. March 26 is Kate's birthday. She's asleep, on her side with her back toward me, breathing softly. So is the figure next to her – Ben. He's sprawled out, his furry head on my pillow. I sit on the edge of the bed and he opens his eyes, looks surprised.

"Fooled ya, didn't I?" I whisper. "You're in my spot." I shove him over and slide into bed.

Chapter 57 One Year Later

Lo and behold, human nature came through for me. My shotgun was never found – or at least never turned in. Probably stolen by the poachers who found Duplantis. The investigation of his death has hit a dead end and wouldn't ya know it, I seem to be in the clear. For now.

Of course, I could be thrown in the hoosegow before the sun goes down. I live with a rope around my neck, but I don't let it bother me.

The boy whose father I killed still haunts me, but not as often. The last time I saw him was a few months ago when I took Ben for a walk to Frazer Park, to the hanging tree. Ben sniffed all around it and peed on it. Crows above us shrieked and then went silent, examining me as if they recognized me. I looked up in the tree at them and for a second thought I saw the boy – sitting on a branch in his Spiderman shirt and underwear. Then he was gone.

I wondered what the kid's name was. What if it's Teddy? I couldn't take that. I feel bad enough knowing what I did to his father – an innocent man I strangled to death with a rope. The guilt is suffocating.

How do I live with myself? Well, I look at it this way. A typo in an address placed me in a crisis that I handled the best way I knew how. I killed a man I thought was bad who was in the act of killing

Mario, then I killed Mario in self-defense (he would've killed me if I hadn't struck first).

My third killing, leaving Duplantis tied to a tree on a mountain in Montana, was a copout – letting the universe decide his fate without having to do it myself. But causing someone to die, however you do it, is killing.

So, bring it on. I'm ready to face a judge or jury and leave my fate to them. If they catch me.

Memories and stories we tell of our past help form our future. Like ruts in a wagon trail that become deeper over time, our memories become entrenched and we go where they lead us.

The concussion I got when I slammed my head into the tree on that game trail knocked some sense into me. It's corny to say but I appreciate life more, and my love for Kate and Jasmine is deeper, stronger. In short, I'm striving to be a better husband and dad. Not as big a jerk.

Of course, I'm as cynical and cranky as ever. Still get bored and restless. Still forgetful.

I'm no longer sober though. Kate and I had another sit-down at the kitchen table and she realized she missed drinking, too. She'd quit to help me stop. We decided to resume imbibing together, judiciously under control. She keeps a close eye on me, or tries to. The reins are still tight, but getting a little looser.

Jasmine, my dear daughter, is back from Ecuador, working at a local law firm, living at home in the bedroom in which she grew up. We argue still but she's become more reasonable. Or I have. All I know is, we both seem to laugh more.

We discussed the kidnapping incident one time only. I just said there were parts of my past that I'm not proud of and would not go into. Ever. She thought the whole thing was just strange and asked me a couple questions, but I refused to answer – taking the fifth.

As for dog Ben, he's quieter now, rarely commenting on my actions. Still refusing to do what I tell him, as usual. I once read where animals can get bored like people. If so, I may be boring him. It wouldn't surprise me.

Oh yeah, my gun locker is gone. I had to give it up as part of my armistice with Kate. But I kept the brass knuckles (don't tell her). They're buried in the escape bag I planted in the cemetery. You never know.

At night I still drive for Uber, ferrying strangers to and fro. I'm trying to be a less talky, less inquisitive Uber driver. But it's hard.

As for finding a killer story, I've given up on it for now. I'm not so driven to write a book anymore. I mean, what's the point?

It's not complicated. You do what you can in life. Try to love someone. Be decent and honest. Leave your campsite clean. Don't hurt or kill anybody (I'm not perfect). And avoid getting eaten by wild animals. What else is there?

So, I try to be optimistic and happy – as deathly boring as that sounds. When an Uber passenger gets in my car now I say, "So, what's going well in your life?"

And the minute I get bored with the response I cut in, "Got any personal problems I can help ya with?" I can't help myself.

Don't miss out!

Visit the website below and you can sign up to receive emails whenever Tom Vandel publishes a new book. There's no charge and no obligation.

https://books2read.com/r/B-A-BFCK-CHBEB

BOOKS 2 READ

Connecting independent readers to independent writers.

About the Author

Tom Vandel is a longtime freelance writer living in Portland, Oregon. He has a one-man business called Les Overhead where he writes for many clients and causes, serving the entire earth. He has written one other book: Driving Strangers - Diary of an Uber Driver. Prior to working in advertising, he lived in New Orleans where he was Credit Manager for a furniture store by day and bar denizen at night.

Read more at www.lesoverhead.com.

CPSIA information can be obtained
at www.ICGtesting.com
Printed in the USA
LVHW112153161120
671891LV00029B/162